HOW TO BECOME A
PIRATE
HUNTER

To James —

You're a natural born friend to my daughter and naturally born for greatness!

Marty Reed

HOW TO BECOME A
PIRATE
HUNTER

MARTY REEDER

SWEETWATER
BOOKS
AN IMPRINT OF CEDAR FORT, INC.
SPRINGVILLE, UTAH

ISBN 13: 978-1-4621-1980-6

Published by Sweetwater Books, an imprint of Cedar Fort, Inc.
2373 W. 700 S., Springville, UT 84663
Distributed by Cedar Fort, Inc., www.cedarfort.com

LIBRARY OF CONGRESS CATALOGING-IN-PUBLICATION DATA

Names: Reeder, Marty, 1978- author.
Title: How to become a pirate hunter / by Marty Reeder.
Description: Springville, UT : Sweetwater Books, an imprint of Cedar Fort,
   Inc., [2017] | Summary: "Eric has low confidence in his abilities and
   usefulness until Charlotte moves in. She tells Eric that she has the power
   to recognize other people's natural born abilities; furthermore, she tells
   Eric that he was naturally born to be a pirate hunter"-- Provided by
   publisher.
Identifiers: LCCN 2016055658 (print) | LCCN 2016059188 (ebook) | ISBN
   9781462119806 (perfect bound) | ISBN 9781462127764
Subjects: LCSH: Young adult fiction. | CYAC: Pirates--Fiction. | LCGFT:
   Fantasy fiction.
Classification: LCC PZ7.1.R433 Ho 2017 (print) | LCC PZ7.1.R433 (ebook) | DDC
   [Fic]--dc23
LC record available at https://lccn.loc.gov/2016055658

Cover design by Priscilla Chaves
Cover design © 2017 by Cedar Fort, Inc.
Edited and typeset by Jennifer Johnson

Printed in the United States of America

10 9 8 7 6 5 4 3 2 1

Printed on acid-free paper

DEDICATED TO STEVE AND DONA REEDER, NATURAL-
BORN PARENTS, FRIENDS, AND MENTORS—A STAR TEAM
TETHERED BY BONDS THAT REACH BEYOND WORLDS.

Prologue
WIND OUT OF SAILS

"Well," Eric's high school counselor asked again. "What do you want to do after you graduate?"

Eric hated this question above all others, because adults seem to care about little else when it comes to adolescent children. And without a good answer . . . well, that quickly turns a conversation awkward.

A couple of cookie cutter jobs flashed through Eric's mind: firefighter, doctor, professional athlete, astronaut, and dozens of others. He sighed. Those are the same answers elementary school kids give, not sophomores in high school. Besides, none of them fit him. Not any job he knew fit him. In spite of this, Mr. Pickney, his counselor, waited for an answer, so he threw one out. "Newspaper reporter."

Mr. Pickney nodded. "Eric, if you want to be a newspaper journalist, your writing skills are going to have to improve. You are barely getting by in your English classes."

Eric squirmed and finally confessed, "I don't know what I'm going to do."

"Okay . . ." Mr. Pickney responded, "What are your hobbies? What is it that you are good at?"

Eric shifted, liking this meeting less and less. He thought hard but drew a blank. Mr. Pickney raised his eyebrows expectantly.

"I . . . uh . . . I'm pretty good at flying kites," Eric answered seriously.

"Kites." Mr. Pickney tried, as he had been taught, not to demean any adolescent's ambitions. "That's good but, uh, as far as I know, there are currently no careers on the lookout for expert kite flyers."

Eric nodded submissively while Mr. Pickney continued. "Now, what else are you good at?"

Eric winced as he gave the only answer to come to his mind. "I'm pretty good at finding people when playing hide-and-go-seek . . ."

Mr. Pickney frowned. "Eric, I'm not playing around here. This is your future we're talking about. I'm trying to help you."

Eric settled back in his chair and crossed his arms. "I'm not playing around either. That's all I'm good at! I have no talents. You think I'm happy about that future?"

Eric returned to his classroom frustrated, as he always was after meetings with school counselors. *Now*, he thought, *I'll return to my science class, where I will get a mediocre grade, just like the rest of my mediocre life.*

Eric sat down at his desk, studying his classmates with jealousy. Brandon was a great all-around athlete. Jeanie boasted an incredible singing voice. Tina could work out any math problem you gave her. Even Christopher—yes, Christopher—with his poor hygiene and thick-rimmed glasses, was unparalleled with his computer knowledge. While scanning the rest of the room, Eric could pinpoint redeeming qualities of each of his fellow students, regardless of whether they were popular, outcasts, unknown, or even hated. Eric turned his thoughts back to himself.

There isn't one thing I'm good at, he thought. *Not one.* He sighed, succumbing to his useless fate.

"Land ho!"

That phrase usually incited excitement among a crew, but the sleek, two-masted sailing sloop, the *Rosemary*, had been sailing in and out of sight of the mainland to the south of them for a couple of days. At this point, however, the mainland lay shrouded by some low-hanging clouds, so Samuel wondered what the lookout meant. A glance to the west, the direction the ship was headed, revealed the mystery as a slight landfall slipped into view. Samuel gazed at it curiously until he recalled the captain's charts in his mind.

"Must be the Montes de Oca island chain," the second mate, Mr. Gary, murmured as he located the same blur on the horizon. "If it weren't so hazy, we would be able to see the mainland jut out there toward it."

Though Samuel was not in the mood for conversation, he nodded at the second mate's comment, "San Fernando Channel." He sighed, relieved. "We're nearly there."

"And not a moment too soon, either," Mr. Gary appended.

Samuel could not have agreed more. He gazed across the deck of the *Rosemary*, strewn with loose rigging, splintered spars, tackles, and blocks. He turned around to gauge their progress, judging their distance from a lone, barren island a couple of leagues back. Though the breeze remained constant and in their favor, the ship crawled forward sluggishly. Samuel knew this to be a result of the countless leaks she sprang during the turbulent night. Still looking back, Samuel saw the mist to the south building up into a dark, menacing cloud gathering in the east.

Hours earlier, that enormous mass pounded itself into their ship mercilessly. In fact, the captain had just gone below to rest after almost two days without sleep. Samuel could hardly imagine that any of the crew members were in better shape. A couple of times Samuel thought they were done for, but somehow they managed to survive. Even greater was their fortune that they found themselves only a long day's journey from the friendly Port Raleigh. *Yes, the storm was bad luck*, he thought, *but it could have been much worse.*

After a couple more hours of headway, the mist began to clear in the mid-morning sun as the San Fernando Channel edged closer. The jut of rocky mainland fell out into the ocean just short of the island chain stretching off to the north, marking an obvious path between the two land masses.

"Sail ho!"

"See if he can't make out what type of ship, Mr. Gary," came Samuel's mechanical response. Thanks to Port Raleigh's status as a busy harbor, it would be highly unlikely to sail through San Fernando Channel without crossing spars with another ship. Though another ship at this point and in their condition might bring relief, Samuel felt annoyed more than anything. With Port Raleigh so close, the last thing he wanted was to stop and hail another ship. He would rather go straight to port for aid.

"They'll be wantin' to know how we weathered the storm, I shouldn't wonder," Mr. Gary noted, after passing along the proper message to the lookout. His lack of enthusiasm suggested that he did not look forward to frequent stops on the way into port either.

"Looks like a merchantman, sir!" the lookout yelled from his perch in the crow's nest.

By that time they had traveled enough that Samuel could see the ship forming on the horizon himself. He was somewhat puzzled. The ship headed northward, as if bearing straight for the Montes de Oca islands. There were no ports or settlements on any of the islands. Nor did the wind constitute a tack in that direction if the ship simply intended to exit the channel. No, she just ran a straight line between the islands and the mainland.

Mr. Gary came up to Samuel's side, using his own spyglass to assess the situation. "Strange tack, sir."

Before Samuel could reply, the two seamen observed the merchant ship come about.

"Changed her course, sir," the lookout cried out. "Bearin' her way toward us now."

Samuel set down his spyglass disconcertedly. "Mr. Gary, retrieve the captain immediately."

Mr. Gary hesitated. "But, sir, he said he was not to be disturbed."

"Unless an emergency arose."

"I would hardly call this an—"

"Mr. Gary, now."

By the time the captain, somewhat frazzled, made his way to the quarterdeck, most of the crew had taken a heightened interest in the ship that now careened toward them with all sails set.

"What's the problem?" the captain asked, his voice still hoarse.

"It's the ship, sir," Samuel pointed to the horizon. "When we first saw her, she was running a course straight for Montes de Oca from the mainland, then as soon as she saw us, she headed straight for us."

The captain's demeanor suddenly got serious. "Patrolling."

"Yes, sir. That could mean one of two things."

"Royal Navy or pirate. What's the flag?"

"Should be in sight any moment, sir."

The ensuing silence as the men awaited the verdict was only tainted by the continual sound of the bilge pumps, which the men had been working unceasingly since the storm.

"I can see her banner, sir," the lookout cried down. "She's flying . . . she's flying . . . "

"What?" Mr. Gary called up impatiently.

The tone of the lookout's voice told them all they needed to know.

"Bring her about," the captain barked, not even waiting to hear the rest of the lookout's report. Samuel did not hesitate putting the orders into action. Although no one said anything, he could sense the deepening of the somber morale of a crew that had been through too much to be able to support another setback like this, especially with relief so close.

The turn about was sloppy and slow, not a result of an inept crew, but of a ship barely holding together in one piece. "Keep her tight against the wind," the captain warned as he watched the pirates gaining ground on them after their sluggish maneuver. "As tight as she can handle. Those rogues won't catch the *Rosemary* beating into the wind, especially not with a bulky piece of driftwood like that." The captain was putting on a show. Samuel knew it. Most of the crew knew it. But even if they did know it, at least it showed that the captain would not give up easily.

Samuel came up to the captain's side and stood for a moment as they both stared off the back of the ship, monitoring their pursuers. "Not many pirates would be brave enough to plug up San Fernando Channel," Samuel noted. "It's only a matter of time before Governor Rose catches word of their presence and sends someone after them from Port Raleigh."

"Not many pirates indeed. I caught sight of the flag as we were coming about, Samuel," the captain said quietly.

"You recognized it?"

The captain nodded. "It's one of the Willards."

Samuel's heart sank. Impossible. The captain must be mistaken somehow. Even as he thought it, however, Samuel knew the captain could not mistake something that big. If he was right, then that meant that where there was one Willard, there was another close by. He gripped the taffrail. The infamous Willard Pirate Twins blocked their path into Port Raleigh.

They would have done better drowning in the storm.

Chapter 1
USELESS ERIC

Eric stood at the whiteboard in Mrs. Weston's math class. He held the marker limply at his side. "Come on, Eric. This is supposed to be a simple math problem. It's exactly like the problems you did for your homework."

Eric refrained from telling Mrs. Weston how much trouble he had with his homework. While Eric did not consider himself good at anything, the thing he felt least bad at was math. In fact, in geometry last year, he almost felt like he was finding a niche for himself. Unfortunately, as he moved on to Algebra 2 this year, he fell back into his normal pattern of mediocrity. With geometry, he could see shapes, rearrange them in his mind, and use them to plot out and make sense of them. With other math classes, however, pictures disappeared and endless parades of random numbers and letters replaced them in one big, jumbled mess. As if to prove this point, he stared at the whiteboard hopelessly as Mrs. Weston pressured him.

"Barring a miracle, Eric," she said, "I'm keeping you up there until you complete this math problem."

Eric sighed. If he could have calculated his odds of a miracle helping him, he felt confident they would be fairly scarce. Of course, if he could calculate odds, he would hardly need a miracle because he would be good at math anyway. Where was his guardian angel when he needed it?

A knock came at the classroom door, which then opened abruptly. Eric slumped in disappointment upon seeing Vice Principal Olsen standing in the doorway, the furthest thing from a guardian angel he could imagine. Before Mr. Olsen explained his presence, Eric saw someone emerge from behind him as he entered the class. It was a girl.

True, Eric has seen many girls in his lifetime, but he sensed something different about this girl. Physically, she did not stand out much more than any other girl. Plenty of others shared her blonde hair and rosy cheeks. He did notice, however, the way she eased her hair back into a loose bun that shot flares of unruly curled hairs around her head to create of a sort of halo, and the red in her cheeks and lips glowed in a way that compensated for a slightly short stature. Her jeans and light green shirt hardly set her apart in style from anyone else in the room, but the way she walked in them lent her an air of certainty.

While absorbing this girl's presence, Eric realized that, contrary to normal adolescent instincts, what he felt upon seeing her was not love. He knew what love felt like because he had been in love with Sara Parker—until she laughed at him for holding a baseball bat by the wrong end in gym class. So he knew that this was not love, yet that was all he could do to narrow the field of what it was about this girl that captured his attention so vividly.

A mesmerized Eric observed as the girl trailed Mr. Olsen with uncanny confidence. While gliding into the room, she scanned each student. Her sweep ended with Eric, who still stood lamely in front of the whiteboard. If this girl overcame unremarkable physical qualities with a mystical strength of personality, Eric disappeared into his unremarkable self. His short-cropped, tawny hair lay limply across his head, and his bony joints tried to meld into his bland T-shirt and old jeans. Though his height exceeded most boys his age, he hid it well with hunched shoulders and a downward-angled head, accustomed to staring at the ground.

In spite of Eric's camouflage, Eric noticed the girl pause as her line of sight slid past his own. For a split second they connected, and she cocked her head curiously. Then, just as quickly as she reacted upon seeing him, she allowed her face to glaze over with apparent disinterest.

"Sorry to interrupt your class, Mrs. Weston," Mr. Olsen declared, breaking the spell that held Eric captivated, "but I was wondering if I could borrow one of your students."

Mrs. Weston, clearly on rocky terms with Vice Principal Olsen, curtly responded, "No."

Mr. Olsen had not expected that reply. "Oh . . . um, well, I'm going to have to borrow one anyway. You see, we have a new student here, and I wanted to have another student show her around the school."

"Go ask Mr. Lindley. I'm busy with a lesson. Just because my classroom is right next to the office doesn't mean that you can drop in here all the time and steal my students at will." Scattered snickers indicated the students' pleasure at seeing Mr. Olsen getting an earful.

"I didn't come to your classroom because it was close to the office."

"Then what was your reasoning?" Mrs. Weston pushed.

"Um . . . I, um . . . just decided to go by alphabetical order."

"Darren," Mrs. Weston upped the stakes by addressing Mr. Olsen by his first name, providing the more delinquent boys in the room with new bathroom stall vandalism fodder, "my last name is Weston. The letter 'W' is at the end of the alphabet."

"Yeah, I know. Uh . . . I'm going backward in the alphabet."

"What about Mr. Yang, then?"

The vice principal's mouth stood open for a second before he turned and grabbed Eric. "What about this young man? Certainly you won't miss him."

"Eric isn't going anywhere until he finishes the problem on the board."

Though he was as desperate as ever, Eric still had no clue what to put for an answer. On the front row, however, he realized that Tina Ortiz must have been as desperate as Eric was to keep him from standing in front of the whiteboard all day. She scribbled something on her notebook and held it up. As incompetent as Eric felt, he at least recognized a lifeline when offered. He quickly copied the answer onto the board.

Mrs. Weston looked at the answer with widening eyes before glancing suspiciously at Tina, who had by now hidden her notebook on her lap. "Excellent work, Eric," she said deliberately. "That answer seemed to have come out of nowhere. I guess you got a miracle after all." Eric smiled lamely, and Mrs. Weston concluded, "Fine. Get out of here."

As the three worked their way back into the hallway, Mr. Olsen gave a last look back at the glaring Mrs. Weston while adjusting his tie nervously. He ushered the two students farther down the hall, then tapped Eric on the shoulder. "Eric, this is Charlotte Reeves. Charlotte, Eric Francis." The two nodded formally to each other, though each eyed the other curiously while Mr. Olsen continued, "Charlotte just arrived today, so I hope you can give her a good welcome and show her around the school."

Eric nodded.

"Right," Mr. Olsen said, handing Eric a note to use as a hall pass. "Then I guess that's everything. Oh, and Eric, for the bathrooms, girls bathrooms in particular, you'll just have to show her where they are located. You don't have to physically go into them."

Eric rolled his eyes. While he did not have the best opinion of himself, he at least did not think anyone would be idiot enough to have to be reminded of that. After scrutinizing Mr. Olsen's expression, however, Eric recognized the sincerity of the warning, as if it reflected an awkward past experience from the absent-minded administrator.

As soon as Mr. Olsen left, Eric turned to Charlotte and stared for a moment, trying to decipher why she intrigued him so much. His gaze finally broke when Charlotte piped up, "So, are we going to see the rest of the school, or is this hallway all there is?"

"Oh, I'm sorry," Eric snapped out of his trance. "Um, follow me."

Though Eric tried to be a good tour guide, he vaguely sensed that Charlotte cared little about learning the school's layout. Still, though, he could not deny that she paid close attention to at least something about him. As they strolled past hallways and rooms, she had an uncomfortable habit of looking directly into his eyes when he spoke to her, even if she barely acknowledged anything he said.

This only made Eric more nervous, and by the time they reached the cafeteria, he began rambling on about the legend of the lunchroom being the location of the most catastrophic fire in school history when some troublemaking students played with a lighter close to the cafeteria french fries. The fries were so greasy that they immediately flared up and caught onto their neighbors' fries until the whole place was up in flames. "So, anyway," Eric wrapped up the story, "it would have been a huge mess if it weren't for the meatloaf that day. Apparently the cafeteria's meatloaf is really good at extinguishing fires, and once they figured that out, they put the fires out with some well-placed meat loafs. Meat loaves? Anyway, um, it turns out that the cooks weren't too pleased with the whole thing and they—"

"What's your favorite subject in school, Eric?" Charlotte interrupted him out of the blue.

Off guard, Eric stumbled, "Um . . . well, I . . . I don't really have a favorite subject." He shrugged. "I'm really not that good at anything."

Eric could almost swear he saw Charlotte stifle a grin. "Nothing?"

"Not a thing," he answered definitely.

"I find that a little hard to believe."

"So does my school counselor. So do my parents. But it's true."

"Have you ever seen the ocean, Eric?"

The question seemed to be more random than her last question. Having been born and raised in the same landlocked, rural town of Nibleton, high in the Intermountain West, Eric's only experience with the ocean came from seeing it on TV or through pictures. "No. Not the ocean, but . . . um . . . I've been to Badger Lake a couple times . . . for Boy Scout camp."

Charlotte nodded as if his answer cleared something up for her. "Ever been in a boat?"

"I've been on one of those floating raft things," he replied.

"I'll bet you were pretty good on that raft, weren't you?"

Eric frowned. "Um . . . I'm not sure I remember."

"I mean, did you feel at home when you were on it?"

"I had fun playing on it."

"Well, didn't you want to go back and play on it some more?" Charlotte pressed.

"Yeah, but one of the Scouts in our troop punctured it . . . and, well, I've never been back to Badger Lake since."

"Ah, but you never punctured it, did you?" Charlotte pointed out.

Eric nodded his head slowly, still trying to find out where this conversation was headed.

"Well, then, you are good at something, aren't you?"

Eric stopped walking. "Um, I guess, I . . . but I don't see what that . . . I mean, not puncturing a raft isn't really a skill. Most anybody can be pretty good at not puncturing a raft."

"I guess he hasn't had enough experience near water to get an idea," Charlotte mumbled to herself, chewing on her lip. Eric wanted to ask her what in the world she was talking about, but then she said out loud, "You know, that still doesn't mean that you don't have something you are good at."

Eric shrugged. "Maybe, but if that's true, I've yet to see any proof."

"Well, you're just going to have to trust me then," Charlotte said, matter-of-factly. When most people said something like that, they were being nice. When Charlotte said it, however, Eric sensed her complete sincerity. It reminded him of that same confidence she exuded when entering Mrs. Weston's classroom. He could not help but feel that she really did know what she was talking about.

The school bell rang, distracting Eric from his analysis of Charlotte.

"I suppose you have to go to another class now, right?" Charlotte asked.

"Um . . . yeah."

"I don't suppose you could point me back toward the office then, could you?"

The hallway began bursting with students changing classrooms and heading toward lockers. "Um, of course," Eric replied. "Just turn around, take a left at the end of this hallway, and it's all the way down and on your left."

Charlotte nodded. Then she gave Eric a meaningful look before turning around and navigating through the crowded hallway.

Part of Eric felt ready to leave this strange encounter behind and go back to his normal daily routine. Then he realized that he hated his normal daily routine. Something about Charlotte intrigued him, and he had to find out what it was. Finding a boldness not native to him, he yelled, "Wait! Charlotte, wait. Wait a second."

Charlotte's blonde hair bobbed, then swiveled back toward Eric. Students jostled past her as if she were a rock parting water in a rushing stream. Eric could not be sure, but he thought she concealed a smile.

"I . . . uh . . . I think my next class is canceled. If you'd like, I could finish giving you a tour of the school."

"Canceled?" Charlotte now smiled openly. "That's rather odd." Eric realized how dumb of an excuse it was. Before he could retreat, however, Charlotte continued, "I suppose if your class is canceled, I wouldn't mind finishing the tour."

"Well, what I meant is that I think Mr. Olsen wouldn't mind if I missed my next class if I—"

"Let's go, Eric," she interrupted him.

Eric guided Charlotte away from the crowded hallway and outside onto the school grounds. He did not say a word on the way, let alone talk about the school. Once outside, they sat down on a small hill overlooking the field where Mr. Lindley's PE class would soon be congregating. Charlotte waited patiently.

Unsure of exactly what he wanted to know—besides how Charlotte managed to make him feel so strange—Eric went back to their previous conversation. "How come you think that I'm good at something?"

"Everyone's good at something."

"I always figured I was the exception to that."

"Nope," Charlotte countered without hesitation.

"How can you say that? You don't even know me."

Charlotte sized Eric up, gauging if he was ready for what she had to say. "Because Eric, that's what I do. I can see people for what their talents are."

Eric thought this response a little vague. "So you're like an NBA scout or something? If so, you're talking to the wrong guy. I'm lucky if I can hit the backboard, let alone put the ball in the hoop."

"Not just basketball talents, Eric. Any talents. And not just talents either, but I can see what that person was born to do."

Charlotte was right to size Eric up; he found this difficult to swallow. "Wait a second. You're telling me that with any given person you could tell me what they are born to do?"

Charlotte nodded.

Eric barely contained his skepticism. At that point Mr. Lindley's class filed out onto the field, getting ready to play Frisbee. "All right," Eric said, "let's try this out then." He pointed to one of the students lining up on the far side of the field. "What about that guy over there? What is his talent? What was he born to do?"

Charlotte squinted, then shrugged. "It doesn't work that way, Eric. I have to be able to see the person eye to eye."

How convenient, Eric thought. He berated himself for almost believing her. Before he could suggest that they head back to the office, someone interrupted him from behind.

"Eric, shouldn't you be in class right now?"

Eric pivoted, somewhat anxiously, but then smiled as he recognized the speaker. "Al, you scared me. Actually, I'm giving this new student a tour around the school. Here's my note from Mr. Olsen."

"New student?" Al looked over at Charlotte.

"Oh, I'm sorry. Al, this is Charlotte Reeves. Charlotte, Al Lorenzo, one of our school custodians."

Al certainly looked the part of the school custodian. He was carrying around a push broom and had some plastic garbage bags sticking out of his pocket. He wiped his hand on his pants and stuck it out. "Charlotte, pleasure to have you at our school."

Charlotte shook his hand and smiled.

"Well," Al said, "you two go ahead and finish your tour." He then leaned toward Eric and whispered in a way that Charlotte could still hear him. "But do me a favor and don't take her by the north parking lot until I'm finished up there. Apparently some students didn't agree with the cafeteria food, and they abandoned the leftovers on the pavement," he held up the broom, "so I've got to go sweep it off the ground and take it back to the cafeteria for tomorrow's lunch. Cook's orders."

Eric and Charlotte both laughed at what they hoped was a joke. After Al left, the two of them stood for a moment in silence. Eric suddenly realized something.

"You looked Al straight in the eyes, didn't you?" Eric asked suddenly.

"Yes."

"Well . . . ?" he prodded. He expected her to go off of what she had seen from him already, labeling him as someone born to clean or something related to his job as a custodian.

Her easy reply threw Eric off guard. Without thinking twice, Charlotte said that Al Lorenzo was born to be a stage musical star.

Eric's mouth gaped open, while his eyebrows furrowed in disbelief.

"I know it's hard to believe," Charlotte followed up, "and I know that I can't prove it to you, but I promise you that is what Al was born to be. Just because someone is born to be something doesn't necessarily mean they will end up as that same thing."

"No," Eric replied, "you don't get it. I can't believe that you would guess such a random thing . . . and be dead on."

"Oh, so you've seen that he has musical talent?"

"Any time Al comes into our choir class, the teacher asks him to sing for us. You can ask him to sing anything, and it comes out like a pro. He'll even play the piano and make up brilliant songs on the spot. He is the most amazing singer I've heard in my life." Charlotte nodded and shrugged as if this was hardly news to her. "But how could you possibly know that? He's never been able to sing professionally since his mom got sick and he's been taking care of her."

"Eric, I told you: that's what I do."

Eric found himself much more convinced than he was a couple minutes ago. "Then come with me." Eric guided Charlotte down to the playing field where Mr. Lindley's class tossed a Frisbee back and forth. They sat on the sidelines and waited until Charlotte could gain eye contact with one of the students.

"What about her?" he asked as soon as one of the students glanced in their direction.

"Tractor mechanic."

"And her?"

"Canal lock operator."

"Him?"

"Zinc miner."

She didn't hesitate for even one of her responses. Eric listened to her, amazed. Either she was a really good liar, or she really did know what she was talking about.

"Okay, what about that guy right there?"

"Roof thatcher."

"Roof thatcher? Do you mean a roof patcher?"

"No, thatcher. I'm not talking about shingles, I'm talking about a roof made of thatch."

Eric was clearly caught off guard by this comment. "Thatch? What are you talking about?"

Charlotte sighed. "Eric, most people aren't born in the right circumstances for their natural-born talent: like Al—something holds them back. Or with that girl there, she's probably never seen a real live tractor before, so she'll never get a chance to realize what her ability is. A huge majority of natural-born abilities are useless in their time period. When I say roof thatcher, I'm saying that he was naturally born to make roofs for the types of houses built in ancient civilizations."

Eric was fascinated by this explanation. "So that guy over there, if we gave him a house and a bunch of thatch—whatever that is—he'd be able to roof it no problem."

"Exactly. Even though hardly anybody has thatch-roofed houses these days, he would be able to do one in record time with no training at all. He'd surprise himself even."

"But with a shingle roof, he'd be just as good as you or me."

"Not necessarily. Some of the skills for roofing a house with thatch would probably transfer over to roofing with shingles. He'd be a decent shingler, I imagine."

Eric shook his head in amazement. "Just born at the wrong time, then. Well, is there anyone else here that has been born in the wrong time period for their talent?"

"I'm sure," Charlotte said as she focused her attention to the students again. "Most people are, actually." She waited to catch some people's looks. "She's an indigo gatherer, you know, for dye. He's a silkworm breeder. He's a water buffalo hunter. She's a—"

"Wait, who is a water buffalo hunter? Him?" Eric pointed to an athletically built young man running across the field with ease.

"Yeah, water buffalo hunter."

"I think you're wrong with him. That's Ryan Thompson."

Charlotte raised her eyebrows. "I don't care who it is. All I'm saying is that he was naturally born to be a water buffalo hunter."

"No, you don't understand, Charlotte. Ryan is the quarterback for our high school football team. Not only that, but he's the best in the state, one of the best the high school has ever had. Colleges all over the nation are trying to recruit him. He has got to be a natural-born football player."

Charlotte could not be fazed. "Look, Eric, it's not a democratic process. Ryan was naturally born to be a water buffalo hunter. It's that simple." Eric almost interrupted, but Charlotte continued, "You're still not making the connection. What kind of skills would you need in order to hunt water buffalo?"

Eric rolled his eyes. "I don't know . . . be able to imitate the water buffalo mating call?"

"Maybe," Charlotte replied patiently. "But he would have to also be very agile and athletic in order to get close to a water buffalo or to run away from one if need be. Most importantly—since his natural-born ability is not for this time period—he would need to be able to throw a spear hard and accurately, sometimes from a distance, and sometimes while he or his target is on the run."

Eric took a second to think this over. "Wait . . . so you're saying that his ability to throw the ball so well is not from a natural-born football throwing talent, but from . . ."

15

"That's right. Spear throwing talent." Eric sat speechless for a moment and Charlotte took advantage of his silence. "I guarantee that if you gave that guy a javelin he could nail a moving target fifty yards away on his first try. He doesn't know that of course. He simply transferred the relevant talents from his water buffalo hunting skills to something with modern day similarities, such as throwing the football."

Up until then it had not occurred to Eric that he should not believe what Charlotte said, simply due to her matter-of-fact means of telling him. For a split moment, however, he doubted. *Maybe she's making it all up*, he thought. He looked at her curiously as she continued to watch the students playing Frisbee. He found no lie in her eyes. Instead he noted inquisitiveness as she scanned each new face, made contact with their eyes, and learned something new. Then Eric realized something. The look he saw her with now matched the same intriguing one that had captivated him from the moment he saw her.

As he took in this simple yet extraordinary girl's demeanor, she brightened and turned to Eric. "See that girl there?"

Eric looked at the girl who had just run past them. "Yeah, that's Jill Oakley."

"She was born to be a com-generator operator."

"A com-gener . . . what's that?"

"I don't know. It's some kind of job in the future. The future talents are always fun because it makes you wonder what they could possibly be good for."

Eric could hardly believe the conversation he was having. "The future . . . the past . . . so is anyone actually born in the right time and circumstance as their natural-born ability?"

"Yeah . . . but not that often. Most of them you've actually heard of. William Shakespeare, natural-born playwright. Imhotep—the guy who built the pyramids in Egypt—natural-born architect. Cicero, natural-born orator. Genghis Khan, Hernán Cortés, Alexander the Great, natural-born conquerors. Christopher Columbus, natural-born sea explorer. Pheidippides—that Greek marathon runner guy—natural-born distance runner. Michelangelo, natural-born sculptor . . ."

"And painter," Eric added.

"Actually no, but he had such wonderful sculpting skills that many of them transferred over to painting as well."

Eric let out a breath. "Wow. But how can you know about these guys? Obviously you've never got to look them in the eyes before."

Charlotte nodded. "Good question. I don't know from firsthand account. But I have met various other people like myself who have handed the information down over the generations."

"Wait . . . like yourself. What do you mean?"

Charlotte smiled. "Haven't you guessed yet, Eric? My natural-born ability allows me to recognize what other people were born to be. We call ourselves natural-born seers."

Considering all the information Eric just learned, that was relatively easy to believe. "Natural-born seer," he repeated. "So you've met other seers?"

"When you've moved as much as my family has, you run into a lot of people with a lot of different natural-born abilities. Once my eyes come across those of another seer, which isn't often, you can imagine that we immediately connect. The information on past natural-born abilities has passed from one to another throughout time."

It amazed Eric that this whole new world existed all around him without him knowing about it. "How have I not heard of this before?"

"History has left hints here and there. The Elephanta Caves in India are said to have sculptures of every known trade in the past, present, and future—the work of a seer. As part of the birth ceremony, Aztec priests or priestesses would present babies with tools for different trades, trusting the babies to naturally choose the one most fit for them in the future. The seers I've spoken to assume the priest or priestesses deciding what tools to present to the babies were seers."

"Okay," Eric conceded, though he maintained a skeptical tone, "but it still seems like most seers don't advertise."

Charlotte nodded. "It's a powerful thing to be able to read other people's abilities. Powerful and dangerous. Mostly to protect ourselves from being exploited, we keep it quiet. But we still like to use our talent. Lots of seers work in human resource, because they are really good at hiring the right people for the right jobs; others—like you suggested— work as athletic scouts or military recruiters. There are plenty of ways for seers to be relevant without being conspicuous. We may not tell the world about what we see all the time, but that doesn't mean that we're not always watching."

Always watching, Eric repeated in his mind. He suddenly realized something that had evaded him since they began their conversation. *When she walked into Mrs. Weston's room*, Eric thought, *our eyes met. She looked into my eyes. She knows what I was born to do.*

Eric opened his mouth, about to say something, then he clamped it back shut again, as if changing his mind. A million thoughts flashed through his mind at that moment. What if I don't like what I was born to be? What if I don't even know what it is when she tells me? Then the most scary thought of all crossed his mind. What if I don't have a natural-born ability?

Eric tried to remind himself that Charlotte said everyone was born to do something, but she certainly had not mentioned his ability yet. What if he was the first person she met who did not have a natural talent in anything at all? What if she was just being nice by pretending he had one? If anyone could be the exception to this strange rule, it would most certainly be him, he knew.

But he wanted to know—wanted it badly. Eric tried to muster the courage to ask, but his mouth refused to open. He simply could not handle it if he asked and she told him he had no natural-born talents. He tried one last time to force the question out. It rose in his throat, his mouth set itself to speak, and then suddenly Mr. Lindley called over to them.

"Eric, what's going on? You need to get to class . . . take your friend with you. I don't want you getting into trouble on my part."

The moment passed. Eric succumbed, stood up, took Charlotte back to the office, and sat in his classes for the rest of the school day wondering if Charlotte's gift could even be real or not. If it was real, Eric wondered if he had missed his one chance at rising above mediocrity.

Samuel watched the events around him in horror. Nearly three days had passed since they managed to elude the pirate ship blocking the entrance to Port Raleigh. Their escape in a half-ruined boat constituted a miracle in and of itself. By the time they bore down on the barren island just out of the shipping lane, the pirates backed off, not willing to leave their post for such small prey.

Despite their dire circumstances, the captain made the most of their first day by anchoring at the small island and fixing the leaks the *Rosemary* sprung earlier. Then the horror began on day two. Since most of their drinking water had been ruined in the storm, the crew had gone to refit the ship with water from the island. Unfortunately, the island held no natural spring, only pools of stagnant rainwater from the storm of two days previous. Thirst overcame caution. They hauled the water aboard.

Samuel now looked around in disbelief. Half of the crew lay overwhelmed by the potent disease contaminating the bad water. They sprawled pathetically before him on the deck of the ship suffering for what would be the last hours of their lives. Although a distressing scene, nothing upset Samuel more than the knowledge that the captain also waned, bedridden in his cabin.

The captain put up a spirited fight against the merciless epidemic, but the final stage of the disease now left the veteran seaman's fate as only a matter of time. This unnerved Samuel, not only due to the respect he harbored for his captain, but also because he recognized that, as first mate, charge of the ship fell to him next. Samuel had never been an ambitious sailor, and such a turn of events would then bestow upon him with the unenviable position of deciding how to rescue what was left of the crew—if there was any crew left.

Weighing his options took a disturbingly short amount of time. Samuel knew that if they stayed at their anchorage for much longer, the rest of the crew would fall victim to either this unseen foe or die from simple dehydration. He also knew that if he pressed toward Port Raleigh, he would run straight into the awaiting arms of the Willard Pirate Twins . . . something even less desirable than death by illness.

Samuel paced the deck desperately. Having experienced some narrow escapes on the high seas before, he racked his brain for a solution. No matter how he framed the problem, however, no solution came. Usually, he saw at least some hope for survival—some chance, no matter how small, of living to see another day. He stared over the glassy ocean water, searching for anything to alleviate their condition.

The black ocean water reflected back only deep nothingness.

Chapter 2
ERIC'S NATURAL-BORN ABILITY

Mr. Dutch wondered, not for the first time, whether being a student driver instructor was worth the effort. Yes, he found the extra money convenient, but on the other hand, a possible heart attack and subsequent visit to the hospital probably cost more than his earnings. "Eric, you're floating all over the road. This is not an open parking lot. This is a busy street."

"Sorry, Mr. Dutch," Eric mumbled. Not only did he lack talent at driving, but in this particular session Eric happened to be distracted by the person in the backseat. He had not seen Charlotte since the day before, but he thought about her a lot. He certainly could not hide his surprise that she also had just been assigned to Mr. Dutch—coincidentally at the same time as him.

Much to Mr. Dutch's relief, the car arrived at the school parking lot, and the two students got out. "Do both of you have a ride home?" Mr. Dutch asked. Eric thought the instructor eyed him particularly close.

They both answered in the affirmative and Mr. Dutch left them sitting on the curb of the parking lot waiting for their parents to come pick them up.

"That was really great driving, Charlotte," Eric said to break the ice.

"Thank you. Yours was good too."

Eric did his best not to snort. "Yeah, right. Good if eight near accidents are ideal."

Charlotte smiled. "Actually I was thinking that it was good considering something else."

Eric took a deep breath at this statement. "Good considering that I have no talent whatsoever?"

"Eric!" Charlotte replied sharply, "You know that's not true. I'd have thought our conversation yesterday would've taught you something."

"I get that most people are born with certain abilities."

"That's right. And you just happen to fit under the category of one of those people," Charlotte gently chided.

"Are you sure?" Eric thought he knew the answer, but he still feared the response.

"Oh, I'm sure," Charlotte said without hesitation. Eric detected the tiniest trace of a grin on her face.

"So . . ." Eric rubbed his hands together and took a deep breath as Charlotte waited patiently. He continued slowly, ". . . so you've looked into my eyes and seen what I was born to be?"

She gave him another nearly imperceptible grin. "Yes."

Eric waited for her to continue, but she held back. "Well . . . ?" he finally asked when he could wait no longer.

Charlotte laughed at his discomfort. "Eric, can't you even guess?"

Eric racked his brain, but this reminded him of his meetings with Mr. Pickney. His mind went blank. Despondent, he shook his head. "No, I can't."

The smile left Charlotte's face and she gently reached out and touched Eric on his hunched shoulder, forcing him to look into her eyes. "Listen to me, Eric. You are just as talented as anyone else out there. You just haven't been in the right circumstances to prove it."

"Why?"

"Because. You are a natural-born pirate hunter."

A part of Eric wanted to laugh, but he knew from the look on Charlotte's face that she would not stand for such a thing. So he allowed the other part of him to take over, and he went silent as he digested her declaration.

"Eric?" Charlotte prompted.

Eric snapped out of his momentary lapse in thought. "I'm sorry. I just . . ." He shook his head.

Charlotte could finally laugh at his reaction. "Eric, you are one of a kind."

"'One of a kind'? Are there not that many . . . natural-born pirate hunters?" He seemed tentative to actually say the words himself.

"Well, probably not, actually, but I just meant in general you are one of a kind."

Eric mulled over this new information. "Now Charlotte, you're not kidding around with me or anything, are you? I mean, you aren't making something up just to make me feel better about myself, right?"

For all of Charlotte's playfulness, her subsequent expression was devoid of deceit. "Eric, there are probably a lot of things you couldn't trust about me, but when I tell you that you're a natural-born pirate hunter, please know that I take that responsibility of telling someone what they were born to do very seriously."

Eric allowed his belief to trickle into his expression. "Wow," he said. He waited another second before repeating, "Wow." He gave Charlotte a look of hope that she must not have seen in him since the moment she first met him. "Um . . . what, exactly, is a pirate hunter?"

Charlotte's giggle rang like a string of chimes. "I imagine that it would be someone who hunts down pirates. You can feel free to correct me if you think my instincts are off."

"Right," Eric nodded apologetically. "Of course . . . you probably don't have a book with brief summaries of every known natural-born ability."

"No . . . at least, not yet."

"Wow," Eric finally smiled. "Someone who hunts pirates. A pirate hunter." The look on Charlotte's face suggested that she never tired of watching people's reactions to discovering their abilities. "Well," he declared, "I guess that makes sense why I haven't had a hint of it before. I've never been near a body of water long enough to prove it to myself." He then looked over to Charlotte. "Ah. That's why you were asking all those questions about the lake before."

Charlotte nodded, seeming pleased at how well Eric put it together. Then it came. Eric's newly revived face suddenly became crestfallen. "Pirate hunter . . ."

"Yes," she replied, pushing him to come to the inevitable conclusion.

"Then . . . then, that means I won't be able to ever become what I was born to be. I'm one of those, one of the ones you talked about, that was simply born in the wrong time period." Charlotte said nothing and let him follow his thought process through to the end. Eric shook his head in disbelief. "So, really, nothing has changed at all. I'm still useless. The only difference is that now I know why and I also know that I won't be able to make myself useful."

In the way only Charlotte could, she shook her head condescendingly and said, "Eric, that is ridiculous. If your argument were true then that would mean that most everyone in the history of the world has been useless."

Still skeptical, Eric said, "That's just a nice way of saying, 'Yep, Eric, you're never going to know what it's like to reach your full potential.'"

"Whoever said that you won't know what it's like to reach your full potential?"

"Right, Charlotte. How many towns do you know of nowadays that have problems being pillaged and plundered by pirates on a regular basis?"

"None. Certainly not in our time period."

"Oh, is piracy going to be a big problem in the near future? Am I going to be chasing after pirates in speedboats? While you're looking into the future, could you tell me how many times I'm going to have to take the driving exam?"

Charlotte folded her arms and turned away. "Let me know when you're done making cynical remarks and are ready to listen to me."

Though Eric felt pessimistic, Charlotte had proven to him more than once that his wisest course of action would be to pay attention to her. "Sorry. I'm listening."

"Now, Eric, you've believed everything I've told you so far, haven't you?" Charlotte said as she turned back to him.

Eric paused before responding. There were a lot of sensational things Charlotte had been telling him since he met her, but Eric found that, to his surprise, he could truthfully respond in the affirmative.

"Well, as with before, you're just going to have to trust me with what I'm about to tell you." Eric nodded. Charlotte scrutinized him, then continued, "What if I told you that there is a way for you to actually realize your full potential as a natural-born pirate hunter?"

"I can't see how that's possible, but I'm certainly open to suggestions."

"Eric, what is my natural-born ability?"

"You're a seer. You see other people's natural-born abilities . . . I thought."

Charlotte shook her head. "That's a by-product of being a seer."

"So . . . what can seers do then?"

"I help other people see the potential of their natural-born ability through personal experience."

Eric took a second to think this statement over. "Wait a second. What, exactly, are you saying?"

Charlotte gave another of her mischievous smiles. "I'm saying, Eric, that if you want to travel to a place where you could see what it'd be like to be a pirate hunter, then I can do it."

Eric stared at Charlotte in awe. "You're not kidding, are you?"

Charlotte laughed again. "Eric, how many times do I have to tell you that I am positively serious about this whole thing?"

Before the astonished Eric could respond, his mom pulled up to the curb where they were sitting. "I, uh . . ."

"Come on, Eric," his mom called from the car. "We've got to pick up your sister from gymnastics practice and get home before dinner burns in the oven."

Eric was about to move obediently into the passenger seat of the car when Charlotte grabbed him by the shirt and whispered urgently into his ear, "Eric, think about it, because it can be done. If you agree, then I will first need to know the exact location of your birth and on which phase of the moon you were born."

The best reaction Eric could give to this enigmatic statement before slipping into the car was a nod.

Two nights later, Eric sat on his bike in the middle of an open and dark parking lot, reconsidering his actions. Due to a seemingly point-less purpose of life, Eric came to the conclusion that whether Charlotte could hold true to her word or not, he had nothing to lose in giving it a shot. Now that he thought it over again, however, he knew that he did, in fact, have something to lose. He could lose every scrap of self-worth he had accumulated up until that point in his life if it didn't work. *Oh well*, he thought, *too late to back out now.*

Charlotte pumped her bike up to Eric's side and got out a scrap piece of paper, holding it up to the light from the street lamp a few yards away. "I thought maybe I had gotten the wrong address . . . I didn't know you were born in a parking lot."

"I wasn't born in a parking lot," Eric replied. "This is where the old hospital used to be until they tore it down. Will it be good enough, or do you need to know where the exact room was?"

"No, this is good enough."

Not wanting to seem too distrustful, Eric checked his tone when he asked how she could know for certain.

Charlotte smiled. "The same way you'll know how to catch a pirate. I just know."

For some reason, Charlotte's sense of ease did not comfort Eric. Charlotte apparently decided to keep him talking before he would chicken out of the ordeal entirely because she spoke out, "So you're sure tonight's phase of the moon is the one you were born on?"

"Why does the phase of the moon matter, anyway?" Eric circumvented her question with another one.

"Good question. Who knows? There was a seer back in the 1800s who wrote a book called *Solar Biology* that combined his seer ability with astronomy in a way that inspired a lot of what we now know as modern astrology and tied in the phases of the moon with—"

"Astrology? You're telling me that the guy that helped put horoscopes in the paper is what you're basing all of this moon stuff on?" Eric asked.

"Easy, partner. I'm basing it off of my own ability and experience. As for him, I think his seer science was better than his astronomy skills, so I pay closer attention to the comics page of the newspaper than the horoscope. Still, though, the guy made some interesting points. He theorized that the magnetic pull of the moon during different phases had a formative effect on a newborn's brain at the moment of birth. So, the phase of the moon, combined with other astrological factors at birth, pushes a baby's development toward certain natural-born tendencies."

Eric glanced over to the spot where the moon would be rising at any moment. "Well, who knows if that guy knew what he was talking about . . . but we'll find out if I'm right about my phase of the moon soon enough." Charlotte followed his gaze to the mountain silhouette that hid the moon.

Eric turned back to Charlotte and said, "I was kind of surprised with how easy it was to figure out. I did a little reading on the phases of the moon on the Internet, then I kind of worked it out in my mind. My dad checked it out in the almanac just to make sure, but we're pretty sure I'm correct."

"Of course," Charlotte replied confidently, "knowing the phases of the moon would be practically essential for someone on a sailing ship on the high seas."

As much as Eric wanted to believe the truth of this statement, he held back giving all of his trust to a girl he had known for less than a week. He joked away his doubt. "Either that or I was really naturally born to be the man on the moon."

Charlotte smiled wryly at his attempt at humor, then declared, "Okay, moon man, your home should be coming up any second, so we need to be ready." Charlotte stepped off her bike and motioned him to stand in front of her, then grabbed his hands.

There was what Eric deemed an awkward pause. He tried to remedy the silence. "I was half expecting you to start muttering incantations."

"Nope. No words. In fact, all I really need is to be able to look into your eyes."

"And be touching me . . ." Eric held up one of her hands attached to his.

"Not necessarily. That's only if I plan on coming along for the ride."

"What?"

Charlotte shrugged innocently. "Oh, by the way, I'm going to be tagging along. I've sent a couple of people to experience their natural-born abilities, but I've never actually gone with someone. I'm hardly going to pass up the opportunity to see a natural-born pirate hunter in action, am I? That is, unless you protest."

After all Eric had heard in the past couple of days, this bit of information could hardly impact him too much. He shrugged, then said, "Fine. I'm sure I could use all the help I can get." At this point a shimmering light pierced the darkness of the night as the moon commenced its climb over the horizon. Eric watched it, then looked into Charlotte's eyes for a moment. Nothing happened. He waited a second longer then finally said, "We're still here, Charlotte. If you ask me, you just went through a lot of trouble to meet me in the middle of the night and hold my hand. But, hey, well done. You succeeded." He about released his grip on her hands, but Charlotte squeezed them tightly together.

"Ha," she quipped, followed by her familiar grin. "Don't flatter yourself pirate hunter. We have to wait until the whole moon has risen.

If I was making this all up just to hold your hand, I would have chosen to do it on a night with a new moon so there wouldn't be enough light to see your ugly face."

Charlotte's jab caught Eric completely by surprise. He laughed hard. "Charlotte," he began, but would never finish. The moon had, in that second, cleared the last of the horizon on its ascent into the night sky, its waxing gibbon face seeming to throw an extra silvery sheen about the world beneath it. As soon as this happened, everything dissipated—the star-filled sky, the parking lot, the streetlights, the bikes. Everything but Charlotte, who stood in front of him, and the pale gleam of the moon in his peripheral vision.

Chapter 3
ONBOARD THE ROSEMARY

M an overboard! Man overboard!"

The abrupt shouts startled Samuel out of his sleep—if it could be called sleep. For days, Samuel and the surviving crew members of the *Rosemary* lived in a nightmare. As he stirred, he felt mildly surprised someone actually stood on watch to shout out the alarm. The crew still had assignments, of course, but with life ebbing out of the ship, fewer and fewer had either the energy or will to complete their duties, and Samuel had no desire to enforce those rules.

After stepping out of the captain's cabin, the darkness told him that night had fallen. The time of day hardly mattered though, since time quickly lost more and more meaning to him. As soon as Samuel breached the quarterdeck, the officer of the watch approached him. "Captain, sir! Two persons spotted overboard just off the port stern. I heard the splashing a few moments ago."

Samuel still adjusted to his new title of captain. Considering the circumstances under which he received it, he could not covet it. He reached the port stern and gazed out into the calm cove of the barren island. Behind him he could hear the bustling of other crew members whose curiosity conquered fatigue and who came to investigate the commotion. The light from the waning crescent moon revealed the silhouettes of two forms no more than a ship's length beyond them, between the island and the *Rosemary*.

"Deserters?" Samuel questioned the officer, then without waiting to hear a response, he said loudly enough for the rest of the crew to hear, "Let them have the island then. The accursed plague that gave us all our trouble came from there anyway."

28

"I don't believe they are part of our crew, Captain," the officer spoke hesitantly.

"What?"

"Begging your pardon, Captain, but no one—as far as I could tell—was above decks before I caught sight of them, sir. And ever since I called 'man overboard,' they've been swimming toward the ship, not the island."

"Knew they were caught, and so they turned around to swim back to the ship," Samuel mused to himself.

"I suspect not, sir," the officer mumbled with reserve.

"Well then, explain your reasons and be done with it," Samuel retorted on edge. Neither his body nor mind felt fit for such exertion over a matter he cared little about considering the current state of his crew.

"Well, sir, it's just that I could hear them talking as they came toward us and one of them sounds . . . well, Captain, one of them sounds like a woman."

In spite of his obvious exhaustion, this last statement forced Samuel to perk up. "But we didn't have a woman on board our ship. How could . . . ?"

"Shhh, listen, Captain . . . they're speaking again."

The clear voices carried over the water easily enough to where Samuel and the crew eavesdropped. "This is incredible, Charlotte," one of the voices sputtered between strokes. "If the water didn't taste salty, I'd have thought you knocked me out and threw me into that pond over by County Hall."

"Ha," a silvery voice responded haltingly as the two made progress toward the ship, "I think the pond by the county hall would have a difficult time fitting a boat that size." The officer of the watch dropped all formalities and nudged his captain after Charlotte's reply. Had Samuel not been so surprised to hear a female voice seemingly out of nowhere, he would have chastised the officer. As it was, however, he only furrowed his eyebrows and continued to listen.

"I don't mean to complain, but would it have been too much to ask for us to land directly on the boat instead of a football field away from it?" Besides the difficulty of explaining their mere presence, Samuel and the officer stood mystified by their strange conversation marked by unfamiliar words and accents.

"Oh, Eric, you make it sound like darts or something. You think I control precisely where we land? Maybe it's because you fidgeted so much before the moon came up completely. Or maybe you just needed a good douse of water. This is the first time I've done this too, you know."

"Well, let's just get one thing straight here, I'm not the one who—"

"Here we are," Charlotte cut him off, looking up at the goggling captain, the officer, and the rest of the crew. "Are you going to give us a hand up there, or are you going to sit and stare?" Charlotte's matter-of-fact way of approaching an already indescribable event only did more to freeze the speechless crew. "Look, you can't pretend you don't see us here because we heard the guy call out 'man overboard' . . . though his statement wasn't completely correct, since I'm not a man. I'm willing to overlook that for now."

Samuel wondered for a moment whether he was truly hallucinating, his dehydration coming to a point where he imagined this whole scenario in his mind. He decided that this seemed far too bizarre for his own mind to concoct. Even if he were hallucinating, at least he found comfort knowing that the whole crew hallucinated the same thing as well. A splash from the ever-dauntless Charlotte brought him back to his senses.

"Don't just stand there, fish them out!" Samuel took hope in seeing that the crew's sorry physical state still did not restrain their curiosity. A couple ropes fell into the water and the next thing Samuel knew the two swimmers stood on deck before him. Besides their strange clothing and looks, Samuel noted that the two were surprisingly young.

Although he could tell the crew yearned to know more about the strangers, Samuel felt that discretion would be the best course of action. "I want blankets and dry clothes for these two, and then you will all go back below to get your rest. You two, come with me."

The captain's cabin in the *Rosemary* was not large, so when Eric and Charlotte squeezed in they took up most of the extra space. In the mean time, crew members went to bring clothing. Samuel watched them in amazement for a moment. In spite of her ragged condition, the girl stood with a pleased look on her face, her bearing confident as ever. The boy looked around with interest. His eyes glittered upon seeing the ship's maps and navigating instruments sitting out on the desk.

"My name is Captain Samuel Wesley, and this is the merchant ship *Rosemary*. May I ask whom we had the pleasure of hauling out of the sea?"

The antithesis of bashfulness, Charlotte eagerly gave her and Eric's names. Samuel's next question, however, pressed for the answer that intrigued him most. "And now, if I may ask, how did you end up in the sea between an island and our ship?"

"Well, that's the complicated thing . . ." Eric started out. "You see, when I first met Charlotte, it was—"

". . . on the island," Charlotte finished. Eric looked sharply at Charlotte. Samuel noticed a meaningful look pass between them. "We were both marooned there."

"You were marooned on that island?" Samuel motioned toward the dark mass out the windows of his cabin.

"The very same," Charlotte replied.

"But we've been anchored here for days. The island is not large or with vegetation. It's a wonder we didn't find you before."

Eric sighed while looking back at Charlotte. She refused to flinch. "That's obviously because we were hidden during the day. We didn't want the scorching sun to take away our energy."

Though it was a scanty explanation, before Samuel could follow up, Charlotte continued, "Then while we were looking for more food and water on the island tonight, we saw the light from the ship. You know the rest. Of course, you did keep us in the water a bit longer than necessary, but I'm willing to forget about that as long as I don't spend the rest of the night sopping wet."

The diversion worked. "The men are seeing to it that you get dry clothing, though I regret, Miss Charlotte, that they may not find suitable clothing for a lady such as yourself."

Charlotte did her best not to laugh. "I'll have to make do, I suppose. Though I don't know if it would be too much to ask to get a cup of water with the dry clothing. That seawater sure makes me thirsty."

Samuel smacked his dry mouth just at her request, but before he could offer his apologies, Eric jumped in. "I don't think that's an option, Charlotte. The ship seems to have fewer sailors than it should, and those that it has look sick and weak. They're probably pretty low on food and water."

Taken aback at this statement, Samuel took a second before nodding to confirm. Yet even Eric seemed puzzled by his own response, as if
he did not expect to have made it. Only Charlotte seemed unsurprised.
She smiled. Samuel finally found his tongue. "Um . . . that is precisely
the issue at hand. I wish I could say that we rescued you from that
island, but we happen to be in quite the predicament ourselves." Samuel
focused on Eric. "You noticed the state of the crew. The sad thing is
that they are the ones who survived. Over half the crew was taken by a
disease that came as a result of some infected water we took from this
island . . . I see that you were not affected by it . . ." Samuel raised his
eyebrow.

"Luckily we had some fresh water with us when we were marooned,
but we just ran out of the last of it when we saw your ship," Charlotte
was quick to answer. "But that's terrible about your crew. Is there no
place nearby where we can get help?"

Samuel sighed. "That is where the problem compounds. We stopped
at this island because we were driven away from the only port of refuge,
a day away."

"Driven away?" Charlotte asked. "How?"

"A storm," Eric suddenly jumped in again, much to his own surprise. "You must have run into a storm. The broken stuff on the deck of
the ship suggests that you went through some bad weather."

Once again, Eric's comment caused Samuel to pause and wonder
at this boy's insight. "Actually, we did hit a storm to the east . . . gales
of the like I've never seen before . . . that storm must have been what
marooned you on the island. Am I right?" His query left Eric tongue-
tied. Samuel noted the delay, though he moved on without a reply.
"Well, no matter. The storm was actually not what kept us from the
port. We were chased and barely avoided being captured by a pirate
guarding the channel leading to port."

At the sound of the word "pirate," Charlotte glanced over at Eric,
who returned the gaze with widened eyes. The intriguing silence that
followed eventually broke with a knock at the door. The clothes for
Charlotte and Eric had arrived. Samuel directed them to separate quarters where they could change. Then he gave orders to see that the crew
members provided them with places to sleep.

As soon as she changed into her dry clothes, Charlotte searched out Eric. He wore a dark jacket and pants over a tunic that must have been white before time faded it into a grainy yellow. He pulled his similar-colored socks up to his knees to compensate for the pants, which only reached to the middle of his shins, in the way of most sailor clothing. His black, scuffed shoes enveloped the bottom of his socks. Although the clothing clearly belonged to a larger person, Charlotte noticed that Eric seemed more comfortable in it than in his own clothes. She saw that, even though his shoulders still sagged slightly, Eric appeared somehow taller. "Well . . . ?" Charlotte asked.

Eric shrugged. "I don't know. You look good, though the pants are a little big." The large pants and tunic rested broadly on her, but she donned them as if someone tailored them specifically for her. She had used a stray rope to tie down the extra fabric near her waist in a way that looked almost fashionable.

"I'm not talking about clothes, Eric," Charlotte responded.

"What?"

"You heard him mention a pirate . . . well, now is your chance."

Eric shook his head. "Charlotte, I'll admit this: as soon as we stepped onto this ship it felt like . . . oh, I don't know how to describe it . . . it was amazing. It felt like coming home. I noticed things, I had a feel for things, I . . . I just felt at home. So, I believe that I was naturally born to at least have something to do with sailing ships. But no one, not even a natural-born pirate hunter, would be dumb enough to go against a pirate in a little ship like this the way it is now." Eric saw that Charlotte verged on disagreeing, so he cut her off. "Even with a full crew and no damage done to the ship, this is just a little trading boat. She probably has a couple guns at the most. It's mind-blowing that they outran the pirate to this point. This ship was not made for hunting. If anything, it's made for being hunted. That is not just my opinion as a teenager; that's my opinion as . . . well, as a natural-born pirate hunter."

Charlotte acquiesced to Eric's convincing statement. "Well then, where does that leave us? Are we just going to sit and wither away with this crew? Have we no other options? Frankly, I expected a bit more than a slow and painful death when I decided to come with you, Eric."

"Maybe if you would have dropped us off in a situation more friendly to a pirate hunter's needs . . ."

"It doesn't work that way, Eric. What did you expect? Did you expect to be transported straight to the wheel of a huge ship with a crew already prepared and a helpless pirate right in front of you waiting to be caught?" Eric thought on this and then shook his head slowly. Charlotte continued, "No, I hope not . . . if that were the case, then I could be the pirate hunter, pretty much anyone could. You are given the opportunity, but it's up to you to take advantage of it. As you've already been told, there's a pirate in the area. Now it's up to you to do something about it."

Eric threw up his hands. "Well, I've already told you that it can't be done with this ship and this crew. I don't know what you expect me to do."

"Expect you to do?" Charlotte restated, a little frustrated, "Eric, you may not be able to hunt a pirate right now, but you know what I do expect you to do?" Eric shook his head and Charlotte replied, "Be useful."

This declaration forced Eric to think. Humbled, he responded, "Okay, you're right. Doing nothing isn't helping a thing. I don't know what kind of use I can be, but I'll go to the captain and figure out what's going on. Then I'll see if there is anything I could help him with."

Charlotte smiled. "That's all I'm asking."

When Eric approached the captain's cabin he saw no light. He about retreated, but he almost heard Charlotte's reprimanding tone ask him why he didn't even try, so he reluctantly set himself before the door and knocked.

"Yes?" a faint voice called out from within.

"Sorry to disturb you, Captain. I can talk to you in the morning if that works better."

A pause ensued long enough that Eric backed away from the door. Suddenly the latch opened and a weak, pale looking Samuel stuck his face out. "Master Eric?" Eric nodded and much to his surprise, the captain opened the door and motioned him in. "What can I do for you?"

"Oh, I didn't want to keep you from sleeping . . . I just kind of wondered if you could show me the situation we're in right now on a map or something. I can talk to you tomorrow morning."

Samuel probably would have laughed had he not lacked so much energy. "I wasn't sleeping, Master Eric. I haven't slept much lately."

"You haven't?"

"No. In fact, I keep on thinking about exactly what you came to ask me about, and I keep on finding myself in another dead end. I would welcome a fresh viewpoint."

Eric shook his head. "I really doubt I could help with anything, but I am kind of curious to see what's going on."

"Then come over to my desk." Samuel shuffled to his maps and instruments and lit a lamp. Had Eric studied Samuel carefully in the pale lamplight, he would have seen a tall man in a crumpled officer's uniform, curly dark hair that matched his chocolate complexion—a Creole in looks and an Englishman in manners. But Eric found little interest in the man standing next to him, only in the map that lay before him. He instantly devoured it with his eyes as if he feared it might disappear any second. Samuel observed Eric before almost apologetically disrupting his trance.

"As near as I can gather, we are here," Samuel pointed to an empty space on the map, "anchored next to a previously uncharted island. It's small enough to have evaded some maps. Port Raleigh is to the west, here." Samuel's finger slid across the map to where the continent's main land met the sea. "Of course, our problem is that to get to Port Raleigh, it's necessary to go through the San Fernando Channel, between the mainland and the Montes de Oca island chain." Slightly to the north and east of Port Raleigh, Eric noted that the land came out into a sharp peninsula that was abruptly interrupted by San Fernando Channel. Past the channel, along the same line as the peninsula, the land continued in the form of five or so islands, the biggest of the islands being the one closest to the mainland's peninsula. Everywhere between the islands, except in the channel, Eric noticed scattered dots and faint, curving lines in the sea. Before he could say anything, Samuel answered his unasked question. "These right here represent shoals . . . impassable. As you can see they extend north from the Montes de Oca for a little more than thirty leagues."

Eric nodded, completely immersed in the map. "That's why Port Raleigh has such a strong position. It's easy to defend."

"Precisely," Samuel said, "but in this case, it works against itself. If there is an enterprising and clever enough pirate, he can close off shipping to Raleigh completely."

Eric pointed to San Fernando Channel. "All he has to do is camp out right here and wait for the ships to come to him." Samuel nodded. Eric furrowed his eyebrow. "But Port Raleigh should be prepared for that sort of thing by having some war ships on hand to protect the town. That would have to be one brave pirate."

"Brave, yes, but I think I would better describe them as bold."

"Them?"

"Yes. The pirates blocking off San Fernando Channel are the Willard Pirates, twin brothers alike not only in looks but in their notorious reputations. Only someone such as those two would have the capability of gathering enough force and instigating enough fear to pull off something such as this."

"Pirate twins . . ." Eric muttered to himself quietly. Suddenly he could feel a strange sensation of excitement, thrill in his blood. It was unlike anything he had ever experienced before. More than anything, he wanted to go out and face these pirates. He wanted to go out and catch them, anticipate their cruel deeds, outsmart them, and place them in chains and bring them to justice. The thoughts stirred within him for a moment before he recovered his senses. He had to remind himself of what he had just argued to Charlotte: he didn't have the resources to face these pirates. He redirected his thoughts to figure out how to get the *Rosemary* back to port where there should be enough resources needed for such a venture. He scanned the map with new purpose.

"So Port Raleigh is the closest settlement?"

"It's Port Raleigh or nothing, considering our stores and the crew's physical state."

"And the only way to Port Raleigh is through the San Fernando Channel here?"

Samuel shrugged. "If we were to circumnavigate the island chain and shoals, there is a passage to the north, but—"

"But that passage would most likely be covered by the pirates as well," Eric nodded sagely, finishing Samuel's statement for him. Samuel could not help but be impressed by this boy's insight. Eric continued,

"Even if they weren't covering that passage, they wouldn't necessarily have to. Whoever watched the San Fernando Channel could also keep an eye on the north passage. It'd be a simple matter to just spot them coming and cut them off."

"Yes, but I'd wager they do have someone patrolling the north passage anyway. The Willard Twins have traveled in larger fleets lately. They would have enough ships to cover both entries."

Eric smiled and nodded. "These pirates certainly know what they're doing. How many ships, then, do you think they have?"

Samuel thought for a moment. "Three or four. They wouldn't need any more than that. There would only be one or two Royal Navy ships stationed in Port Raleigh at any given time. So four ships, plus their reputation, would be enough to contain that threat. Any more ships than that would be too many men to divide plunder with."

Eric nodded. "So the Twins would be captains of two of the ships and two other pirates in the others."

"Right."

Eric realized something. "That means the two junior pirates will probably be doing the patrolling. One of them here at San Fernando Channel and the other at the north passage. The Twins only need to be in a single place to keep an eye on things." Samuel looked on, intrigued, as Eric worked this through in his mind. "What better place than this first island in the Montes de Oca chain? It puts them right in the center of the action. They can leave it and be to either of the channels at a moment's notice, plus they can keep an eye on the junior pirates." Eric's eyes glittered. "That cove on the far side of the island looks like it would be just about right. Maybe big enough for the egos of two pirate brothers and their ships."

Samuel cracked a smile through his dry lips. "Bravo, Eric. I couldn't have deduced it better myself."

Eric permitted himself a self-congratulatory smile before he fell back into his pensive mode. "Of course, that still hasn't fixed our problem."

"No, it hasn't. In fact, it furthers the case that we are in more of a bind than even before."

"But . . ." Eric thought out loud, ". . . but we do know where they are most likely anchored, and that helps."

"We'll need more than just that kind of advantage," Samuel remarked grimly. "Even with a full crew and an undamaged ship, we'd be sitting ducks for any one of those pirate ships, let alone four of them."

"Yes, you're right . . . we wouldn't stand a chance going head-to-head with the pirates. But the ship isn't in too bad of shape. I saw things scattered around, but the ship itself appears to be okay, and it seems to have a fast design. With a head start, it might be able to outrun the pirates. You outran the ship guarding the channel, didn't you?"

"Well, yes, but in that case we were running away from the pirates . . . not attempting to run through them."

Eric pressed further, "But what if we caught them off guard?"

"I don't know how we could accomplish that when they know there are only two ways to get to Port Raleigh and they're already guarding both of them."

Eric nodded and carefully pored over the map in front of him before venturing a question. "What about these shoals?" He pointed to the shoals connecting the Montes de Oca island chain. "There has to be a way through them. I mean, you can't tell me that along this huge stretch there isn't a single spot where the *Rosemary* could slip by."

Samuel thought for a moment. "The shoals are not well-known since the two channels are obviously the most practical ways in and out. But . . . but I wouldn't doubt that there are several breaks in the shoals. Especially at this point, closest to the main island," Samuel indicated the spot just north of the biggest island of the chain. "The map depicts the shoals as relatively skinny there, giving more likelihood for breaks." Eric's eyes lit up, but Samuel did not seem to share his enthusiasm. "While that may be the case, it does not improve our situation at all."

"Except that if we get through there, we can catch them off guard."

"Off guard maybe, but not in an advantageous spot. While it places us west of most of the pirates, it will also place us north of at least three of the ships . . . and we would still need to go south to reach Port Raleigh." Eric was quiet. "It's a good idea though—nearly worth a shot."

"Wait," Eric said, and pointed to the island on the map. "If the Twins have their base in this cove, then they probably wouldn't see us until we'd be pretty much past them."

Samuel looked at the map, nodding slowly. "You may be right . . . but that's not certain. And besides, you're forgetting the ship that we do know about, here in the San Fernando Channel. That ship would have plenty of time to spot us and cut us off. Even if the rogue doesn't keep his eye on the west, which he probably does, one of the Twins could fire a cannon to alert him once they spot us from the cove."

"Right," Eric conceded, though his morale stayed high. "But if everything else is true, then we only need to get past that last ship before we're home free."

Samuel paused to marvel at the confidence of this fascinating stranger. "I'm guessing you think that you have a way to do that?"

Eric's smile broadened.

Chapter 4
SHOOTING THE GAP

S amuel had not seen the *Rosemary* in full sail for days, but it felt like months. He never would have imagined before last night that the following day he would see his ragged crew setting sails and fixing rigging. That accounted for only one of the several amazing things that had happened since last night. Samuel knew that he owed it all to the strange arrival of Charlotte, that girl who seemed afraid of nothing, but most especially to the keen-minded enigma, Eric.

Samuel watched the young man pace around the quarterdeck with a contagious excitement that penetrated the whole ship. Bemused, Samuel struggled to make any sense of the situation. While the boy undoubtedly wielded impressive instincts for seamanship, it appeared as if he had never been on a ship before in his life. As he helped them get underway this morning, he made suggestions without knowing the name of any of the things he referred to. Samuel wondered whether the young man was putting on an act. It seemed impossible for him to have no experience at sea and suddenly make all these informed nautical deductions and competent suggestions. Even as Samuel considered this, he realized that—act or no—Samuel had nothing to lose by listening to him, and Eric certainly had nothing to gain by sticking with the *Rosemary* through such unfavorable odds. This last thought caused Samuel to question whether Eric really understood the potential consequences of his plan. He stood next to him.

"You do realize, Master Eric, that by acting on your plan, we are depending on a lot of variables. Everything we've speculated will have to be correct, and even then, everything else will have to go perfectly if we have any chance of surviving this."

Eric nodded. "You don't have to go through with this, Captain Wesley."

Samuel looked back to the fading island where a disturbing amount of his crew had died. "Well, frankly, the alternative isn't very tempting."

"For what it's worth, Captain, if anything does go wrong, you can put all the blame on me."

Samuel smiled. "You've got yourself a bargain. However, you should know that if we do somehow succeed, then I'd be obliged to give you all the credit."

Eric grinned. "Well, we would have to get to that point first."

Charlotte finally found a moment when Eric had a break from making suggestions in preparation for what lay ahead of them. "My goodness, Eric," she said, "I don't know what you told the captain last night, but it sure put this ship in an uproar."

"Yes. In fact, we'd have left by now, but we found out that flood tide will be a little after midday. That would give us the best chance for passing over the shoals, so we decided not to leave until later this morning."

Charlotte contained her grin. "Look at you, Eric. You seem right at home here. Are you glad you decided to come?"

Eric tried not to smile, but it broke through. "I'll tell you at the end of the day." Then his face turned serious. "But really, Charlotte, what we're doing right now is the final resort. The chances of success are kind of slim. So, if you have the ability to go back, now is the time."

"What about you?"

Eric shook his head. As he and Samuel worked out details and the crew sparked to new life, Eric had considered the danger of his situation. It was strangely real—a danger he had never before known in his sheltered life—and for a few moments, it worried him. But then he heard the clank of rope and tackle and felt the stirring of the early morning breeze, and he thought about the pirates out there needing to be brought in. There was no way he could back down now. He might as well try suppressing the winds of a hurricane. "I'm staying. It wouldn't feel right to send them into this mess without coming along."

"They'll get along fine, Eric. These guys are sailors. They'll understand if you go."

Eric shook his head again. "I know they're sailors, but I'm afraid they won't understand the plan I have in mind . . . I mean, I've explained it, but I don't know if they'll be able to pull it off without me to help them."

Charlotte's eyes twinkled. "You mean . . . you consider yourself useful?"

Eric nodded reluctantly. "Yes. I guess you could say that. But that still doesn't mean the danger isn't real. So, Charlotte, please, I'd feel better if you would go back now. And maybe you could find a way to make up a story about me being gone to my parents until I'm through here."

Charlotte put on a mock look of dismay. "Not even a day into our adventure and you're already trying to get rid of me. Is my company that bad, Eric?"

"You know that's not true. I just feel responsible for you."

"Well, don't. You weren't the one who got us here. That was me. I'm sticking around whether you like it or not for a couple of reasons. First of all, I wouldn't miss this excitement for the world, and second of all, I can't leave . . . and neither can you."

"What do you mean?"

"I mean I don't have the ability to send us back home. At least, not yet."

Eric could not help but show a little bit of distress. "You don't? You mean I'll never see my home and family again?"

"Settle down, Eric. Don't be ridiculous. I wouldn't have whisked you away from your family for all time without at least a warning. What I mean is that I won't be able to send either of us home until the moon reaches the reciprocal phase to the one we used to travel here last night."

"Reciprocal phase?"

"The phase you were born on is the one that sends you, the phase opposite of that is the one that brings you back—reciprocal phase."

Eric nodded and then did some calculations in his head. "But that's not for another two weeks . . ."

"Very good calculating, Eric, though I was already familiar with how long it takes for the moon to reciprocate its cycle."

"So you have to stick around with me for two weeks before we can go home again? What will my family say?"

"They might wonder why you got a tan in the hour or so since you were gone, but they won't think much else beyond that.

"What?" While not fazed by the proximity of two ruthless pirate twins, Eric felt himself starting to dismay over Charlotte's confusing calmness at this new information.

"When we go and come by the reciprocal phases of the moon, it brings us back full circle, time-wise, to where we started. No more than a few minutes or hours will have passed when we come back."

Eric calmed down a bit more at this clarification. "Wait," he followed up. "When you sent other people but didn't go yourself, how did this work?"

"The same, I just didn't hold their hands. They would disappear, and I had to wait in that same spot for them to work out their two weeks. For me, though, I usually only had to wait for less than an hour before I felt their tug and could stare where they would be standing seconds later." Charlotte suppressed a yawn, as if these engrossing details were boring her.

"If I hadn't just left a parking lot and landed in an ocean twelve hours ago, I would have thought you were crazy," Eric said. "But I have to admit, you sure sound like you know what you're doing."

Charlotte rolled her eyes. "Thank you for your strong endorsement! By the way, since we're on the subject, I hope that your sailor mind can remember the coordinates to that little island we just left, because we have to return to that same spot too for it to work."

For some reason Eric felt assured that he could find the island again, coordinates or not. Though more at ease, Eric remembered something. "When were you planning on telling me this? Now you have to risk going up against these pirates with the rest of us."

Charlotte pursed her lips. "Eric, you don't possibly think that I would have chickened out of this. If you'll kindly recall, I am the one who knew this whole time what I was doing. Besides," she smiled, "it's hardly a risk with you running the show."

Eric stood stunned at Charlotte's stubbornness. "I hate to tell you this, but with or without me, it's going to take a miracle to get out of this without being captured . . . or killed."

"I guess I will have to continue to be the one who has faith in you, since you're unable to do that yourself."

"Charlotte, you have no idea what—"

"Sail ho!"

Immediately, Eric stopped talking and maneuvered himself to see past the *Rosemary* into the ocean waters beyond. Samuel joined him in a matter of seconds. The mainland peninsula now came into view to the southwest. Just to the north, the first island of the Montes de Oca island chain crept over the horizon. Almost directly in the middle of the two pieces of land, Samuel and Eric spotted a white object that would soon show itself to be the patrolling pirate ship inside the San Fernando Channel. The crew stood at their stations, watching with a reverenced silence. They knew what the ship meant. They also knew that this time they would have no retreat to the east.

Charlotte, who feigned disinterest at first, posed a question to Eric. "Why isn't he sailing straight for us? I can tell he's getting closer, but he keeps on going back and forth."

Eric did not take his eyes off the ship. "He can't come straight for us. The wind is coming from directly behind us and he can't sail into the wind. The only way he can approach us is by sailing at angles into the wind, back and forth."

"Beating into the wind," Samuel jumped into the conversation.

"Beating," Eric repeated, as if committing it to memory.

Something must have dawned on Charlotte. "Oh, I see. You are going to take advantage of the wind direction, keep getting closer, then as soon as the pirates turn one direction, you try to rush past them on the other side."

Samuel smiled. "You're not the only one to have a pretty good eye for sailing, Master Eric."

Eric smiled as well, then turned to Charlotte. "That's what we want them to think we're doing."

Charlotte, who had happily believed she guessed their strategy, deflated. "Why aren't you really going to do it? Won't it work?"

Samuel fielded her question. "Don't take it too hard, Miss Charlotte. It is a good strategy, and had we no other option, we would most likely attempt it. But look." Samuel lifted his finger up and pointed to the ship, which was now coming closer and closer. "See how, even as he is sailing back and forth, he is edging toward the south?"

Charlotte squinted. "Yes, I see it. What does that mean?"

"It means," Eric jumped in, "that they want to force us to pass them on the north side. They could stop us either way, but they aren't taking any chances. They're making sure that even if we got a little past them, they'd still be between us and Port Raleigh, which is to the south past the peninsula. Then they'd have to sail alongside us until we tried to move south."

Charlotte worked this out in her mind. "Then if we aren't going to speed past them, how do we plan on getting to Port Raleigh?"

"If we can't sail through them," Eric answered, "then we'll have to sail around them."

The three observed the pirate ship approach, every time sliding just a little bit more to the south, subtly opening the channel to the north. As the pirate ship took one final turn to the south, Eric looked at Samuel, who then ordered the coxswain to attempt a pass of the pirate ship on its north side.

The pirate ship responded to the maneuver and the race was on—they breached the point of no return. The pirates clearly anticipated their tactic because they instantly flipped their course to the south and ran parallel with the *Rosemary*. "Well," Eric remarked, "it looks as if they are taking the bait."

Samuel stood with him. "The question is whether the bait will get away."

"I'm sorry," Charlotte jumped in. "I don't mean to interrupt this mysterious talk between you two, but if I understand correctly, you have successfully guessed that they'd guess this move. What, then, did you guess we'd do from here? Even I can tell that the pirates have cut off our southern passage to Port Raleigh."

"Right about now, they believe we're figuring out our mistake," Eric explained. "They'll start to close in on us and leave us few options but to go to the north. Our job is to get them to believe they're close enough to catch us."

Charlotte nodded. "That'd open up the San Fernando Channel because you'll have drawn them away from it. Okay, I can see that. But how do you plan on getting past them into the empty channel? That leaves us in the same predicament as before."

"Not if we don't plan on going through the channel," Eric replied.

"What other options do we have? Flying?"

"Well, that would be nice . . . we're not exactly sure of our other options. We'll see what they are when we get there."

Charlotte gave Eric an impatient look. "What is that supposed to mean?"

"See the first island in the Montes de Oca island chain?" he pointed to the green mass of land to the west and slightly north. Charlotte nodded. "The plan is to go around that."

"But I thought there were reefs there or something. That's why San Fernando Channel was the only way in and out."

Eric nodded. "We're hoping that there aren't reefs the whole way."

Charlotte thought about this for a moment. "But what if there are? What if there's no way through?" Eric was silent. Charlotte thought it through. "Then that pirate ship would be right behind us . . . there'd be no escape."

"So let's hope there is a way through those shoals."

"You're risking everything on the slight chance that we can get through shoal-infested waters?" Eric never witnessed a distressed Charlotte—this was as close as he would get. "Are you sure you know what you're doing?"

For some reason, though under normal circumstances he might, he did not panic. "You know what? I think I do."

"Yeah, unless you can't get us past that reef."

Eric grinned and then shrugged his shoulders.

"Now what is that supposed to mean? You little—"

"Captain," Mr. Gary called out from the quarterdeck, "she's getting awfully close. We'll be within range at any moment. Should we start runnin' north?"

Samuel about replied, but then Charlotte noted with interest that he glanced over to Eric. Eric did not say anything, but he gave an almost imperceptible shake of the head. Samuel turned back to Mr. Gary. "Not yet. Hold your course. We want to make sure they follow us."

Mr. Gary nodded after a moment's hesitation, bringing his spyglass back up to his eye. Samuel tried to show restraint, but he tensed visibly as he watched the ship coming closer and closer. Suddenly a puff of smoke emitted from the pursuing ship.

"Here comes one, sir," Mr. Gary stated nervously. The whistle of the cannonball's approach followed the crack of the opening shot. The splash a couple ship lengths short showed that they raced still out of reach. "Now, sir?"

Samuel could not help but glance once again back to Eric. This time Eric spoke out, "Let them get a whiff of us first, Mr. Gary. We don't want them to march back to their post."

Minutes that felt like hours to Samuel and Mr. Gary dragged on. They spent the whole time in an uncomfortable silence, both of them fidgeting and glancing back to Eric. Eric, for his part, put on an admirable show of patience, almost indifferent to the situation.

Another puff of smoke came from the pirate ship. This time the sound afterward followed it much closer. The scream of the ball approaching brought a shout, and everyone on deck threw themselves down. Everyone except for Eric and Charlotte standing next to him. The splash landed close enough that water scattered on the deck. The captain and first mate, realizing the shot missed, picked themselves up, still somewhat shaken, but marveling at Eric's dauntless pose.

Eric waited for a second longer, then looked at Samuel and nodded. Samuel immediately barked out orders for the coxswain to swing directly north. The crew responded, and before the next shot came, they no longer headed west.

"Lovely day for a sail," Charlotte said, attempting to break the tension now that they found themselves temporarily in the clear.

Eric nodded, not really listening. He walked to the back of the quarterdeck and watched the pirate ship. Samuel joined him. "I doubt they thought twice about not following us," Samuel said. "No self-respecting pirate would back down from any ship after getting as close as they are now, no matter what orders they might have otherwise."

The pirate ship's actions confirmed Samuel's statement, changing course so as to swerve just behind the *Rosemary*'s stern. Eric eyed the pirate ship for a couple seconds, as if convincing himself they would not make an abrupt turn around, then nodded. "Well, the channel is now open, if only we can get to the other side to take advantage of it."

The two ships cruised in line, racing northward with the main island of the Montes de Oca to the west of them. Slowly but surely, Eric had the coxswain angling more and more toward the north edge of the island. At first Samuel feared that they had allowed the pirates to get too close to them, but soon he recognized that the *Rosemary* outdistanced the rival ship. In fact, after gaining a few ship lengths, Eric had the crew discreetly draw back on sails. They took care to only shorten sails out of view from the pirates, lest their pursuers suspected the ruse. The pirates, for their part, showed no signs of suspicion. They eagerly pressed forward, sensing their prey just within their grasp.

With the pirate ship now only a secondary concern, Samuel trained his eye on the approaching shoals. The first Montes de Oca island flattened out to the north until it converted to a long, sandy spit that eventually disappeared in the sea. The shallow nature of the sea at that point manifested itself clearly, even from a distance. Samuel observed the white foam from waves crashing all up and down the submerged reef. These white caps traced in a long line north, every now and then building up into small and scattered coral islands, before finally meeting up with the second island in the Montes de Oca island chain a little more than three leagues farther up.

As they approached the seemingly impenetrable wall, Samuel noted the unease of the crew. Samuel scanned the shoals for any signs of a break. Though he identified where the shoals narrowed, he failed to perceive any hint of passage.

The coxswain also watched with his keen eyes. It flew against his instinct to sail headlong toward shoals, seeing as how he spent his entire maritime career learning to avoid them. After some unsure moments the coxswain finally asked, "What part of the shoals should I be headin' for, Captain?"

The recent confidence Samuel gained from tricking the pirates began to deflate as he faced the possibility of sailing into a dead end. Rather than blame Eric when it did little good at this point, he instead asked for Eric's opinion. Eric, also scrutinizing the approaching reef, shook his head. "We'll have to get closer. I can't tell yet."

The minutes, once again, dragged on. All eyes glued themselves to the thrashing white foam spuming above the shoals just in front of them. Samuel and the anxious coxswain periodically glanced at Eric, but Eric refused to return their looks. "Take us a little more south," he muttered after an extended silence.

Samuel swiveled south. "Do you see a break?"

"No, but I'm sure there isn't one north."

The ship fell silent after the adjustment. The shoals loomed closer. During this time someone cried out that the pirates had backed off.

Samuel waited until he could not delay longer. "Master Eric, we tried. We knew this would be part of the risk."

Eric's eyes squinted. He licked his lips in concentration. "Eric?" Charlotte asked.

"There," Eric said intently, pointing. "Right there is the break."

Everyone swung their heads to where he pointed, but they saw nothing more than the same monotonous, white-crested waves. "I don't see it, Master Eric," Samuel said. Though he tried to hide it, skepticism seeped through his statement.

Eric refused to be fazed. "It's there. There is a line of shoals in front of the main section. That's why the reef looks continuous, but you can slip into it from the north. I don't know if it will take us all the way through though."

Samuel returned his gaze to the breakers. It all looked the same to him from that distance. He could not tell the difference.

"I know it's tough to see, Captain Wesley, but you have to believe me. I can guide us through it if you would like."

Samuel could not be sure whether Eric simply saw what he wanted to see or if he truly pinpointed a gap. In the end, he shrugged. "It's either that or returning to the awaiting arms of our friends back there." He gestured toward the pirates, who had pulled back into the wind, watching carefully. "I'm sure they expect us to turn back any second now because they see what I see." Samuel took a deep breath. "Go for it, Master Eric."

Eric swung into action. "Let's slow down. Tie up some of the sails! Coxswain, go straight for now. I'll head to the front of the boat and call out instructions. I need you to trust me and obey every order exactly. Do you understand?"

The coxswain glanced nervously between Eric and Samuel. "But, sir," he addressed Samuel, "If we run the *Rosemary* aground, even if she don't sink right away, we'll be sittin' ducks for them pirates. They won't even have to board us, they can just come close as they dare and shoot us ter pieces."

Samuel's response was concise. "You will obey this young man's every word to the letter." He waited for a moment to let the order sink in, and then added, "Because no matter what course we take, we'll end up a prize for either the sea or these pirates. This young man is the only option we have left, so we're trusting him unequivocally."

"Aye-aye, Captain Wesley."

Eric imparted a nod of gratitude to Samuel before rushing to the forecastle. He climbed onto the bowsprit for a view of what lay ahead. Then he turned back and called to the quarterdeck. "Hold your course perfectly straight, then when I give the word take her hard south! Don't hesitate a second. The turn has to be complete!" Eric turned back and monitored the *Rosemary*'s progress. Seconds passed in agonizing silence. Samuel tracked the approach to the reef and felt the urge to close his eyes. *Any moment now*, he thought to himself. Crashing waves roared in their ears. Their proximity surpassed reality. Any captain sensed the unnatural position of navigating a ship that close to shoals. Then the reef surged up on the larboard side of the ship. Samuel could actually see the rocky corals underneath the flood tide waters, and they just barely skimmed along its side. In front of them, as far as he could see, the shoals pitted the sea. *Any second now*, he told himself again. He braced for the crash.

"Now!" Eric hollered from the bowsprit.

The jittery coxswain swung the wheel for all he was worth. The ship creaked and moaned in response. Samuel dared to look and saw a small path open up in front of them as they turned into it. His sigh of relief only lasted until he asked himself how long the path could last, how long before it simply closed off into the rest of the shoals.

"Southwest when I say!" Eric's shout interrupted Samuel's thought process. The coxswain deferred impatiently, unnerved by the shoals fencing in the *Rosemary*.

"Now!"

Once again the coxswain slid the wheel and the *Rosemary* responded. Samuel saw another path open up in front of them. They hardly settled on this new course for a dozen seconds before it gave way into a nice, open space. While nice to have the breathing room, Samuel noted they only cleared a section of the shoals and had more in front and to the sides of them. He figured that the coxswain felt temporary reprieve as well, judging by the blood returning to his knuckles on the helm.

"West again, please," Eric's orders carried across the ship.

The short-lived relief built into renewed tension as the next line of shoals approached. The coxswain muttered something to Samuel, but he did not hear it. He focused, instead, on Eric's next instructions.

"Next turn to the south-south-west when I say."

The whole crew stood in anticipation. "Now!"

The new line of shoals approached. Samuel waited once more for the sickening crunch of the ship hitting ground, but again the shoals passed along both sides of the ship as a type of spectral threat without even grazing the hull.

Three commands later and the crew saw the open sea on the other side. They held their breaths, as if worried that one exhale too many might ruin their good fortune. After a final swerve to the west, they thought they saw a clear passage to the other side. The path appeared to widen, to open up. The coxswain sighed, wiping a sweaty palm on his trousers. Some of the crew stirred again. Samuel felt confident enough to glance back.

"Wait!" Eric's voice pierced the deck. "The very edge of the path is blocked off!" Samuel took in a sharp breath and squinted his eyes to the edge of the shoals. The sun glinted off the water at an angle that kept him from confirming Eric's claim, but the young man had no reason to lie. The path was blocked. They had failed.

Eric must have sensed their despair, because he spoke out across the silence. "But there has to be an opening somewhere. I'm guessing these paths were made from seawater moving back and forth, so it has to be like a river emptying from one body of water to another . . ." Samuel wanted to believe Eric, but even if it were true, their time ran low. Eric yelled out as he scanned the reef on all sides, "Keep an eye out for— hang on a second!"

The screech in Eric's voice betrayed his excitement. "There's a small channel turning off to the west-north-west coming up. It looks like it . . . yes . . . it should take us the rest of the way! But we'll have to enter it perfectly. Listen carefully, and I'll guide you. There's a slight bend in the channel, so we'll have to be very careful. Wait for my exact instructions on when to turn. Understood?" Eric's voice started turning hoarse from yelling, but he displayed an acute calmness that belied the situation.

The coxswain immediately craned his neck to peer over the starboard side of the *Rosemary*. "Captain, he's lost his mind, sir. There's no channel there."

Samuel looked for himself.

"Is that understood?" Eric repeated his original question.

"You see what I'm saying, Captain?" the coxswain said. "I think we best hold our present course." Samuel did not respond.

No one answered Eric.

"Captain," an upset Charlotte postulated, "aren't you going to answer Eric?"

Samuel felt torn. "Miss Charlotte," he said quietly, "I can't see anything."

Charlotte fumed. "Do you mean to tell me that after all Eric's done today, you're going to ignore him now at the most critical time?" Samuel could not even look into Charlotte's eyes. "I never took you for a fool, Captain Wesley," she said, then turned on her heels and shouted out to the forecastle, "They won't listen to you, Eric!"

Eric perked up, as if about to reply, then he turned and surveyed their course again. Having gauged the situation, he agilely hopped onto the deck and raced to the quarterdeck. As soon as he climbed the stairs he wasted no time speaking. He simply ran to the wheel, shoved the unsuspecting coxswain aside and gripped the helm. For a split second he waited, then he gave the wheel a precise turn and held it. The *Rosemary* careened straight for the reef. Samuel and the rest of the crew braced for impact—but it never came.

As soon as Samuel dared open his eyes, he blinked to ensure he really was not seeing things. From all appearances, the *Rosemary* floated across the shoals. Eric said nothing as he coolly held the wheel as if he had been born with it in his fingers. "How in the devil . . . ?" Samuel mumbled to himself, wondering if they were caught up in some sort of black magic.

"The channel is super narrow, Captain. It has just enough room for the *Rosemary* to fit between her, but not the width of the deck, only the width of the ship lower down, where it meets the water. That's why it looks like we're sailing straight over the shoals."

"That's . . . that's impossible. Why, going off course a foot, maybe even inches, would put us aground."

Eric nodded while gripping the wheel firmly. "That's why holding her steady is kind of important."

Samuel marveled for a moment before he realized something. "Wait. Didn't you say there was a bend in the channel?"

"Yes."

"Well, then you'll need someone up in the forecastle to warn you when we get to it. If you don't turn exactly with the curve, we'll be at the mercy of the reef."

"No need, Captain," Eric said. For all his confidence, he was not boasting.

"What?"

"I saw the channel myself. I know when to turn. Someone else would only confuse me."

"But—"

Eric suddenly pushed up on the wheel a couple spokes, paused for a long second, then slowly pulled down on it, performing a deliberate turn over the next dozen seconds. All the while the shoals sped past the very seams of the *Rosemary*'s sides. Then, almost as abruptly as they entered the shoals, the menacing threat disappeared from all around them, and they found themselves gliding across the open water.

For a moment, the crew hesitated, allowing the reality of what happened to sink in. A rousing cheer erupted from the crew, an impossible feat from the emaciated group only hours earlier. Eric held the wheel for a moment longer before swinging the *Rosemary* due south and handing it over to a completely befuddled coxswain.

"We should probably pack on some sail, Captain," Eric stated calmly. "We'll want as much momentum as we can get going past the island. I'd rather not make it through the shoals just to have the Twins catch us."

Samuel barely found his voice for calling out the orders. Even when he did, it took some blatant commands before the crew stopped gawking at Eric and sent themselves above to adjust the rigging. Probably the only person on board who did not stand in awe at his accomplishment was the coxswain, who maintained the wheel with a sour look on his face. It only soured more when they overtook the path they originally meant to use for exiting the reef. From the other side, without the glare from the sun, Samuel clearly noted a low line of sharp shoals that clearly would have slammed them to a halt had they attempted to challenge them.

As the crew adjusted the sails and the coxswain and captain set a course for passing the island, Charlotte came up to Eric. "As I was saying earlier, Eric, lovely day for a sail, don't you think?"

Eric, though happy to be past the shoals, still maintained his focus. "We still have to outrun two more pirates before I'll agree with you."

Charlotte gave Eric an expectant look. "Okay," Eric gave in. "If you'll look back you'll see the ship that was supposed to be patrolling the San Fernando Channel on the other side of the reef." Charlotte nodded as she saw the beaten boat doing its best to sail back to its station, knowing it would never arrive before the *Rosemary* passed. "Now, there should be another ship over to the northwest somewhere . . . let's see . . . ah, there." Eric pointed, and they both saw a ship to the north of them moving back and forth between the mainland and the furthermost island chain, patrolling the north passage.

"I see they are so involved in their duty, they haven't even seen us sneak behind them yet," Charlotte noted.

"Exactly. Even if they do see us, they're too far to the north to be a problem."

"Two down . . ." Charlotte quipped.

"And we believe there are only two to go."

Charlotte took in the scene around them and pointed to the island they now began to pass. "There, right?"

"Probably."

"Will it be close?"

Eric thought for a moment. "I hope not. If all goes well, they shouldn't know what's going on. If they don't see us until we're about even with where they are, then we should be able to outrun them into Port Raleigh."

Charlotte sighed. "Is this day ever going to end, Eric?"

"If it does, I hope it's a happy ending."

"Captain Wesley," Mr. Gary called out for Samuel, but also looked in the direction of Eric. "We'll be coming in view of the cove once we round this next bend of the island."

Samuel beckoned Eric to join him. "What do you think, Master Eric?" he asked while gazing at the coastline to their left with his spyglass.

"It's probably best if we stay close to the coast as much as we can so we don't pop into view of the Twins until the last possible second. We'll need every second we can get."

Samuel nodded, visibly nervous. He passed along the instructions to the coxswain, who—still stinging from the events in the shoals—obeyed with a dour expression. The *Rosemary* eased up along the coastline to the point where its passengers could make out the details of the palm trees on the shorelines.

Eric gazed intently as the cove opened up to their view. The longer it took for the *Rosemary* to see the pirate ships the more chance they had of outrunning them . . . unless it happened that they had assumed wrong and the Twins weren't even in the cove and instead patrolling somewhere nearby, ready to pounce on them. This thought began to plague Eric the more the cove opened up and they saw nothing. In his mind, he started to work out a strategy on how to estimate the Twins' current location and how to avoid them. Yet he knew that if they were not in the cove, one of them would most likely be stationed to the south, which meant that the path to Port Raleigh would be blocked and they would be effectively surrounded by all four hostile ships. As the last edges of the cove revealed themselves, Eric succumbed himself to this predetermined fate. *I knew it was a risk*, he told himself, *and now I have to face the worst-case scenario of my gamble.*

A shout about seeing some ships from the lookout interrupted Eric's thoughts. He perked up. "Did he say, 'ships'? . . . as in more than one?" Eric asked.

Samuel, who had also observed the unveiling of the cove, nodded. "I think he did."

Sure enough, as the last bit of the cove opened up, in the far corner sat two large, intimidating ships. Eric laughed. It was a laugh of pure joy and relief. Samuel gave an uncertain smile. "What?"

Eric pointed to the two huge wooden structures. "We've got them, Captain! Look. That one over there is on its side on the beach . . . and the other one isn't even close to ready to chase us."

Samuel used his spyglass to confirm Eric's description. "Bilgewater and barnacles, you're right! They're cleaning the hull of one of them— that's why it's on its side. The other one is anchored away nice and snug, without even a scrap of sail ready." Samuel now joined Eric in laughter. "Why, I'll bet the anchored one is carrying all the ballast from the ship they're cleaning. Even if she were ready to sail, she'd be almost as heavy as two boats. There's no way she'd catch the *Rosemary*." Samuel shook his head in amazement, taking in all the events from the entire day. "Eric, you—"

Eric suddenly excused himself from the Samuel's side and ran down on deck. The meager four cannons that the *Rosemary* carried had been loaded and run out since morning in the event that they would be used in a desperate situation. They seemed as if they would serve useless at this point until Eric solicited the help of a couple crew members. They did not take much convincing considering the miraculous escape they just witnessed him orchestrate.

Eric guided them to the gun closest to the quarterdeck, facing the island. "Help me aim it for that ship, the one at anchor."

The men knew how to use the pulleys to move the cannon. Eric told them exactly where he wanted it. "Okay up a little, down a little . . . there, perfect!" They grabbed the powder and put in what they figured as distance. Eric added just a touch more. "Now, I just yank on this to fire?" They nodded in the affirmative. Eric held onto the cord and watched the pirate ships sitting to the east of them. By now the *Rosemary* had been spotted by the pirates and a commotion set the cove to life. Regardless, the pirates were sitting ducks and they knew it. Eric watched, waited, and then jerked the cord. The cannon roared in response.

The *Rosemary*'s crew gathered to the side of the ship to watch the shot. An extended pause of anticipation dominated as the shot flew across the distance dividing the two ships. They all had a clear view of the cannonball's arrival as the top of the pirate's foremast snapped off, while splinters, rigging, and sails dropped to the deck of the ship.

Before the sounds of the damaged incurred by the successful shot reverberated back to the *Rosemary*, the whole crew erupted in cheer. Eric observed the pirate ship and nodded firmly as the crew gathered around him with shouts of congratulations. He appeared to not notice them; instead, he whispered, "That's your warning, Willards. You haven't seen the last of me."

It took Samuel five minutes to calm the crew down, though he could hardly blame them considering his own state of astonishment. Finally, the crew settled into their duties, remembered their fatigue, and watched with great relief as Port Raleigh inched closer. Eric eyed the two pirate ships behind them until they shrank beyond scrutiny. Then he watched as the receding twilight spilled past the *Rosemary* and settled through the open San Fernando Channel. The wind gusted as constant and strong as ever. Eric let it twirl his hair back and forth as he closed his eyes and felt the enchanting motion of the ship under his legs. Finally he opened his eyes and walked over to Charlotte, who stood patiently at the opposite end of the quarterdeck.

"You know what, Charlotte?"

"What, Eric?"

"It sure is a lovely day for a sail."

Charlotte smiled. "I knew you'd see it my way."

Chapter 5
PORT RALEIGH POLITICS

The governor's mansion, an opulent column-bordered brick residence, sat atop a hill overlooking Port Raleigh's harbor. As Samuel, Eric, and Charlotte entered, amidst a flurry of official and formal introductions, Eric could not help but keep glancing back through the doors and windows at the half dozen or so fine ships anchored just off the pier with the last bits of sunlight outlining them.

Finally they entered a study, and a puffy man wearing very meticulous dress and a freshly powdered white wig welcomed them. "Captain of the *Rosemary*, I assume?"

"Yes, Governor Rose. Captain Samuel Wesley at your service, sir."

"This is most miraculous indeed, Captain. For a moment, when we first sighted you entering the harbor, we thought that maybe the Twins had vacated, but the fort reported to us that they were still patrolling. How in the devil did you manage to get past them?" Governor Rose's cheeks glowed a soft red color as he spoke.

"First, Governor, I have the honor and privilege of introducing you to two recent passengers of the *Rosemary*, Master Eric Francis and Miss Charlotte Reeves."

Governor Rose nodded toward them civilly, though impatiently, then pushed, "But the Twins—however did you manage to get past them?"

Samuel smiled. "That is why I took the time to introduce you to my friends here. You see, it was through Master Eric's remarkable planning that we gave the pirates the slip."

The governor's eyes inflated at this announcement. He looked Eric up and down while Eric stood in an unassuming manner, glancing around the study with his eyes fixing on some maps on the wall and desk. The governor then turned back to Samuel and whispered somewhat obviously, "What . . . this mere boy here?"

"Don't let his appearance deceive you. This 'mere' boy managed to make buffoons out of the Twins' fleet with a damaged ship and half a crew."

Samuel, by now, captured the governor's full attention. He next related the whole story of the *Rosemary*'s woes with the storm, pirates, and disease. Finally, he introduced his encounter with Eric and Charlotte, the plan, and then the events of that very day as they drew the patrolling pirates out of the channel, miraculously crossed the shoals, circumvented the Twins, and even how Eric took a parting shot at them before entering Port Raleigh. Throughout the whole telling, Governor Rose stared more and more intently at Eric. Had Eric been listening to the praise Samuel had been heaping on him, he probably would have been quite self-conscious under the attention. As it was, however, Eric found himself too submerged in scrutinizing the room's maps to really register much from their conversation.

"That is quite the adventure," the governor finally exclaimed. "Truly marvelous. Why, you all must be terribly exhausted . . ."

"That is part of the reason for our delay in reporting to you, Governor Rose," Samuel replied. "We took some time to refresh ourselves with clean water and fresh food."

"Rightfully so," Governor Rose said, then turned to Eric. "Now you, young man. Tell me, what is your nautical background that makes you so much of an expert as to sail circles around the Willard Pirate Twins?"

"Um . . . we were very lucky," Eric tore his eyes away from the desk, a little uneasy with the question.

"Fortune can only take you so far," the governor said, his eyes still locked on Eric. "Isn't that so, Captain Bellview?"

A voice came out of the corner of the room as a response. "I'm inclined to agree. I too would like to know more about this intriguing young man."

The three guests of the *Rosemary* flinched in surprise at seeing another person in the room. A man in a sharp naval uniform, with a strong, handsome face, and short black hair stepped out of the shadows. He approached the group gracefully, the whole time keeping a close eye on Eric. "My apologies for the intrusion. I am Captain Lawrence Bellview of His Majesty's Royal Navy."

Samuel nodded in recognition. "Ah, Captain Bellview. Then those must be your two ships-of-the-line in the harbor. Your reputation precedes you, Captain. I am honored." Samuel bowed respectfully.

"Thank you, Captain Wesley, though I must say that a preceding reputation is nothing compared to a current one. You and your friend here certainly have the honorable reputation in this port." Bellview's smile bordered on dangerous. "Which leads to the governor's original question. To what, Master Eric, do you owe your masterful maritime knowledge, especially at such a young age?"

Though the words were formal and complimentary, Charlotte noted an edge of cynicism in their tone that annoyed her. She jumped in, "Master Eric's knowledge is a product of his natural-born abilities."

Governor Rose had not expected Charlotte's response, but he recovered quickly. "Undoubtedly, it would have to be somewhat natural—considering his young age. But there must also be a significant amount of navigational background . . . 'Francis' eh? I don't seem to recall any prominent Francis family member involved in the navy. Where is it that you come from, Eric?"

"Uh . . . Nibleton."

"Nibleton . . . never heard of it. In which county is it located?" Governor Rose's seemingly innocent question sniffed of suspicion.

"I don't see how that's any of your business, Governor," Charlotte snapped, detecting his skepticism. "I was hoping we came here to be congratulated, not interrogated."

Charlotte's frank manner once again jolted Governor Rose, who apparently had not expected anyone to see through his seemingly innocent questions. "Of course. My apologies, Miss Charlotte. I had no intention of offending."

An awkward silence reigned before Eric spoke out, "Sorry for my ignorance, but Captain Bellview, can I ask how you slipped past the pirate twins to enter Port Raleigh?"

Though it was a sincere inquiry, Bellview paused before answering, as if analyzing the motives behind the question. "I have not had occasion to slip past the Twins seeing as how I arrived here just before the pirates blocked off the channel."

"So, you've just been sitting in here this whole time?"

Bellview's face reddened. "No, not just sitting. I've been refitting my ships and preparing them for battle and waiting for an opportune moment to strike."

"I see," Eric replied, leaving an opening at the end of his statement.

Captain Bellview's eyes became slits. "And what would you have me do, little boy? Sail out with my two ships against the Willard Pirate Twins' four? Even ship to ship the Willards would outgun us. My duty is not to recklessly lose two of His Royal Majesty's ships-of-the-line." Eric remained quiet. "I'll give you credit. Sneaking past the Twins was indeed an extraordinary feat, but getting past them and capturing them are two very different things."

Eric nodded slowly. "Then your ships can be ready to go at any moment?"

"Of course," Bellview remarked. "What kind of captain would I be if they weren't?"

Eric sensed that he verged on overstepping his bounds, but his eagerness plowed him forward. "Then, Captain, the moment has arrived."

"What moment?"

"The one you said you were waiting for—to go after the pirates."

Captain Bellview, though annoyed, mustered a snort. "Oh really? So the added strength of your tiny crew was all I needed to reach my opportune moment? Please child, I believe it's past your bedtime."

Eric brushed off the captain's demeaning remark. "The moment has arrived because tonight the pirates will come to us."

This announcement was news to everyone in the room. They quieted enough that Eric knew that he held their complete attention. "The Willard Twins won't be happy with what happened today. Even though the *Rosemary* wasn't a big prize, just the fact that it got past them at all will be a blow to morale. From what I know about pirates, and from what I've heard about the Twins, they'll be too proud to let us get by without punishment. They'll want revenge, and soon . . . probably tonight."

As involved as Eric found himself in his explanation, he barely stopped to breathe. "Because they'll be in a hurry, the attack won't be thought out. Even if they attacked with all four ships, they know they'd be up against at least the fort's cannons as well your own, Captain Bellview." Bellview tried to maintain a skeptical expression, but he obviously felt intrigued by Eric's analysis. Eric continued. "Because of that, they'll most likely try a land attack so they can take out the fort. Then the pirate ships can enter the harbor and have the jump on your ships, Captain. After a quick battle, they'll control the fort and the harbor. By morning they'll have beaten any other opposition from land and have Port Raleigh under their control."

As Eric paused to gauge his audience's response, Captain Bellview remarked, "Even if you were right in your wild assumptions, then the reason the pirates are even doing this would be because of you, of what you did today. You do realize that, don't you?"

Eric smiled. "Of course. In fact, firing at the Twins in their cove was meant to make sure of it. The added sting of that cannon shot, along with the rest of the day's embarrassments, would be too much for any pirate to let go without punishment."

Governor Rose stepped in at this point. "Hold on. You are attempting to inform us that you did this on purpose?"

Eric seemed a bit surprised that his audience had not considered this option before. He replied, "I kind of had to. Trying to chase them down after coming into port would've been hard enough. While I was in the area, I decided to force them to make a rash move. Now that we have a good idea of what they are going to do, that gives us the advantage."

Captain Bellview progressed from annoyance to anger. "So now you've been planning this the whole time?"

Eric glanced back at Bellview, as if for the first time. Bellview's manner had him confused. Without knowing how to respond, Eric decided to ignore the outburst and continue. "If they want to take the fort by land, they'll have to bring a ship secretly along the coast to the east of the fort. They don't want the fort to see the ship, so they'll keep their distance." Eric suddenly shifted the whole group over to the governor's desk where a map that Eric had been eyeing lay open. "But they know that they'll have to go far enough to get past the marshes from the Spenser River Delta, right here." His finger lay down on the patch of bushy, watery symbols to the east of the fort. "That means we can pretty much guess exactly where they'll land . . . right here." Eric's finger slid to the spot just out of the marshes but still a mile or so east of the fort.

"All speculation," Captain Bellview muttered.

Eric proceeded unfazed, caught up in the excitement of his own planning. "This is what we can do. Captain Bellview, you can take one of your ships and place it on the west side of the fort until after it gets dark, then sail out and come down on the pirate ship once it drops off its crew. It should be pretty easy to capture it since it'll only have a few pirates left to guard it."

"A skeleton crew," Samuel aided, his eyes lighting up with excitement as the plan unfolded.

"Right, a skeleton crew," Eric confirmed. "Then, governor, we can bring men from the fort along with some cannons and trap the dropped off pirates up against the marshes. They won't expect it and will probably try to escape, but their ship will be taken by then. Just like that, we'll be able to take care of the pirate land forces."

Samuel grinned from ear to ear. "Master Eric, you will never cease to amaze me."

Eric put his hand in the air, "You'd better wait until you hear the whole thing. Now, with the captured pirate ship, we'll have three ships against the Willard Twins' fleet—now down to three with the loss of their ship—plus we'll have the fort. Captain Bellview can take his ship and the newly captured pirate ship to the northwest, cutting off any retreat from the pirates. Once they come into range of the fort and it starts to fire on them, Bellview's other ship can jump in on the battle from the harbor. The pirates will be outnumbered, surrounded, and left with their only options of sinking or surrendering."

An awe-struck Samuel muttered, "Brilliant."

Once again, Eric brushed off the compliment. "Captain, governor, this all depends on you."

A long pause lingered in the room. Eric wondered what took them so long to respond. Though it all made sense in his mind, he had a small twinge of doubt. Was there something drastic he overlooked, something that a kid from another time would not think about? He looked back and forth between Governor Rose and Captain Bellview, but found their faces hardened. Finally, Bellview's tightened jaw allowed some words to escape. "If you were hoping for me to throw my ships into harm's way, all under the wild suspicions of a youth, then you are disillusioned," Captain Bellview replied quickly, apparently addressing himself to Governor Rose, but with his fiery eyes locked on Eric. "In fac—"

"Captain," Governor Rose interrupted, "if you'll allow me to respond to Master Eric . . ." Captain Bellview swallowed his words, not so much out of respect but out of surprise. Governor Rose continued, "Son, our gracious king has set up the most powerful navy in the world. Within this navy, officers have studied strategy, built up years of experience, and been hand-picked according to their abilities."

Samuel sensed where this was going and could not help but to mumble in an undertone, "Or more likely according to their family connections . . ."

Governor Rose's mounting voice ignored the murmur, though it stung. "If you think that for one second, I'm going to let a lad pop into my study from out of nowhere and have the audacity to dictate to my captain about how to perform his duty, or dictate to me how to defend my port, then you are sorely mistaken. Because you are so young, I will blame this insolence on your ignorance and will overlook it."

Eric stood aghast at these comments. Though maybe he should have been offended, instead he found himself irritated. It frustrated him that he felt so sure of the pirates' next step and that the means for carrying out his plans sat right in front of him, but that these two men allowed their pride to stand in the way. Eric sighed. He attempted a different tack. "I'm sorry if I sounded rude, Governor and Captain. The last thing I would've wanted to do would be to offend either of you. But for the good of Port Raleigh, the Royal Navy, and the kingdom, I ask you to please listen to my warnings." Eric gauged their response before slipping in, "I'd be totally fine with giving you credit for any success, and I'd also be willing to take blame for failures." He remembered this line going over well with Samuel, who nodded in affirmation at the statement.

Captain Bellview scowled derisively. "I don't like your condescending tone with us."

"Sometimes that's the only way an idiot can understand what's being told to him," an angry Charlotte spouted with her typical disregard for tact.

The governor and captain both gasped at her blunt statement, but she still had more. "I can't believe that you are going to let your stupid arrogance get in the way of taking advantage of expert advice, especially when it costs you nothing to at least test his plan."

Captain Bellview verged on exploding. "I will not be addressed in such a manner by a girl, especially one as discourteous as this one, and most certainly when it is dealing with affairs of strategy where she has no right to meddle."

Charlotte rolled her eyes. "Right. You'd like to keep the market of botching things up among the males only . . . probably a good idea, except you shouldn't assume that all females would be as liable to screw things up as much as you."

Bellview, who would have considered himself too much of a gentleman to even so much as snort in front of a woman, was moments away from slapping Charlotte. Samuel had the sense to step in. "Sirs, please don't be affected by this young lady's manners. She has been marooned for a time on an island with little to no stores . . . but I would make my plea as well. I too had skepticism in this young gentleman's abilities when it came to the sea. Yet I found myself in a dire situation so I felt I had no choice but to listen. In every aspect was he right, and in ways that I can only describe as miraculous did he save our lives by bringing us into port. My recommendation is that when he talks, you should listen. You will not regret it."

Captain Bellview, still driven by rage, slighted, "Now a Creole merchant skipper is telling us what to do? What's next, an African slave?" Samuel stared down Bellview with his whole body tensed.

Governor Rose held his hand up, silencing Bellview once more. He took a deep breath and his heavy brow lowered. "This . . ." he stated deliberately, motioning toward the three visitors with his hand, ". . . this is the gratitude we receive for providing a safe harbor. They criticize our method of dealing with the pirates, they would report to His Majesty our alleged deficiencies, and they tote this youth as their hero, when in fact he would be nothing if there had been no Port Raleigh for him to escape to."

The governor breathed deeply several times before adding, "No, my friends, I do not hold a grudge. I recognize that you've suffered difficulties and are not in your proper mindset. Maybe it is time you went and caught up on your sleep." None of them moved, so surprised at how their warm reception had suddenly become quite brisk. "You are dismissed," Governor Rose hissed, his voice edged with danger.

The three exited the room and were escorted out of the mansion. Not until after they cleared the mansion did they start speaking.

"I've decided that I don't like them very much," Charlotte remarked, in her usual frank tone.

Eric shook his head. "This is all my fault. I thought that I'd have the resources here in Port Raleigh on hand when I coaxed the Willard Twins into a fight. You and your crew were so open to my suggestions, Captain Wesley," he turned to Samuel, "that it didn't occur to me that no one would listen to me once we got here."

"I'm still listening to you, Master Eric," Samuel said. "I've seen too much of your skills today to dismiss anything you say. Besides, those men are so entrenched in their prejudices, they're endangering the whole town."

"Yes, I appreciate that, Captain," Eric nodded. "You did stand up for me in there."

"Please, don't call me 'Captain.' Call me 'Samuel.'"

"Very well, Samuel," Eric smiled sadly.

Samuel thought something over. "However," Samuel added, a new glimmer emitting from his eye, "I would like to call you 'Captain,' if I may."

"Me?" Eric suddenly laughed. "Thanks, but I prefer 'Eric.'"

"With all due respect," Samuel replied, "if you are to be commanding a ship, you should be addressed with the proper title, Captain."

"Commanding a ship?" Eric questioned. "What ship? I can't see Captain Bellview handing any of his over."

"For what it's worth, you still have the *Rosemary*," Samuel offered.

"The *Rosemary*?" Eric scrutinized Samuel, who looked back as if to say, "Why not?"

Samuel could see Eric's mind working. "Yes . . ." Eric muttered, "Yes, the *Rosemary*. We couldn't do all of my original plan without Captain Bellview's ships, but we could at least keep Port Raleigh from being pillaged."

Samuel guessed Eric's new plan, which Eric then voiced out loud. "The pirate ship dropping off the land forces will be left with a skeleton crew, which means that we could easily subdue the pirate ship using surprise and a decent-sized crew on the *Rosemary*."

"Of course, without the help of the men in the fort that still leaves the pirates on land unchecked to come for Port Raleigh," Samuel pointed out.

Eric smiled. "Not necessarily . . . what's to stop the fort from helping us?"

"What do you mean?" Samuel asked.

"It's not like Governor Rose sent a message to the fort telling them to ignore all pirate attack warnings from newcomers. If someone goes there to raise the alarm about the pirates, there's no reason for the officer in the fort to not listen to us as long as we have our facts straight."

A slow smile crept across Samuel's face. "If that worked and we got the troops from the fort, then the land force of the pirates would be trapped, on one hand by the fort's men and on the other by the sea, since they would have no ship to retreat in."

Their conversation now surpassed an idea in Eric's mind—it was a plan. "We'll need a decent-sized crew and someone will need to go to the fort and raise the alarm—it'll have to be convincing."

"You leave the logistics to me, Captain Francis," Samuel said. Charlotte noted that Eric's involvement with churning things over in his mind kept him from protesting the title of captain. "If the lads have boasted over your actions earlier today as much as I suspect they have, we'll have every available sailor on the wharf begging for a spot on the *Rosemary*. Once you have a crew, then I'll set out to the fort to warn the officer of the attack."

Eric nodded thoughtfully.

"What should Eric and I do until then?" Charlotte asked.

Samuel smiled. "You might get an hour of rest in on the *Rosemary*— you'll need it. It's been a long couple of days and it's likely to be a long night."

Charlotte glanced at Eric, expecting a struggle. She saw the resistance in his eyes, but to her surprise, he relented. "You're right. Come on, Charlotte. We'd better get back to the *Rosemary*. We'll see you there, Samuel."

"Aye aye, Captain Francis," Samuel saluted smartly.

Joshua and Jedediah Willard would never serve as the paragon for brotherly love, but their family relation implied a respect for each other that they might not have felt otherwise. The oppressive silence in Jedediah's cabin might have suggested the contrary.

After a while, Joshua spoke out, "You were right. I chose a bad time to overhaul the ship. I admit it. You were right."

Jedediah lifted his eyes, seemingly emotionless. "That isn't what irritates me." He remained quiet for a moment, gazing off into the distance. "No. It's what that ship's captain did."

Joshua's face returned to the scowl more appropriate to his role. "Don't let the actions of a worthless maggot of a ship's captain bother you. He got lucky, that's all."

"No," Jedediah said plainly. "It wasn't luck. He knew exactly what he was doing."

"Jedediah, it couldn't have been anything but dumb luck. That guy slipped right through leagues and leagues of impassable reefs without so much as a scratch."

"That's exactly why it wasn't dumb luck."

"According to Captain Pete's report, the ship tried to run the San Fernando Channel, but he cut her off. The ship then fled north, but since Pete was right on her, he drove the pest straight into the reef where, by some rare piece of fortune, she managed to slip by."

"Think about it, Joshua," Jedediah replied patiently. "The ship got close enough to put Pete on the hunt, then kept just out of range for a four-league chase. Just out of range, mark me. Then the ship happened to plunge into the reef right in the only spot possible to make a crossing. Even Pete admitted to believing the ship was floating over the shoals at one point. That isn't luck. That's seamanship. Nor is it luck that left the south entrance to Port Raleigh open. Captain Pete had been purposefully drawn out of his position for that reason. And it wasn't luck that the cannonball hit my ship in the yardarms."

Joshua stared blankly for a moment before responding, "You're right." He gritted his teeth and seethed before saying, "What makes it worse is that there's nothing we can do about it now with that little rat holed up in Port Raleigh."

Jedediah remained silent, but his eyes flickered.

"You think there's something we can do?" Joshua read his brother's expression. "You want to take Port Raleigh . . ."

Jedediah still betrayed no change in his emotions. "We told ourselves to keep it as an option . . . to scout out the situation."

"And our odds are favorable, you think."

Jedediah stayed pensive. "The Royal Navy has sat in the harbor this whole time. The Royal Navy captain obviously doesn't trust himself against us. The whole town has been on alert for the past week. They have to be tiring of watching out for us. Their supplies are diminishing. Their morale is down. On the other hand, that ship's captain remains untouched in the harbor. If we don't do something soon, our crew's morale will take a hit for his flaunting of our seemingly impenetrable blockade."

Joshua's eyes flared. "It's time to take Port Raleigh! Yes, brother, we can take it. Then we'll wreak our revenge on that captain."

"That is our only wildcard. The ship captain who got through, he might suspect an attack."

By this time, Joshua's excitement at the prospect of the taking of Port Raleigh kept him from letting this observation sway him. "How could he? The little rat was too much of a coward to come face-to-face with us."

"It doesn't take a coward to send a cannonball right into the thick of a group of pirates that outgun, outship, and outnumber you."

"Only when he knew he was uncatchable. Come on, Jedediah, we can take them!"

Jedediah fell quiet, thinking.

"I get to lead this one, Jed," Joshua said, as if guessing his brother's thoughts. Jedediah lifted his face, but Joshua cut him off. "I need to make up for my mistake with cleaning the ship's hull. You have to let me lead this one. I want revenge. I'll personally take that little weevil, dismember him, and fire his body parts into a mass of his own crew members as a lesson."

Jedediah's silence lasted another long moment. "On two conditions."

"Name them."

"One, I make the plans. Two, if I call for a retreat at any time, you obey indiscriminately."

"There will be no need to retreat, Jedediah. We clearly have—"

"Those are the conditions or there's no attack," Jedediah stated.

"Fine. But we go tonight, as soon as all the ballast is replaced in my ship. I'm not going to let that pompous captain spend even one night in celebration."

As if deciding against his better judgment, Jedediah agreed. The Willard Twins would be on the move that night.

Samuel trekked to one end of the wharf and sent Mr. Gary to the other end searching for willing crew members for this new, daring expedition. Everyone of the original *Rosemary* crew enthusiastically signed on, despite their exhaustion from the week's previous events. Apparently the couple of hours of recuperation between their arrival and this point served as sufficient. But Samuel knew their willingness came from more than just fresh food and water. All still burned with curiosity and awe at this mysterious young man. He knew they would not let an opportunity to participate with him in action pass by them if they could help it.

Samuel also noted that his previous assumption bore truth. The recovering *Rosemary* crew members had been busy in his absence. They infiltrated every tavern along the wharf relating the day's magnificent events to other sailors. The reaction of these sailors ranged from astonishment to skepticism, but Samuel found that, regardless of their opinion, most allowed their curiosity to at least find out for themselves under Eric's command. Thanks to the pirates' blockade, they had been cooped up in harbor for over a week and itched for action. Even several sailors from the Royal Navy volunteered, though technically they had no permission and risked flogging if discovered.

Samuel met up with Mr. Gary half an hour later, and they compared lists. They soon realized the need to refuse a score of volunteers because there would be no room for the *Rosemary* to effectively fit them all. Once they finalized their list, Samuel left Mr. Gary with the job of assigning duties to the motley gathering while he went to the fort.

As a longtime seafaring man, Samuel recognized that Lieutenant Curtis, the officer in charge of the fort, ran a "tight ship." His men's uniforms looked sharp, they all stood at their posts with a rigid discipline, and each considered his job—however menial—as serious as the most important. One of the soldiers marched smartly while escorting Samuel to the lieutenant's quarters. When the two arrived, Samuel entered and his escort returned to his post.

"How can I help you, Captain Wesley?" Lieutenant Curtis kept his eyes on his desk. Samuel saw that he carefully filled out the fort's inventory list. His short brown hair sat in a frozen wave across his head, as if held there by his will alone. Samuel could tell that the lieutenant would be slightly short of stature when standing, though he doubted that it affected the discipline within the fort.

"Um, first mate, Lieutenant Curtis . . . not Captain," Samuel corrected his statement.

Curtis raised his head. "First mate? I had heard that your captain perished."

"He did, but someone else has taken my place as captain of the *Rosemary*."

Though this comment would usually require an explanation, Curtis returned to his inventory list. "You said you had an urgent message. What is it?"

"Most urgent, Lieutenant Curtis."

Curtis set down his quill and faced Samuel. "Go ahead."

"Port Raleigh is to be attacked tonight by the pirates."

Curtis initially reacted with silence. He seemed to calculate the repercussions of this news. "How do you know?"

Samuel anticipated this question. In order to avoid the same skepticism that they received from Governor Rose and Captain Bellview, he ventured a different answer. "After evading the pirates on our way into Port Raleigh today, we saw them congregate at the Twins' base on the first Montes de Oca island."

"That could mean something," Curtis tapped his finger on his desk thoughtfully, "but they could also simply be meeting to discuss how to shore up their blockade so another ship like yours couldn't get past them."

"That is exactly what we suspected, Lieutenant," Samuel added. "But then, as they were breaking up, just off the horizon, we tracked one of the ships traveling south by southeast. The other three started to slip west by southwest."

"And you suspect this formation peremptory to an attack."

"That is the only sense we could make of it, Lieutenant," Samuel held his breath. This is where he would see if his careful coloring of the truth would pay off.

"Very well. I will put my men on extra alert tonight. I suppose you have informed Captain Bellview as well?"

"It's more complicated than that, Lieutenant Curtis."

Curtis indicated his willingness to listen to more.

"You see, we suspect that the pirates know they will face heavy losses if they attempt a direct assault on Port Raleigh. The Willard Twins are anything but fools. We felt that the ship sneaking off to the south by southeast was particularly suspicious. The only possible reason for the Twins to split up their forces unnecessarily is if they are planning to have a land force take out the fort before the other three ships dispose of Captain Bellview."

"Mr. Wesley, you keep on saying 'we.' To whom are you referring?" Curtis asked.

Samuel had not expected that question. "Um . . . the new captain of the *Rosemary*, actually. He is a master strategist and seaman. It was thanks to him that we got past the Twins in the first place."

Lieutenant Curtis mulled this over. "Well, your logic does seem to make sense. What are you . . . and this master strategist . . . suggesting?"

"Catch the landing force off guard," Samuel regained his confidence for his final pitch, recalling Eric's explanation as best he could. "The pirates will want to land out of sight of the fort, but they will want to avoid the marshes. That means we can pinpoint exactly where they will land. If you have a force waiting for them at that spot, you can catch them on their landing. I have the second mate of the *Rosemary* preparing a crew at this moment. The *Rosemary* can take the pirate ship after they've launched their land force, cutting off any attempted retreat."

"Pretty ingenious, Mr. Wesley," Curtis observed. "And you say this was concocted by your new captain?"

"Yes. As I said, he is a master strategist."

Lieutenant Curtis looked at Samuel in the eyes. "Mr. Wesley, I appreciate your warning. However, I'm afraid I can't clear out my fort in order to stifle a supposed pirate attack I cannot confirm myself."

Samuel stood speechless. This was the last reaction he hoped for. "Begging your pardon, Lieutenant Curtis, but what do you mean?"

"By doing this, I would be trusting to your word alone. And though I would be more than willing to trust you on my own, putting the fort at risk by emptying it for a force that I can't even confirm would, frankly, be folly."

"But . . . Lieutenant Curtis, I assure you that my information is—"

"I mean no disrespect, Mr. Wesley, but how can I be certain that this isn't a ploy to weaken the fort so that the Twins can slip into the harbor uncontested?" Samuel about protested, but Curtis cut him off. "Hearing about your miraculous effort in getting past the blockade is only more suspicious. How can I know you weren't captured and induced into providing this false information at a threat to your family or a friend so that the port would be left open? This new captain of yours, how do I know he's not a pirate, or even one of the Twins himself holding the crew hostage and sneaking into the port trying to open it up for his brother on the outside?"

"Lieutenant!" Samuel cried out, shocked and dismayed. After a moment's meditation, however, he realized, that as outlandish as Curtis's speculations seemed, they rang of plausibility. Putting himself in the lieutenant's shoes, Samuel decided that he had asked the lieutenant to believe an awful lot coming from just one man he met only moment before.

Samuel composed himself. "You have a point, Lieutenant Curtis. I am expecting much. I assure you that none of those scenarios you just mentioned are true, but I understand that you need more than my word to go on." Samuel paused while he considered a compromise. "Sir, having your whole regiment in place to meet the pirates would offer the greatest chance for success, but it could not hurt to send a couple patrols out to watch for the arrival of the pirate ship. If the ship does come as I have suggested, then you can have men here at the fort prepared to join the battle at a moment's notice. If it doesn't come, then you have protected the fort and lost nothing."

Lieutenant Curtis considered Samuel's proposal, nodding slowly. "Very well, Mr. Wesley, you also make a good point. If such a ship is sighted, I will do my best to keep them from advancing on the fort. Though be aware that, even in the event of a pirate attack, I still plan on holding at least half my force in the fort in case it is a diversionary tactic."

Samuel grimaced. Knowing the amount of pirates likely to be part of the landing force, he wondered whether it would be sufficient to quell the attack. Curtis saw the look on Samuel's face and added, "But I will send two cannons with the scouting patrols . . . and we'll pray that we last out the night."

Samuel realized that he had secured the best he could get. "I'll be off to the *Rosemary* then, Lieutenant Curtis. Hopefully we'll see each other victorious before the night is through."

Lieutenant Curtis briskly stood up and saluted.

Samuel could not display too much surprise upon seeing Eric up and about when he returned to the *Rosemary*. He chastised him. "Captain, I told you to get some rest!"

Eric smiled at the juxtaposition of Samuel making demands and calling him "captain" at the same time. "Don't worry, Samuel. I napped briefly, but as soon as the crew boarded the *Rosemary*, I couldn't help but get involved."

Samuel sighed.

"What did the fort say?"

"Lieutenant Curtis is a stubborn man. The best I could do was convince him to have some patrols on watch with a pair of cannons, ready to send for more troops if the pirates arrive. Though he said that, even if a ship were sighted, he wouldn't send more than half his men."

Eric nodded as if he expected as much. "Smart man. Making sure it's not a diversionary tactic."

Samuel managed to contain his surprise at Eric using the exact same phrase as Lieutenant Curtis. In the mean time, Eric calculated something in his mind. "That's fine. It should be enough."

Samuel lifted his eyebrows incredulously. "You're the captain."

The last vestiges of daytime had disappeared from the night sky as the blackness gobbled up the violet remains of the sunset. Eric read the appearing constellations, and then stated, "Well, Samuel, I think it's time we started moving."

Amid the excitement of inevitable action, Samuel passed the word to Mr. Gary, who immediately barked orders. The *Rosemary* captured the soft night breeze, sailing underway in a matter of minutes.

Due to the day's events, the governor had not eaten dinner until nighttime had fallen. Captain Bellview remained with the governor in his dining hall in quiet conversation. Toward the end of their meal, the Royal Navy captain stood up to gaze out the large, floor-to-ceiling windows onto the harbor.

"Who do you think he really is, Bellview?" Governor Rose queried, his corpulent fingers delicately slicing a mango.

Bellview twitched but stayed quiet. Only the sound of Governor Rose slurping on the mango seed broke the silence. Bellview kept his hands latched behind his back while he pivoted, "I don't know, Rose, but it looks like he's leaving."

Governor Rose dropped his mango and briskly paced over to the window. In the glittering starlight, he detected the small ship, *Rosemary*, setting her sails and vacating the harbor.

"The fool!" Rose muttered under his breath. "Let's hope the pirates put an end to his stupidity this time around. That's what he gets for impudent cockiness."

Bellview could only nod his consent, though he remained quiet and pensive. Though he would never admit it out loud, the real reason he did not like this young man was because he showed the bravery that he, a Royal Navy captain, lacked.

Chapter 6
TWIN ATTACK

The sergeant knew better than to complain. Complaints only found their way back to Lieutenant Curtis, who would then really give you something to complain about. So he kept his mouth shut. At the same time, however, the old soldier knew that his patrol and the other one questioned why they had been chosen to drag cannon over a rocky and vegetation-infested path for nearly a full league. At the crest of the hill where they manned their station, which took in a vantage point of the empty beach below, the sergeant tried to convince himself that Lieutenant Curtis would not put them through this as a simple drill. Knowing Lieutenant Curtis, however, even the old soldier could not be sure.

The quiet lapping of the waves on the shore started to sooth the sergeant. *If this were a drill*, he thought, *then Lieutenant Curtis certainly gave some strange instructions for it.* He recalled the lieutenant explaining to him to place themselves on the high ground next to the beach just past the marshes, which they had now done. Though, admittedly, the sergeant never thought they would get to that point with all the effort they made to move the cannon over the uneven ground.

Once in position, the sergeant's instructions informed him to watch for a pirate ship approaching from the east. When they sighted a pirate ship, he needed to send someone on horseback to alert the fort. In the mean time, the entire pirate force should land before the patrols commenced an attack, starting with their artillery. They were to hold their position at all costs until reinforcements came.

Strangely, the sergeant hoped the exercise was not a drill after all. A whole week with pirates sitting on their doorstep put the sergeant, and the rest of the soldiers, ill at ease—they wanted action. Unfortunately, by the time they arrived to their post and the sun had set, they had seen nothing. Darkness gathered and the sergeant became more and more skeptical. He started planning the unenviable task of dragging the cannon back to the fort in the dark.

Due to the growing darkness, the sergeant had one of his men position himself on the beach in order to sight the ship as soon as possible. A scrambling of rocks put the two patrols on the alert.

"Sergeant!" a voice hissed, attempting as much silence as possible in his excited condition.

"What is it?"

"Ship coming, sir! Looks like one of the pirate ships to me, sir."

"You sure?"

"Don't know any other ship that big t'would come sneakin' about at this hour."

The sergeant squinted his eyes and thought he could see a form materializing in the darkness to the east. "Go! To the fort, raise the alarm! Tell the lieutenant exactly what you saw!"

The young soldier wasted no time hopping onto the nearby horse and galloping off. "Get those cannon loaded and ready," the sergeant ordered, his adrenaline starting to rise.

Not until this point had the sergeant realized the precarious nature of his situation in being left to hold off the approaching mass of pirates with a meager two patrols. He hoped the young courier would hurry. He hoped that the pirates would take their time disembarking. And he hoped, while watching the menacing ship grow larger over the black horizon, that the reinforcements that came would be enough.

Charlotte's loose blonde hair lifted and fell with the currents of warm air seeping past the *Rosemary* as they skimmed along under a cloudless sky. She had no idea how Eric and Samuel had any inkling of where they headed; moreover, she did not care. She simply felt pleased recognizing that not only did Eric know, but that he actually felt useful. Telling someone their natural-born ability and watching how it affected them brought a certain level of satisfaction. To personally witness them

meld into their natural element and learn for themselves surpassed anything she had imagined.

Once they passed the black silhouette of the fort, sitting on its high
position overlooking the bay, Charlotte overheard Samuel ask Eric for
directions.

"Set a tack that will take us east by northeast," Eric replied.

Samuel passed along the proper instructions then returned to Eric's
side. "Why not simply east?" he asked. His voice held no distrust. He
simply asked because he had confidence in his new captain and wanted
to learn.

"With the wind coming from the northeast, we'd have a better
advantage on the pirates by coming around to their back side, sneaking
up on them from the east."

"Of course," Samuel whispered to himself. "The weather gage."

"Weather gage?" Eric asked.

"Yes. The advantage of the wind."

Eric mentally stored away yet another term. Samuel went to the
coxswain to pass on more detailed instructions. Charlotte took the
opportunity to steal next to Eric.

"Sure is nice to have Samuel around to give you all these neat toys
to play with," Charlotte said.

Eric smiled. "Well, I did want to play with Captain Bellview's toys,
but the *Rosemary* will do fine. And yes, we are really lucky to have
Samuel helping us. I can't help but think he was born to be at least a
pirate hunter helper."

"Not quite. He was born to be a charioteer."

"Charioteer? Like a driver of those two-wheeled roman things
pulled by horses?"

"He would've made Ben-Hur look like roadkill."

"Now that you mention it, he does act pretty impatient at the wheel
of a ship, like it doesn't react quick enough to what he wants." He eyed
his companion for a moment before adding, "Not me. Give me a nice
ship any day and I'll be happy."

Charlotte grinned. "Eric, not only do you have a nice ship, but
you're finally out on a mission doing what you were born to do. No
more running . . . you're hunting! Aren't you excited?"

Eric's eyes glittered. "I'm really nervous."

"Ha!" Charlotte laughed. "You don't look a whit nervous."

"I know, but I am. It's just that my excitement is covering up all the nervousness. I've never felt so alive in my life." Eric, who looked as if he were hovering, suddenly brought himself back down to earth. "Charlotte?"

"Yes?"

"Thanks."

Charlotte could tell his heartfelt gratitude reached deep. She had not expected it.

"My pleasure," she responded. And she meant it.

A half-hour later, Eric swung the *Rosemary* around in a half circle in order to creep behind what he hoped would be the awaiting pirate ship. The young captain harbored no disillusions. He knew that he would need to arrive just after the pirates disembarked. If he got there too early, his presence would tip the pirates off and they would attack his ship with their fully manned one or they would retreat. If he got there too late, the pirates would have met resistance at the beach and would have either retreated or beat them. In spite of these undesirable options, Eric used the sunset to reckon how far the pirates would need to have sailed to arrive at their landing point and when they would have left. After determining these factors, he felt certain that he timed his approach perfectly.

Eric was right.

As they crawled eastward, parallel with the shore, Eric's sharp eyes distinguished the shape of a large ship revealing itself before them. Seconds later, the forms of the last boats transporting a massive land force raced out of sight toward the beach. In no more than six minutes, Eric estimated, they would come alongside the opposing vessel. He quickly called a meeting with the officers of the *Rosemary*.

"Gentlemen," Eric felt awkward addressing this group of experienced adults, but the looks on the faces of Samuel and Mr. Gary encouraged him. He took a breath and spoke, "Silence is key. They can't know we're coming until we're ready to board her if we don't want her guns to tear us to pieces. Have those grappling hooks ready. As soon as I say so, we board her. I don't expect they'll put up much of a fight. They'll probably only have a couple dozen crew members. We'll check the ship from stern to bow first. Once the top of the ship is under control, you can send patrols below to make sure it is cleared out there. Lock the pirates up somewhere, and then get the ship's guns ready to fire." Eric could hardly believe how closely the surrounding men heeded him. "Mr. Gary," he called out.

"Yes, Captain."

"You stay here and be ready to cut the *Rosemary* loose if we run into more trouble than expected and we need to retreat."

Mr. Gary gave a reluctant murmur of agreement, though he clearly preferred to be a part of the action. "I know you'd rather join us, but I need someone reliable on the ship."

The squatty sailor nodded appreciatively.

"Oh, and Mr. Gary?" Eric added.

"Yes, Captain."

"See to it that Miss Charlotte stays aboard the *Rosemary* with you." Eric glanced behind him, as if afraid Charlotte would hear him.

Mr. Gary grinned. "I'll be needing more men at my disposal if that's the case, sir." The rest of the men chuckled.

"You take as many as you need," Eric smiled, though his heart was beating so loud he wondered if those close to him could hear it. He looked forward and saw their destination looming larger. "Very well, men. Pass the word, make the preparations, and we'll catch ourselves a pirate ship in no time."

The men mumbled their dues to Eric and then dispersed. Eric stood apart and noticed Samuel catch a couple men before they left. Samuel whispered something to the men and Eric recognized a deft gesture made in his direction. A moment later, he realized the two men were flanking him on both sides and keeping a close watch on him. Eric realized that Samuel had given them the charge of being his bodyguards during the action. At first resentful, feeling that he should not receive more preferential treatment than anyone else, at least it put him more at ease considering he had never experienced a conflict like this before.

The pirate ship grew closer and closer. Eric wondered when the pirates would recognize the *Rosemary*'s presence. The tension mounted while the crew members held their breath. Eric listened for the pirate voice crying out, alerting the others of their presence—any second now.

Everyone suddenly flinched at a loud noise, one that did not come from the pirate ship as they expected. Instead, the loud crack came from a quarter mile away, on the shore. They all instantly recognized the blast of a cannon.

Eric breathed freely. Lieutenant Curtis's patrols had started the battle on the shore. Eric now knew that the pirate ship was theirs, since the ensuing battle on shore would keep all remaining pirate eyes diverted from what might approach them in the rear.

By the time a second cannon fired and some musket shots spattered across the swelling waters, the *Rosemary* had slid skillfully in line with the much larger pirate ship. Eric monitored the closing gap between the ships and then motioned for the grappling hooks. The hooks flew through the air in an explosion of ropes and metal. They sunk into their target, and the two ships fused together. Finally, a voice cried out from the pirate ship and the sound of pattering feet showed some action.

Eric's excitement rose to such a point that he about scaled onto the other boat without a second glance back. "Sir," someone caught him from behind.

"Yes?" Eric quipped impatiently.

"Won't you be needing a weapon?"

Eric scanned himself and realized that he almost challenged the opposing pirate crew with his bare fists alone. "Of course," he replied, immediately regretting the lost time it would take to go to the armory and back.

Samuel appeared at Eric's side, his mouth grinning through his dark complexion with the fire of impending battle. "Take mine, Captain."

The situation proved too urgent for Eric to refuse. He snatched the proffered sword. Holding the weapon in his hand, feeling its heft, and hearing the sound of pirates just across from him trying to muster defense sparked something within Eric. Before he had time to second guess his actions, and with a roar not native to his timid nature, Eric enthusiastically called out for the charge. He lept forward, grabbing the nearest rope leading to the tall pirate deck above them. He took some satisfaction in knowing that his abrupt movement caught his appointed bodyguards off guard and forced them to scramble behind him.

As Eric clambered up the rope with his sword awkwardly in one hand, he felt inspired to see the massing crew members of the *Rosemary* surging upward onto the pirate ship. By the time he breached the deck and wielded his sword in front of him, dozens of other crew members had hopped onto the deck and started their sweep of the ship, stern to bow as he had instructed.

Incredible as it seemed, the battle ended before it really started. The isolated groups of pirates on the ship were focused on the battle at shore, so they remained entirely ignorant of the surprise attack until the ships had fused together. Though a few of them tried to scramble to form resistance, the overwhelming number and speed of the *Rosemary*'s crew made it clear that it would be instant death to attempt to fight. Eric hefted his sword in front of him, recognizing how much at home it felt in his hand. Still, his insides took a moment before normalizing. Born for it or not, going into a battle makes you terribly anxious, he realized.

After surveying the carrying out of his instructions, Eric advanced to some of the crew members grouped on the quarterdeck. He was peripherally aware of his bodyguards shadowing him on his way. As soon as he arrived, his crew members parted to let him pass, and he saw what must have been the main body of pirates left to guard the ship, subdued and surrounded.

Eric took only a passing interest in them. "Disarm them, take 'em below, and lock them up. Then join the others in loading the guns."

One of the pirates spurned Eric's statement and held out the handle of his sword to the group. "I ain't surrenderin' the ship till I can give up my sword to yer cap'n."

Eric realized the pirate was abiding by the sea tradition of offering his sword to the victorious captain. Regardless, it was unlikely that this pirate was the pirate captain since that one would be on land directing the attack. Eric also knew they had no time for formalities, as the noises of the battle on shore mounted. "Take them below. We don't have time for this."

Eric's crew members moved on his command, but the pirate suddenly reversed his sword and fended them off. He turned toward Eric. "I'm not lettin' a little cabin boy tell me what to do! Now bring me your cap'n or I tell my men to fight to the last man!"

Eric noticed that the other pirates did not share their leader's enthusiasm, but he did not have time to point out fallacies in the pirate's argument. Every second wasted talking became another second lost with the battle on shore. Determined, Eric used one swift motion, swinging his sword, and hitting the menacing pirate's blade just above the point where he held it. The sword clattered helplessly to the ground, and then Eric's weapon hovered inches above the pirate's heart with a precision that surprised even him. "I am the captain, and I accept your surrender," he said coldly. Without moving his eyes from the pirate's, he then called out to his crew for a third time. "Take them below, now!"

The other pirates immediately released their weapons. The leader, who stood under the threat of Eric's sword, could only look at Eric with his eyes wide open and mouth agape. Seconds later, the crew grabbed him and hauled him below decks. Eric took a deep breath. The rush of the moment now having passed, he marveled for a minute that only a few days ago he sat in Mr. Pickney's office feeling pointless.

Those still on deck who witnessed Eric's feat gawked until Eric came back to himself and commanded them to prepare the ship for sail. In the middle of the melee, he saw Samuel coming up from below.

"Guns are ready, Captain Francis," he reported.

"Excellent," Eric responded. He dispensed instructions to his first mate as the image of Mr. Pickney's office disappeared from his mind.

Captain Pete Shivers never sought to be a pirate. His ambitions went no further than getting a lot of money in a short amount of time—piracy simply turned out to be the best way to satiate his greed. Soon his pirate peers granted him a post as a captain, not so much for valor in battle—something he tried to avoid at all costs—but for a cunning ruthlessness in stabbing the right people in the back at the right time (often literally). Not too much time afterward, he ran into the Willard Twins. He made no pretenses; the brother duo scared him to death. But he could not ignore their unprecedented success rate. His greed overcame his fear, and he joined them.

That brought him to this beach less than a league away from Port Raleigh's fort.

The week they spent shutting down the shipping lanes to Port Raleigh proved exceptionally lucrative. If they would have cut cable at that point and retreated to their own hidden corners of the Caribbean, they could set themselves up pretty nicely with their haul. But the Twins had more in mind.

Pete knew the Twins had Port Raleigh in their sights when they first entered the San Fernando Channel, but he could not help but think that the actions of that small ship that slipped past them earlier that day had instigated this current attack. He also felt relatively certain that they gave him the most difficult job of the attack because he had allowed the ship to escape from him in the shoals. Pete at least had the brains to not point out to the Twins that the little ship had also passed both of them as they sat like beached whales in their cozy little cove.

So, while he did not find pleasure with the assignment of taking the fort, he also could not disguise his enthusiasm for the riches they would shovel into their cargo holds after taking Port Raleigh.

The minute his forces landed on the beach, however, Captain Pete Shivers second-guessed his decision. As soon as the pirates grouped together and performed a weapons and gear check, a loud blast of a cannon shot bombarded them from the heights above the beach. Pete had no qualms with putting life before reputation—he was the first one to scramble to the nearest patch of palm trees and cuddle at their base. Whether he really shrieked like a girl or not remained a topic for debate among the pirate crew for quite some time afterward.

Cowardly though it may have been, Pete's move saved him from the second blast of cannon shot, which pounded a small crater in the spot he had stood only moments earlier. A couple musket shots followed, then another barrage from the cannons.

The pirates did little better than their leader. They ran for any sort of cover in the area, from rocks to trees to simply laying on the ground with their hands over their heads. Their fate may have been nothing more than ignominious deaths in the sand had Pete's second-in-command not shown considerably more poise than his superior. The ugly beanpole of a man growled at the scattering pirates and called for some return fire, all the while looking for the captain.

Pete watched with a pang of jealousy as the fearless man dodged cannon and musket fire, calling out the captain's name. Pete still did not respond until he witnessed his second-in-command approach a particularly terrified pirate, crouched in the fetal position and crying like a baby, and address him as captain. Pete stood up nervously, collected himself as best he could, and called out, "Over here, you swab!"

The second-in-command immediately located the sound of his captain's voice and joined him in the midst of the palm trees. After Pete mumbled something about getting a better vantage point of the enemy's position from his location, the second-in-command asked the captain for orders. "I've started some return fire, but I need to know your plans," he barked.

"How many are they?" Pete stammered, trying to buy some time to think.

The second-in-command returned a curious look before answering, "I can't be sure, Captain. You're the one with the vantage point of scouting out the enemy . . ." Pete grimaced at this jab, but the second-in-command continued before Pete could respond. "There seems to be at least two cannon, which hints of a large force, but we've only seen some scattered musket fire."

Pete hated these situations. The whole reason he had joined the Willard Twins was because their reputation alone usually led to immediate surrenders, which kept him from any real fighting. A quick review of the situation called for an immediate retreat. Their attack on the fort was supposed to be a surprise, and they had already met resistance at their landing. Obviously the element of surprise had been ruined. However, even after Pete arrived at this conclusion, he realized that retreat was not an option. Certainly not because he had a "never-say-never" attitude—his second-in-command could tell anybody as much. Certainly not because he worried about his reputation—being a pirate lent him an admirable reputation in the first place. Captain Pete Shivers knew he could not retreat because the Twins would kill him if he came back without taking the fort.

Pete sighed. On to battle, then.

He took what little comfort he could in the knowledge that Jedediah Willard informed him that they had granted him enough men to outnumber every soldier of the fort. Even if the whole of the fort's soldiers lodged in front of him, he should be able to overrun them with a bit of pressure.

Pete addressed to his second-in-command. "Get every one of those lily-livered cowards off the ground and form a counterattack. We're not about to get pushed around by some worthless lobster backs." Pete felt pleased to see that his second-in-command had not expected this decision.

"Aye, aye, Captain Pete!" came the sharp response.

Moments later, Pete's second-in-command ran along the beach, rallying the pirates to form for an attack. Pete took a couple timid steps out of his secure position before he gained enough gumption to yell at the troops himself. Pretended bravery or not, it did the job. The pirates reformed at the behest of their leaders and did a decent job of returning fire. The few who did not stand became convinced after Pete forced a shot from his pistol inches away from the foot of a cowering pirate (fortunately, no one guessed that Pete really planned on killing the man for effect, but his jittery nerves caused him to miss the easy shot).

Once the men formed into squads, the second-in-command hurried over to Pete. "Captain Pete, I think the opposing force must only be a couple patrols. We haven't seen significant musket fire from them since they started the attack."

This news heartened the pirate. "What are we waiting for?" he responded. "Attack, attack!"

The second-in-command ran in front of the pirates, waving his sword and screaming for the charge. Captain Pete found himself caught up in the act. He clutched his cutlass, waved it menacingly, and ran toward the embankment where the enemy waited. Only steps behind him followed the large pirate force.

Pete's enthusiasm lasted until a pirate next to him went down with a musket ball to the head. At that point, he grabbed a pretended wound on his knee and backed out of the thick of the fighting. He heard a much greater retort of musket fire than he expected from the opposing soldiers. Something was not right.

Just after that, two pirates lugged someone back to Pete's position. The pirate captain remembered himself, seizing his knee in feigned pain as they approached. "Who you got there, lads?"

Then Pete recognized his second-in-command placing a hand over a wound seeping with red blood from his left shoulder. "Are you okay, Captain?" the wiry second-in-command asked with a grit that inspired Pete's jealousy once more. Pete attempted to echo it in his response. "Oh, just a scratch. I'll probably have to amputate. What happened to you?"

"It was just a couple patrols, sir, just as we guessed," he said, ignoring the question. "But as we were about to overrun them, they got a fresh force from the fort. That pushed us back temporarily, but we've still got numbers on them. I expect they'll be overrun soon."

This information relieved Pete quite a bit. So much so that he forgot to keep on nursing his injured knee. "Excellent." He remembered the rest of the plans and gave his orders. "Once they're beaten, we'll move on quickly to the fort. The Twins'll expect it to fall at any moment now. We'll need the gunners at the fort when it's fallen." Pete took one of the men who had carried his second-in-command. "Get some men and take a boat out to the ship. We'll need the gun crews we left there to join us so we can—"

Pete's command cut short as the very ship he was referring to suddenly lit up with the flash of cannon fire. "Those mangy bilge rats are a bit late in helping us out," he deadpanned.

Suddenly a shrill sound caused the small group to freeze. Following the high-pitched whistle came a heavy thud. Then they felt the tiny stings of hurtling rocks and sand. Pete heard screams emanate from his pirate forces a little higher up. "What the devil . . . ?" he muttered.

He at least found comfort in seeing that his second-in-command was just as confused by this occurrence as he was. "Those imbeciles are hitting our forces," he muttered through clenched teeth. A second barrage landed right in the thick of the swarming pirate forces.

Captain Pete Shivers would be the first to admit that he was not the most competent of leaders, but he did pride himself in those things he managed to get right. "I left the blasted gunners on the ship!" he growled. "It shouldn't be that difficult to aim for the side where all the opposing fire is coming from."

After a couple more rounds from the ship hit dead into the bulk of the pirates, mayhem broke out. The pirates could no longer hold ranks. They started to scatter in the face of cannon fire on one side and the fort soldiers' continued onslaught of musket fire on the other. In light of the recent reversal of fortune, Pete did nothing to stop them. The only consolation he gleaned from his hasty retreat was that a small rock ricocheting from a cannon shot hit him in the knee and not only gave him a bruise that would justify his pretended wound from before, but it also kept him from being in the first boat retreating back to the ship. This unfortunate boat achieved an ignoble fate after being demolished by a particularly acute shot from the ship. The other boats knew better than to try their luck. The pirates stayed on the beach, placed their weapons in the sand, and turned themselves over to the approaching soldiers. The battle ended.

Though Pete would much rather be captured by the Port Raleigh garrison than return to the Twins defeated, he could not help but glance back at his ship with regret. The treasure stored away inside of her crossed his mind first. The second thing he thought was that whoever took their ship had brilliantly turned to tide off the battle and cut off their escape in one blow.

The person accredited with Captain Pete Shivers's two regrets did not even witness the end of the battle. Eric, at that moment, anchored the *Rosemary* underneath the shadow of the fort a little less than a league away.

Chapter 7

TURNING ON
THE TWINS

Almost as soon as Eric dispensed his orders to Samuel and pointed out where the gunners would find the greatest mass of pirates to target, he jumped over to the *Rosemary* and pushed off toward the fort. A short while later he heard the first shots of the cannon, and he was satisfied that the battle would be over soon. His satisfaction lasted only a few seconds.

"Eric Francis! You've got a lot of nerve keeping me on this ship while you go about jumping from ship to ship and running around with a sword in your hand as if you were a little kid on a playground!"

Eric turned to see a vibrant Charlotte approaching him with a stern look on her face. Even though he expected such a verbal backlash, he could not help but take a step or two backward as she approached. "Now, Charlotte, I feel responsible for you, and if something were to happen to you, I—"

"Oh, that's ridiculous!" she exclaimed. Though the darkness kept Eric from seeing it, Charlotte's anger harbored more bark than bite. "Did it ever occur to you that I should be responsible for myself?"

Clearly out of his league in this conversation, Eric responded with an even voice. "Charlotte, considering how it was my plan in the first place, it wouldn't be fair to let you blindly go into something that might be dangerous."

Charlotte huffed and glared at Eric before speaking. "Natural-born pirate hunter or not, I could still hold my own against you in a fight, Eric Francis, so you watch yourself." Eric wasn't sure if he noticed a hint of a smile twitch at the corners of her mouth. "I'll tell you one thing,

Captain Francis, the next time you leave this ship, you're not doing it without me."

Eric barely subdued a snicker at Charlotte's stubborn nature. "Charlotte, I wouldn't even dream of it." Charlotte did not realize that Eric knew that his next stop was going to be the fort, and there would be no danger there, so he had no need to keep her cooped up—nor would he dare attempt it.

The boat from the ship took them to a small cove below the fort. Eric guessed, and correctly so, that a path would lead up to the fort from this point. They disembarked and he and Charlotte made their way up the steep trail, followed closely by a couple of armed sailors who escorted a pirate prisoner that Eric brought from the other ship.

After a couple minutes of tiring climbing, they crested the hill and arrived at the fort. They announced themselves at the entrance and were subsequently brought before Lieutenant Curtis, who had expected them after seeing the *Rosemary*'s approach. "Lieutenant Curtis," Eric said. "Thanks for sending your men to fight the pirates. By this time the pirates should be captured and the battle won."

Lieutenant Curtis's eyes twinkled. "Captain of the *Rosemary*, I presume?"

"Yes, Captain Eric Francis." Eric shuffled, feeling unaccustomed to formalities. "And this is Charlotte Reeves, a friend and advisor." Charlotte's eyebrow raised at Eric's introduction.

Lieutenant Curtis bowed politely to Charlotte, and then looked over Eric again with a slight smile on his lips.

"May I ask what is so funny, Lieutenant?" Charlotte asked, irritated by Curtis's cryptic grin.

Lieutenant Curtis's face quickly transformed to seriousness. "I apologize, Miss Charlotte. I did not mean to mock. I just realized why your first mate, Mr. Wesley, was being so careful when he mentioned his superior earlier this evening. I now realize that, for the purpose of maintaining credibility, he was hiding the fact that his captain was no more than a boy."

If Curtis had hoped to appease Charlotte, this comment had the opposite effect. "Boy or not, he is a natural-born pirate hunter, and more suited for this job than you or any other kind of librarian would be!"

"Librarian?" Curtis queried.

This strange quip confused Eric until he realized that Charlotte had just given away Curtis's natural-born ability. Librarian? Eric thought, looking over Lieutenant Curtis. That explains his organizational skills. Eric turned to Charlotte, who still glared down the bewildered Lieutenant Curtis. "Easy, Charlotte. He didn't mean it in that way."

Curtis nodded. "Indeed, Miss Charlotte. I was only trying to say that Mr. Wesley was being very careful about mentioning his captain, so I assumed that there was something suspicious about the whole situation. As it turns out, he was only trying to maintain credibility by not revealing that the youthful age of his captain." Charlotte about snapped again at this comment, so Lieutenant Curtis raised his hands. "This is hardly an issue anymore, however, as I've seen that Captain Francis's strategies and deductions were all perfectly sound, regardless of his age. As soon as I realized this, I couldn't help but smile at my own ignorance of the situation. Please forgive my impertinence."

Charlotte's muscles relaxed. She sighed and reluctantly said, "You're forgiven, Lieutenant Curtis."

"Now, Captain Francis," Lieutenant Curtis said, the mood in his voice turning businesslike. "You left the battle early for a purpose, I presume. What is it?"

"The Twins should still not know that their plan hasn't worked," Eric stated. "They could not risk being in visual range with the fort until they knew it had been taken. They'll have heard the cannon and musket fire but will assume that it was the fort falling to the pirates. Now that the sounds of battle have ended, they'll be trying to enter the harbor at any moment. Obviously without the fort to attack them or warn anyone in town, they'd be able to take out the Royal Navy ships in a rush and Port Raleigh would be theirs."

Lieutenant Curtis nodded. "But since we do have control of the fort, we can keep the Twins from entering the harbor."

"Yes," Eric replied expectantly, "but I am hoping that we can still do more than just keep them away. I'm hoping that we can take one or two more of the Willard Twins' ships this evening."

Charlotte saw the gears working in Lieutenant Curtis's head as soon as Eric made his proposal. "If that is the case, then we'll have to let the pirates enter the harbor before we start to fire into them."

Eric confirmed Curtis's speculation with a nod.

Curtis continued. "Then, after we have opened fire and battered them well enough, you will take the *Rosemary* and close in on the ship that is most damaged."

Eric smiled.

Lieutenant Curtis seemed to be gazing off in the distance as he considered this plan. "But do you have enough men for this? Even if you're only battling against one of the pirate ships, they will still have a very large crew, if not the leadership of one of the Willard Twins themselves."

"True. But I'm hoping that surprise will give us an advantage. Beside the surprise of the fort opening fire on them, what if the recently captured pirate ship, under the command of Mr. Wesley, and the *Rosemary* hid behind the fort, out of sight from the pirates? After you have started your cannon attack on the Twins, we'll both attack the weakest ship. If that attack goes well, we might be able to catch another damaged pirate ship as they retreat."

Lieutenant Curtis's eyebrows raised. He took a moment to consider Eric's proposal. "I think it's brilliant. Risky, but certainly brilliant." After another moment's consideration, he nodded, and then said, "Very well then. You'd better get into your position. I'll see to it that my men don't fire on the ships until they are well into the harbor."

Eric made no indication that he was going to leave. "There is one more thing."

"Oh?" Lieutenant Curtis wondered what it was that he had overlooked.

"In spite of their recklessness, I think the pirates won't want to enter the harbor until they can be sure the fort is taken."

Curtis nodded slowly as he processed this statement. "You think they'll wait for the pirate ship to come and report to them?"

"I'm not so sure they will lose time waiting for the other ship. I think they've simply prepared a signal."

"Of course!" Curtis tapped his finger on his mouth. "But we don't know the signal." Eric shook his head, and Curtis continued, "If only we could have one of the pirates from the captured ship to interrogate . . ."

At that point, Eric made for the door and called in the escorts with the pirate they held captive. "I thought the same thing, Lieutenant, so I brought along a prisoner." Curtis could barely hide his astonishment.

Eric continued. "This particular pirate has difficulties listening to a me so I hoped you might have more luck."

Lieutenant Curtis nodded. The guards roughly guided the pirate captive into the room. Eric had chosen to bring the same pirate who involuntarily surrendered his sword to Eric on the ship. The pirate stood in a stupor, angry and embarrassed about being captured, but even more ill-tempered about the young captain who had shamed him by subduing him and dragging him around as his prisoner.

Lieutenant Curtis stood up to the pirate, drilling him with a no-nonsense gaze. "The other pirates we talked to mentioned that there was to be a signal given from the fort to indicate that you had taken it."

The lie was simple, but effective. "Yeah," the pirate replied dully, "But seeing as how we've been captured, there won't be no signal."

"That's right," Curtis continued. "The only signal the Willard Twins will see from this fort will be dead pirates warning them what awaits them." Lieutenant Curtis let this grim image sink in before he added, almost nonchalantly, "But, for the sake of curiosity, what kind of signal was it going to be?"

The pirate snuffed disinterestedly. "Well, that's why myself and my crew weren't to go to land until the battle was over, cause we're the gunners, and they needed us unharmed to send out the signal from the fort once we took it."

"Oh, so the signal was going to be some cannon shots? How many, exactly?"

The pirate was about to respond, but his slow-thinking mind finally caught up with what was going on. "'Ere, now! I know what you're trying to do. You want me to tell you the signal so that you can lure the rest of them pirates into the harbor. Well, sir, I may be many things, but I ain't no rat. I'm not tellin' a soul."

Curtis's lip stiffened. "You will be killed along with the rest of the pirates for your crimes, but I can promise you a humane death if you talk. We already know the signal; you just have to tell us how many shots."

Impelled by the only shred of dignity he had left, the pirate kept his mouth shut.

Curtis waited the pirate out for a moment, but it availed nothing. He turned to Eric with building frustration. Eric stood thinking.

"It couldn't be many cannon shots. There weren't that many gunners on the ship when we took it. Enough for three or four cannons at the most."

"Well," Curtis demanded, turning back to the pirate, "Which was it, three or four?"

Though the pirate said nothing, the question clearly summoned an almost imperceptible facial reaction.

Eric approached the pirate, still thoughtful. "No . . . too many. They wouldn't want it to seem like a salute." The pirate looked at Eric sharply. Eric continued. "One shot maybe?" The pirate stared Eric down seriously. Eric smiled. He looked the pirate dead in the eyes as he spoke. "No, it couldn't be one shot. One shot could be mistaken for a warning shot." The pirate's eyes flickered; his mouth twitched. Eric turned triumphantly to Lieutenant Curtis. "It's two shots, Lieutenant Curtis. That's our signal."

The pirate's mouth hung agape for a moment. Lieutenant Curtis smiled while nodding his head incredulously.

With this information gathered, Eric quickly wrapped up their business. "Very well, Lieutenant. I'm sure you know what to do. I'm going to get the *Rosemary* into position and wait for Mr. Wesley's arrival. Good luck, sir."

Curtis saluted sharply, and just before Eric and Charlotte left, Eric turned and added, "Not that I need to tell you, Lieutenant, but it has to be two shots precisely. One more or less could tip off the Twins and cause them to retreat before we can spring the trap."

Curtis saluted again, "Aye, aye, Captain Francis."

The captive pirate watched Eric go in awe before he was finally able to recover his senses. Forgetting his place as prisoner, he looked over to Lieutenant Curtis, "Who the devil is that boy?"

Curtis laughed. "Funny, I was thinking the exact same thing."

On their way back to the *Rosemary*, Charlotte grinned.

"What?" Eric asked. He had to take a break from working out the particulars of his upcoming strategy.

"You knew what the signal was, didn't you?"

"The signal for the Willard Twins from the fort, you mean?"

"Yes. You knew it."

"Well, I know it now," Eric answered, not sure exactly what Charlotte was insinuating.

"No, Eric," Charlotte followed up. "Don't play this game with me. You knew even before we entered the fort."

"That's ridiculous. Then why would I have Lieutenant Curtis interrogate the pirate if I already knew?"

"Because you are smarter than you will admit, Eric. Ever since the governor and Captain Bellview treated you the way they did, you are being much more careful when dealing with adults. In this case, instead of running the risk that Lieutenant Curtis wouldn't believe your speculation on the signals, you decided to help him make the discovery right at that moment."

"I suspected, Charlotte," Eric replied, his response curt. "Our little interrogation only confirmed what I suspected."

"Whatever you want to call it. You needn't be so moody about it, Eric. I'm only trying to give you a compliment."

Eric gave Charlotte a cautious "thank you." The following seconds ensued in silence as they scrambled down the rocky path toward the boat they left a short time earlier. Then Eric spoke out. "I just didn't feel good about tricking Lieutenant Curtis. He seems like a very honest man. I guess I'm just angry at myself that I had to resort to such a level."

Charlotte almost comforted Eric, but she held herself back. She knew that Eric had done what he needed to. As she mentioned, it was likely the only way to guarantee that Lieutenant Curtis would believe him. Eric had made a calculated decision. But Charlotte could also not deny that he had deliberately deceived Curtis, good intentions or not. *Well*, she thought, *Eric proved that he recognized the fault in his decision.* Even though he and she knew that he did it for a good cause, Charlotte figured it would be better if she let him feel guilty for what he did so as not to numb his sense of what she saw as admirable integrity.

By the time the two had boarded the *Rosemary* again, the recently captured pirate ship, captained by Samuel, had anchored next to the *Rosemary*. In a matter of minutes, Samuel joined Eric and Charlotte on the quarterdeck. He first reported what they already suspected, that the battle had been won and the pirates on the shore subdued. Eric then revealed to Samuel his next plan of attack.

After the incredible events of the past couple of days, Samuel thought the time would come when he would cease to be amazed by Eric. But that moment had not yet arrived. Eric's daring once again left Samuel speechless before he finally saluted and muttered a respectful, "Aye, aye, Captain Francis."

Eric spent the next few minutes debriefing his officers, telling them of the daunting task before them. Charlotte could see that the officers were not stupid. They knew the risk in the endeavor, yet the sheer audacity of the plan lit a fire in them that made it too irresistible to pass by.

Only dozens of yards away, Samuel must have just finished the same discussion, because his crew mobilized and made preparations on the ship. Several men transferred over to the *Rosemary*, since she only carried a skeleton crew, and she likewise prepared for battle. The crews accomplished all this behind the protective shadow of the fort, out of sight from where the pirate twins would approach.

By the time the preparations for sailing drew to a conclusion, Eric could only stand and wait impatiently for the fort to see the approaching pirate ships, let them enter the harbor, and then give the go-ahead signal to the *Rosemary*. The crew, which had bustled only moments earlier, found themselves forced to await the command to put the ships in motion.

Eric should have been tired, and he felt that somewhere, deep inside, his body bordered on extreme fatigue. It had been a very arduous night, day, and night. But his adrenaline, combined with the exhilaration of accomplishing something that he excelled at, something he was born to do, somehow managed to push him past his exhaustion. In a way, he felt that if he slowed down he might wake up, or in some other way lose this surreal, once-in-a-lifetime opportunity. This explained why waiting for the signal resulted in such a difficulty—he simply wanted to move to the next challenge and keep moving until his dream ran out from beneath him. Eric's anxiety soon dissipated.

A deep and solitary shot fired out from the fort into the silent night. The crew rustled, in spite of his warning for them to remain still until his command. The echoes of the shot rolled across the waters until it died out and silence refilled its void.

Then the second shot rang out—music to Eric's ears.

Although the slab of land on which the fort sat blocked a view of the entrance to the harbor, in his mind Eric could see the approaching pirate ships. He knew their location. From the wind that ruffled his hair, he knew how fast they would be going. He felt relatively certain that he could even pinpoint the exact moment when Lieutenant Curtis would open fire from the fort.

Eric closed his eyes as these calculations and images methodically worked their way through his mind. Fourteen more minutes and the cannon barrage would begin. Eric then saw what would be the confusion on the pirate ships: the falling spars and rigging, the splintering wood, the explosions, the mayhem as the pirates would first try to push through the cannon shots, then eventually fall back.

Seven more minutes.

Eric considered his chances again. He knew that taking one of these ships would not be as easy as taking the last pirate ship. Still, he felt the pirates would be taken off guard, and because of this, he and his crew ran a decent chance at succeeding.

Suddenly an unexpected occurrence interrupted his thoughts.

From the window of a room where he had been locked, the pirate captive witnessed the two secret signal shots that he would have fired if his fellow crew members could have taken the fort. He then saw the dark silhouettes of the approaching pirate ships, oblivious to their danger. Anger swelled up inside of him.

The pirate did not abound in loyalty toward his cause. Piracy encouraged little of thinking generously about others. Still, as he watched the approaching ships, the pirate stewed over how he had been made a fool, and not by a competent Royal Navy officer, but by a nobody. Now he not only would experience the shame of being put to death as a pirate, but he would also be known as the man that had been captured by a lad. The very thought almost drove him insane with disgrace. He could not accept such a fate. He refused to.

"Unlock the door! Hurry! I've some information fer your commander 'bout the pirates. There's no time. Take me to him right now!"

The guard knew that Lieutenant Curtis interrogated the pirate earlier, so he easily believed that the pirate might have felt it would be in his best interest to share information in order to negotiate his death sentence. Driven by the urgency in the pirate's voice, he fumbled with the keys in order to open the door quickly. The lock had barely clicked before the door was suddenly kicked open, smashing against the guard and toppling him to the ground.

The guard only needed a second to recover, but it was a second too late. The pirate had not hesitated once free of his cell. He rushed forward, unchecked, toward the ramparts of the fort. The guard's cries alerted the troops, and they immediately opened fire on the flying figure. He evaded every shot. Advancing quickly and unexpectedly, the pirate bowled over a gunner, who barely had time to turn and see what the commotion was about. With the gunner out of the way, the pirate then grabbed the cord attached to the cannon.

Because the pirate stood still at this point, the errant shots of the fort's soldiers finally hit their mark. The other gunners nearby heard the thudding of each musket ball as they pounded into the pirate's body and some groans emitted from his throat. Though mortally wounded, before dropping to the ground and taking his last breath, he tugged hard on the cannon's cord.

The loaded cannon roared as a result, sending its shot far into the air, while the recoil managed to smash back into the already failing body of the pirate. By the time the soldiers of the fort reached the pirate, they heard his dying words: "No shame in that death."

Eric could hardly believe what he heard. Though he expected a shot from the fort, this one had come at least seven minutes early. The Twins could not have entered far enough into the harbor to give them the barrage they would need to receive before diminishing them enough for an assault by either him or Samuel.

Eric could not be sure of what happened, but the fact that subsequent shots did not follow immediately afterward helped him realize that Lieutenant Curtis had not ignorantly "jumped the gun." *It must have been an accident*, Eric thought, *a trigger-happy gunner*. Eric felt that Lieutenant Curtis would train more disciplined gunners than that, but whatever the reason for the shot, the timing crippled his plan. If the pirates suspected anything, they very well could pull back right then.

Charlotte heard the unexpected shot like everyone else, and after watching Eric fret, she surmised what it insinuated.

"The pirates saw the earlier signal," she said. "They'll just assume this shot was an accident."

Eric threw this idea around in his mind. *Yes*, he told himself, *the pirates could think that.* They might dismiss the shot. After all, there was no reason for them to think that the first stage of their strategy had been foiled. These pirates were supposed to be reckless. They would be too intent on revenge for the run of the *Rosemary* earlier that day to turn back because of one inadvertent shot.

Eric forced a smile to Charlotte. "I guess we'll find out soon enough."

They did find out soon, though much sooner than he hoped. A minute after his statement, the sharp silence that pervaded the tense night air suddenly ripped into a veritable thunder that exploded from the fort as it let loose all its firepower. A short interval of calm followed it before the scattered roars of individual shots continued the salvo of artillery fire.

Charlotte looked at Eric hopefully. "That's good, right? They're firing on the pirates."

Eric thought it over. "It's too early."

"But why would Lieutenant Curtis fire too early? He seemed like he knew what he was doing."

"He does," Eric confirmed. "Which means the only reason he would open fire early is because the pirates turned around at the misfiring of the lone cannon shot. He's trying to hit them with what he can before they get out of range."

Charlotte discerned the disappointment on Eric's face. His careful strategy seemed to be falling apart. Charlotte was about to consoled him, but Eric suddenly took some initiative. "Mr. Gary!" he called out.

"Aye aye, Captain Francis." Mr. Gary and the crew had been watching their curious captain from a distance, wondering to see his reaction to the series of sounds emanating from the fort.

"Set sails! Those pirates aren't leaving without seeing the *Rosemary* in action!"

"Aye aye, Captain Francis!"

Mr. Gary set the crew to work with an unquestioned confidence in his teenage superior. Since they had been waiting at their stations in eagerness, the crew set the *Rosemary* moving within a matter of moments.

Charlotte watched for a minute before she spoke. "Eric, wasn't the plan to board the pirates after they had been pounded pretty badly by the fort?" Even now the fort's guns shot less and less often, indicating that the pirates had worked their way out of their range.

Eric nodded.

"Do you think they've been hit badly enough to fight them?"

"No," Eric said with grim certainty.

Though tempted to prompt Eric for a more detailed response, Charlotte could tell by Eric's mood that he would explain when he felt ready. Right now, his focus lay before them.

The *Rosemary* had practically jumped out of its hidden position in the small cove behind the fort. Samuel, in the newly acquired pirate ship, started moving forward himself, but he had not been prepared for the *Rosemary*'s abrupt start.

As soon as they cleared the rocky cape blocking their view of the events in Port Raleigh's harbor, Eric's confirmed his suspicions. The three spectral shadows of the pirate ships retreated into the darkness to the north. The fort, by now, reverted back to the silence that dominated the area only ten minutes earlier.

The sight of the ships brought new life to Eric. He called for more sails.

"Eric," Charlotte could no longer keep to herself, "we're one tiny ship and those are three large ships."

"And we only have four guns and they probably have thirty-six guns each," Eric answered.

Charlotte nodded. "Just making sure you were aware . . ."

Eric nodded distractedly, his eyes never wavering from the targets in front of them. His persistence paid off when the speed of the *Rosemary* carried them close enough to fire a shot. Though the shot came short, they still gained on the pirates. After a couple more minutes of chase, they actually hit the trailing pirate ship with a scattered few of their shots. The damage for the pirates ranged from minimal to none, but Eric clearly presented them with a challenge.

Charlotte felt relieved to see that once they sailed within range, Eric shortened the sails and kept at an even distance from the pirates, shooting his sparse cannon shots as frequently as possible. At first, the pirates endured these shots, hoping the *Rosemary* would come close enough that they could chase him down and board him, but Eric did no such thing.

Finally, after the *Rosemary*'s constant harassing, the middle pirate ship began to pivot back, as if to chase down the irritating *Rosemary* and teach her a lesson. Eric's eyes lit up. "Come on, you oaf!"

Eric's sudden excitement intrigued Charlotte.

"Mr. Gary," Eric called out, "make ready to come about on my mark."

"Aye aye, Captain Francis!"

"Gunners!" Eric yelled down to the deck.

Some scattered "aye ayes" told him he had their attention. "When we come about, get ready to fire on that ship that is bearing down on us!"

A curious Charlotte listened to these instructions as she might listen to another person speaking a foreign language to her. After giving his orders, Mr. Gary came to her side. "That friend of yours is the most reckless captain I've ever known." His eyes glittered. "But he's a brilliant one!"

"I guessed that much, Mr. Gary, but would you do me the honor of telling me why he is so reckless and brilliant?"

"I just figured it out ma'self," he said, "But he's harpin' away at these pirates, trying to bait 'em into chasin' after him. Well, you can see that one of the pirates is taking the bait. So Captain Francis is going to stay just ahead of them, fire some shots to goad them on, and lead them—"

"Right into Samuel as he catches up with us in his ship."

Mr. Gary nodded with a huge grin on his face. "Yep. Then we both join up against the rogue, give 'im some hard broadsides, then board 'im on both sides."

Charlotte finally understood Eric's improvised strategy. She looked out and saw the pirate ship that had pealed away now almost completely turned around and bearing down in their direction. The *Rosemary*, by this time, deliberately turned about herself. As she did so, she lined up her cannons with the pirate ship.

"Not yet!" Eric instructed the gunners. "Wait for it. Wait! And—"

Eric stopped short when he and the crew suddenly saw some bright flashes pierce the night, not from the ship that decided to chase them, but from the one next in line to it. A few seconds later they heard the rumble of cannon shots. The most astounding result, however, was that the cannon shots were not aimed at the *Rosemary*, but at the other pirate ship, the one that had—as Mr. Gary put it—taken the bait. The pirates had dealt one of their own ships a close range, and possibly very damaging, broadside.

The repercussions of such an unexpected maneuver followed immediately. The ship that had turned to chase the *Rosemary* now came to a dead stop. Some wondered whether it would return the fire; instead, it slowly swiveled back around, following its previous course like a reprimanded dog with a tail between its legs following its master.

Charlotte guessed that Eric had to be frustrated from his second attempt to ensnare the pirates being foiled by another unforeseen occurrence. In reading his expression, however, she saw no anger there. Instead, Eric simply contemplated what occurred in curiosity. As the pirate ships finally disappeared into the dark night, Eric murmured, "Those are two brilliant pirate twins."

Though Governor Rose and Captain Bellview were steeped in pride, they could not be accused of being idiots. The two knew that a pirate attack had taken place, just as Eric had predicted. Not only that, but they also recognized that the fort took part in the defense of Port Raleigh. Rather than humble them, Eric's timely and brilliantly planned defense only managed to anger them more.

"Bellview, this is getting ridiculous," Governor Rose noted. "Do you realize what this means?"

Captain Bellview brooded.

"I'll tell you what it means," Governor Rose continued. "It means that this upstart young captain now has the backing of Lieutenant Curtis and the fort. He has just gone from crazy maroon who managed to creep into harbor with a skeleton crew to hero of the day with all of the military might of the town backing him."

Captain Bellview still did not respond.

"The second I try to reprimand him for going against my orders, every sailor from the wharf, every soldier from the garrison, if not the whole infernal town, will come up in arms against me. He's turned everyone against us! I should have suspected he had some second agenda hidden away somewhere. Who do you think he's working for? It might be that fatheaded moron, John Arnold back in London. That sorry excuse for a parliament member has always been looking for a way to undermine me, ever since I took this post out from underneath his nephew. Or it could be someone closer, like Governor Terrance, over in Nevis. Or . . . Bellview, are you even listening to me?"

Bellview stayed motionless.

Governor Rose threw his hands up exhaustedly. "What good is it to be governor if no one listens to me? And you, what good is it to be a captain if members of your own crew are serving on a backstabber's ship? What can we do?"

Captain Bellview stepped away from the window, where he had just witnessed the silhouette of the *Rosemary* reattach itself to the pier—welcomed by a crowd of flickering torches and celebration.

"We do, Governor Rose, the only thing we can do," Bellview finally responded. "We accept them as returning heroes. We set up a meeting with them tomorrow morning on their ship in order to congratulate them and provide them with due and appropriate accolades."

Governor Rose squinted in displeasure. "You can't be serious. You mean, we actually go before that pompous brat and give him the pleasure of seeing us grovel and snivel at his feet?"

Captain Bellview's eyes flickered in a way that might have scared even himself. "I never said that we actually talk to the ingrate. I merely mentioned that we set up a meeting."

At that moment, Governor Rose realized that Bellview had brewed some sort of plan. Rose lifted his heavy brow. "I'm listening . . ."

Chapter 8
SNEAK ATTACK

To Jedediah and Joshua Willard,

Though we will never submit to your forces, we are willing to negotiate the end of your blockade of the San Fernando Channel. The young man, who is captain to the ship that was able to sneak past your blockade, happens to come from a very well-to-do family in England and is sure to garner a hefty ransom. We will be willing to offer him up in exchange for an appeasement of the blockade you have imposed upon Port Raleigh.

If you are inclined to agree to this proposal, then the matter must be handled delicately. Because the boy's family has a good reputation back in England, he is beloved by the people here, and they would never allow him to be handed over to pirates. In reality, the boy is corrupt, immoral, and detrimental to the principles of our local government.

Since the townspeople are unaware of this and will defend him to the last, in order to take him you must immediately take the fishing boat that came to deliver this message, enter Port Raleigh harbor, and board the ship that slipped your blockade (now sitting at the pier on the west side of the harbor). For my part of the deal, besides imparting this information, I have ensured that the young captain will be present on the ship as I will set up a meeting with him there for this mid-morning. He is a young man and will likely be in the company of a young woman. Once you have successfully subdued him, you can ease the blockade and deliver a ransom note to the family, who are certain to pay handsomely.

If you refuse this offer, then you cannot say you were not given a chance to retreat with your lives. If you doubt our resolve, then please reference our brilliant fighting from last night. It will only be a matter of time before we take more ships until we will have you hanging from the gallows at the fort.

Amos H. Rose
Governor of His Royal Majesty's Colony, Port Raleigh

Jedediah Willard immediately recognized several noteworthy things about this letter. First, he found it amazing that after last night's victory, Port Raleigh would try to negotiate. Second, the fact that the governor offered up the very captain he and Joshua hoped to inflict their revenge upon astonished him. Third, Jedediah piqued with interest at their reference to this captain as being a youth. Besides these points, probably the most noteworthy aspect of the letter was that it brimmed with deceit.

After reading through the letter a couple of times, Jedediah found it completely unbelievable that the governor expected someone with the reputation of the Twins to back off their lucrative blockade in exchange for one person, a person whose name they did not even know and who was not guaranteed to bring in treasure. The governor clearly reeked of duplicity, or else he would have delivered the young captain himself instead of giving instructions on how the Twins should accomplish the feat. Why the deception? The most obvious reason is that it was a trap.

For Joshua's part, he fully believed that the invitation was a trap, much like the one his ship fell for last night. For this reason, he wanted to punish his first mate, Walter, for acting insubordinate and turning the ship around after Joshua had retired to his cabin to brood at the failure of taking Port Raleigh. Walter claimed that he could not resist going after the small ship that had brashly pursued them in their retreat from the harbor, and this insubordination caused a stern broadside from Jedediah's ship. Consequently Joshua had come onto deck to reassert order and bring the ship back around. What Joshua could barely admit to even himself is that, had he been on deck with that little ship pestering them, he probably would have done exactly the same thing.

"Sure, it's probably a trap. Who cares? Walter then gets captured. No loss there. Then again, there's even the possibility that it isn't a trap," Joshua argued. "Maybe—for some strange, wild reason—the governor is telling the truth. If it's true, then Walter can bring us the captain and we'll have revenge. Either way, we've rid ourselves of a menace."

Jedediah mulled the letter over in his mind carefully. It was too obvious to be a trap. The governor would never expect either of the Twins to actually go into the harbor on a fishing boat because of his word alone if he intended to trick them. That meant that there had to be some kind of truth hidden beneath the deceit. Jedediah examined the letter again.

The lies glared out at Jedediah and confused him further. It was a blatant lie that the governor attributed the victory of last night to himself. The governor had not been able to do anything for a full week, and then all of the sudden he ended up getting a backbone and some brilliant tactics? No. Jedediah knew that it had all started with the arrival of the young captain. The victory belonged to him.

Then there was the other ruse. The whole idea of turning a young gentleman over to pirates because of his corrupt and immoral nature— even though he heralded from a wealthy family back in England— came off as a laughable lie. Beside the hypocritical nature of betraying someone to pirates because that person is corrupt and immoral, Jedediah had yet to meet a governor in the Caribbean who cared more about cleaning up corruption than preserving their own reputation. If the young man indeed came from an influential family in England, immoral or not, the governor would treat him like a king for political reasons, not try to pawn him off to pirates.

Jedediah considered both these lies in his mind. The governor had nothing to do with the victory—it was the captain. And, secondly, the captain did not come from an influential family back in England. Lies though they were, they told a lot. Jedediah allowed a gradual smile to creep across his face as he recognized the single vein of truth in the letter. While the governor lied about the circumstances surrounding the captain, one thing from the letter was certain: the governor wanted to get rid of him.

"You know my favorite part of the letter, Jedediah?" Joshua said with a grin on his face. Jedediah did not respond, so Joshua continued, "I like how the dolt thinks that we would want the captain to put him up for ransom. It doesn't even occur to him that we really want him so that we can turn him inside out and feed him to the gulls."

"Wrong," Jedediah said, catching his brother off guard. "He doesn't care what we do to him. He just wants the little captain off of his hands."

"Come on, Jedediah," Joshua followed up. "You don't really believe that the governor wants to get rid of an immoral, corrupt kid from his so-painfully-pure town?"

Jedediah shook his head, considering the actual reasoning in his mind. "No. The only explanation for his actions is jealousy. This captain came and immediately did something about the pirates, something the governor couldn't do for a full week on his own. The town loves the captain not because of his family's reputation, but because he shows valor where the governor showed cowardice. The governor doesn't even believe we'll try to remove the blockade. He's just using us to get rid of his new political competition. He wants us to do his dirty work."

Joshua smiled as he realized what Jedediah claimed. Then he realized something else. "Then why don't we do the governor's dirty work? He thinks he's tricking us, but what does it matter? Whether he really tricks us or not, it helps us anyway. This way we can kill two birds with one stone. We can capture the captain and get our revenge, plus we can take away Port Raleigh's strategic defender. The illustrious and 'moral' Governor Rose won't be able to defend against our next attack without the captain helping him out."

Jedediah nodded slowly. "You make a good point, brother. If we heed the governor, trap or not, we've nothing to lose but your mate Walter if it fails."

Joshua pounded his fist on the table. "Then we accept the governor's proposition!"

Ten minutes later Walter, with a sparse crew of nine other pirates, sailed on the small fishing boat into Port Raleigh harbor. The Twins toasted to the good fortune that came their way after a disastrous night.

Eric took no part in the celebration when the *Rosemary* sidled into its spot on the pier. Fatigue finally caught up to him and he fell into a deep slumber below decks, protected fiercely by Mr. Gary, who insisted he be left alone. He did not stir until well into the next morning, his eyes fluttering.

"It's about time you woke up. I kept on taking a pulse every five minutes just to make sure you hadn't died."

Eric looked out past his hammock and saw a smiling Charlotte sitting close by. The morning light had only managed to pierce the darkness below deck in a single shaft at the open hatch, and Charlotte appropriately sat just in the middle of it, her maverick blonde hair once again creating a halo effect around her face. *She may look like an angel at times*, Eric thought to himself, *but I'd never expect an angel to have the kind of attitude she has.* Eric stretched a moment before saying, "I wouldn't have woken up either if it weren't for the racket my stomach kept on making."

Charlotte shifted in the light, and her eyes twinkled. "You did a good job last night, Eric."

Eric dodged the compliment. "I wanted to do better."

"Well, what can you do about it now?"

Eric considered Charlotte carefully. "I can go and get those pirates."

Charlotte's head bobbed lightly. "I was hoping you would say that, for two reasons."

After a short pause, Eric realized Charlotte was waiting for him to prod her. He relented. "Okay, what two reasons?"

Charlotte grinned. "One, because you were born for that; and two, because you're the hero of Port Raleigh and Lieutenant Curtis is waiting to congratulate you. I think he and everyone else here would all be very relieved if you helped them to get rid of the nuisances blocking their channel."

Eric sat up quickly. "Lieutenant Curtis is here?"

"Yeah."

"How long has he been waiting?"

"Ever since he told me not to wake you up because you needed your rest."

Charlotte clearly savored this conversation. Eric almost instinctively scolded her, but he knew that would only please her more. Instead he glanced at her wryly as he placed his shoes on and tried to fix his tousled hair. After a couple of passes with his hand through his hair and a couple chuckles from Charlotte, he finally gave up and the two scrambled up the companionway hatch onto the deck of the *Rosemary*.

The bright, tropical sun already crawled well up into the sky, and Eric felt the humidity sticking his clothes to his body only seconds after he emerged. On the quarterdeck, he spotted Lieutenant Curtis speaking with Samuel. As soon as Eric got near enough for them to notice him, they stiffened up. They both brought their arms to their heads in a sharp salute, and Samuel barked out, "Morning, Captain Francis!"

Eric sensed the innate awkwardness of these two respected individuals saluting him of all people. He brought his arm up to a half-hearted salute and mumbled, "Good morning . . . um, gentlemen."

Though their formal greeting felt uncomfortable, when he noticed their smiles he found himself more at ease.

"Captain Francis, I was hoping to tell you first hand what a remarkable job you did last night, and I bring a report from the fort."

"Please report, Lieutenant Curtis," Eric responded, hoping that he answered correctly.

"The entire pirate crew landing force was captured with very few casualties. They are now under lock and key at the fort." Lieutenant Curtis's eyes then faltered somewhat. "I also would like to apologize for the misfire last night. There is no excuse for the behavior and I hold myself responsible. I am deeply disappointed that such an occurrence would happen in a fort under my keeping."

Because the incident had already occurred, Eric had no desire to dwell on it too much, but he did want to know the circumstances. Before he even asked, however, Lieutenant Curtis said, "Suicidal pirate."

This realization dawned on Eric. He nodded as if he should have expected it the whole time. "Of course. Lieutenant, that's my fault. I should've known he would've tried something desperate after being humiliated."

Lieutenant Curtis quietly appreciated Eric's maturity before replying, "Well, Captain Francis, whoever takes the blame should also take credit for the tremendous victory." A deft reminder of a phrase Eric used earlier. "Some pirate ships slipped away, but one didn't and the whole of the town was most likely saved because of it."

As someone who had avoided the limelight for most of his life, Eric suspected that the conversation might get embarrassing if it continued in this way. "Thank you, Lieutenant. Any other news from the fort?"

Lieutenant Curtis thought for a moment. "Nothing to speak of. Just that your brilliance has inspired confidence in all of us, from the sailors on the wharf, to the soldiers in the fort, to even the fishermen in town. I actually saw one of them take his ship out of the harbor earlier this morning for what was probably the first time in a week."

"Had an itchin' to go fishin'," Eric said, quoting a favorite phrase of his grandpa. He had not really thought of his family since he had been gone—his mind had been preoccupied with other pressing matters. Now, however, he felt a slight pang of homesickness as he thought about his family as the one place he felt wanted before he came here. Eric shook his head. "Where is the good fishing here?" Hoping to continue the conversation as a way of distracting himself.

"Near some shoals on the west side of the harbor. The fish swim around there in masses."

Eric squinted over in that direction. "Then the ship is farther away than my eyes could see, probably."

"Actually, the ship didn't go that way for some reason. He headed more toward the channel."

This statement triggered something in Eric. "Is there some fishing out by the channel?"

Lieutenant Curtis could see where Eric was heading with this question. "Some, yes, but not near as good as to the shoals to the west."

"Then why," Eric mused, "why would a fisherman, cooped up for a week, not only avoid the best fishing spot in the area, but also risk going near to where the pirates are?"

Samuel now became intrigued with the conversation. "He wouldn't."

"Lieutenant Curtis, can you see the fishing spots near the channel from the fort?"

"Most of them, yes."

"So the boat may, in fact, be found in one of those spots . . . if it is fishing, that is."

"Yes, Captain Francis."

Charlotte, who had silently sat in on the conversation, now could not keep herself from announcing, "Then what are we waiting for? Let's go see what that little fisherman is up to!"

The gathering on the quarterdeck took initiative with Charlotte's remark, heading for the gangplank. A messenger running up the gangplank interrupted their movements.

"I'm looking for Captain Francis and any officers that may be with him."

Eric stood forward cautiously. "I'm Captain Francis."

The messenger eyed Eric suspiciously, but judging by the looks of the others present, he realized that Eric told the truth. "Captain Francis, I send my compliments from Governor Rose of Port Raleigh, along with the most sincere gratitude for your role in saving the town from the impending pirate attack."

"Sounds like someone realized they were about to become really unpopular," Charlotte mumbled dryly.

The messenger ignored her statement and continued, "The governor hopes that he can meet with you, discuss your brave actions, and give you your due reward."

Eric's feet shuffled on the deck. His mind dwelled on the fishing boat, and the last thing he wanted would be more awkward pomp and ceremony. "That's fine. Tell him that I'll meet him up at the governor's mansion in a couple hours."

"Oh that won't be necessary, Captain," the messenger suggested quickly. "The governor will come to your ship. In fact, he said he's on his way. I'll inform him that you will agree to see him."

Before Eric could respond, the messenger ran down the gangplank, hopped on his horse, and trotted off toward the mansion. "Great," Eric muttered, "Now I have to sit through the made-up flattery of some self-centered government officials."

Charlotte found herself even more annoyed that Eric. "This is ridiculous. You'll see the governor when you're good and ready. You have more important things to do right now. You gentlemen go and check out the fishing boat. I'll stay here and keep our distinguished dignitaries busy until you get back."

Eric shook his head, albeit reluctantly. "No. I can't make you do that. I wouldn't even make the pirates go through that kind of torture. I'll just wait here and you guys can go check the boat out."

Charlotte insisted more earnestly, "Eric, I'm not going to tell you twice. Go. I'll stay and take care of it."

The fishing boat was only a hunch, but he knew that it would not stop eating away at him until he investigated it. Beyond that, he still lacked the energy to argue with Charlotte, who seemed set. "Fine," Eric gave in. "But you should get some kind of reward for your sacrifice," he appended.

Charlotte grinned. "I've already got a couple of possibilities in mind!"

After mounting the horses that Lieutenant Curtis and his men rode into town from the fort, they set out toward the road leading back to the fort, with Eric sitting behind Samuel since he did not feel comfortable directing a horse himself. A little more than ten minutes into their ride, Eric, Samuel, and Lieutenant Curtis pushed up the final stretch that led to the fort's front entrance. This time Eric approached the opposite side of the fort from where he had entered the night before. Unlike the last night, however, he would never make it through the gate.

"What is it, Captain Francis?" Lieutenant Curtis asked after Eric asked for them to stop and dismounted from behind Samuel. He stepped off the path to get a view of the bay, rather than toward the fort.

"I found the fishing boat."

Samuel and Lieutenant Curtis both dismounted from their horses and joined Eric at his viewpoint. Sure enough, the elusive fishing boat passed almost harmlessly underneath the watchful eyes of the fort. Small and unassuming, it seemed foolish that they had spent so much energy investigating it.

"The direction it's coming indicates that it came from the channel," Samuel noted.

"But where would it go in the channel?" Eric said out loud, though he mainly thought to himself.

Below them the fishing boat passed the point they stood at, approaching the piers of Port Raleigh.

Suddenly they heard the clopping of horse hooves, and a rider crested the hill with a stout man clinging desperately to him. Mr. Gary clearly did not have the build for horse riding, but he clung to one of Curtis's men who had been left at the pier with the fierce determination of someone willing to venture any danger for an important message.

As soon as the rider came up, Mr. Gary plopped to the ground and gathered himself.

"Mr. Gary," Samuel prodded, "what is it?"

"The fishing boat, sir," he said between breaths. "It was stolen."

"Stolen?" Lieutenant Curtis queried.

"Yes, sir. The fisherman that owns it just came to the pier this morning to find his boat gone, sir. I thought you might want to know that information, because it sounded mighty suspicious, as if—" At that point Mr. Gary saw the fishing boat entering the harbor, and he stopped short. "Ah. There t'is. Maybe there was just a mix up." A flustered Mr. Gary tried to gather his breath. "Sorry 'bout the disturbance, but I's just thinking that if there's boats being stolen then there'd be a possibility that . . . well, I'm sorry."

Eric mulled over this information with such inner focus that Mr. Gary wondered whether he had heard him at all. He shuffled awkwardly.

All of the sudden Eric's silence broke. He jumped past Mr. Gary toward the horse and rider. "Can you get me to town as fast as possible?"

Though confused by the impetuous act, the rider nodded. Eric put his arm up so the rider could heft him onto the back of the already sweating steed.

"Captain Francis," Samuel called out. He and Lieutenant Curtis shared looks of bewilderment. "What's going on?"

"We've been duped," Eric replied bitterly. He then urged the rider on, and they were away.

Lieutenant Curtis and Samuel mounted their horses and followed, still baffled at the mysterious events that just occurred—so much so that it took Samuel a minute before he realized that he had left Mr. Gary and turned to pick him up. Though neither could imagine what had happened, if Samuel had learned anything in the past couple of days, it was that trusting Eric's judgments was essential.

By the time they approached the outskirts of Port Raleigh, Lieutenant Curtis noted the elusive fisherman's ship leaving the harbor again. He wondered what in the world had been happening. Minutes later he found out.

When they reached the pier, they met with a considerable ruckus. Sailors milled about and some citizens left their homes and businesses to investigate the commotion. As they traversed along the pier and approached the *Rosemary*, they heard murmurings of pirates.

113

Immediately Lieutenant Curtis checked the harbor for approaching pirate ships, but only saw the small fishing boat, which now wended its way back toward the San Fernando Channel.

Then they saw Eric in a telling position. They urged their horses forward until they stopped at his side. He knelt on the pier and gazed ruefully out on the harbor, disbelief welling up in his eyes. Next to Eric stood one of the faithful members of the crew, who winced as he bent over, favoring a wound to his torso. The sailor's hand didn't completely cover the blood stain seeping through his shirt.

Samuel rushed to the sailor. "You're hurt! What's happened? Someone call for a physician!"

The sailor shook his head slowly. "I'll be fine, Mr. Wesley," the sailor answered, grinding his teeth, "Nothin' too serious. Just a lot of blood." He flinched, though this time the pain was not physical. "And besides, I need to tell you what I told Cap'n Francis, here."

Samuel motioned him onward.

"We failed the little miss, sir."

"What, you mean Miss Charlotte?" Samuel asked. A groan emitted from the otherwise silent Eric.

"Yes, sir. We didn't . . . I mean, it was just a fishin' boat, sir, and we never suspected they was comin' for her. Before we knows it, there's nine or ten of 'em on board, and they catch us all off guard and without our weapons at the ready. They cut a couple of us down, and while they secured the deck a couple went below. They was there for some time, but they finally come up with the little miss." He faltered at this point, and Samuel and Lieutenant Curtis could guess the rest.

"She sure did put up a fight," the sailor added. "I seen it as I lay on the deck. A couple of 'em ought ta have black eyes before the day is through. But, well . . ."

Samuel and Lieutenant Curtis now understood Eric's current state. Not sure whether he said the right thing or not, Samuel put a hand on Eric's shoulder and said, "At least they took her alive."

Eric nodded, though he did not seem much comforted.

"But why?" Lieutenant Curtis queried, his analytical mind racing.

Eric guessed it the moment Mr. Gary came to warn them, but he failed to return in time to prevent it. The whole trip back to Port Raleigh from the fort his stomach turned as he realized his error. He kept punishing himself for not seeing it sooner. Once he reached the *Rosemary*, a quick word from the injured sailor confirmed his suspicions. It left him at a loss of how to express his feelings—frustrated, angry, dismayed, hurt . . . defeated. All of these he felt, but instead of reacting, he could only observe the ship carrying Charlotte leave the harbor, out of his reach.

Since no one answered Lieutenant Curtis, Eric's soft voice finally pitched in. "Don't you see? This was meant for me. They came to take me away."

The sailor perked up at this comment and piped in, "That's right, Cap'n Francis! I remember when they came up, they said something about not findin' the boy—begging your pardon, Cap'n, but that's what they called you—and then another'n said that they'd just have to take the girl."

Samuel summed up. "So they assumed you'd been in the ship when they came, but luckily you were with us."

"I wouldn't say 'luckily,' Samuel," Eric said bitterly. "I'd rather be with Charlotte right now. And they didn't assume. They knew."

Samuel almost asked Eric how they could know for certain that he would be in the *Rosemary* at the exact moment they entered the harbor, but Lieutenant Curtis noted another inconsistency and pointed it out. "Wait; if the fishing boat belongs to a fisherman here in Port Raleigh, how did the pirates come into the harbor in order to take it?"

"They didn't," Eric answered quickly. "That's why this was done with the help of someone on the inside, someone from Port Raleigh. And that explains how they knew I would be on the ship as well."

"But who would do such a thing? Who would get the fishing boat to the pirates and divulge when you would be on the ship?" Lieutenant Curtis asked.

Still resigned, Eric sighed, "The ones who knew I would be on the ship? I expect they will be here any minute. I have an appointment scheduled with them at about the time I was supposed to have been kidnapped."

Lieutenant Curtis and Samuel allowed this information to dawn on them when they heard the noise of an approaching carriage. As the crowds parted to allow the carriage to the edge of the pier, it soon became apparent that the carriage belonged to the governor. When it came to a stop, Governor Rose and Captain Bellview exited. As they began to work their way down the pier, it took them great effort to hide the smirks on their faces. Governor Rose then saw the bustling on the pier and the large crowd before saying out loud, "My, my, what in the world could be happening here? Has something occurred?"

If Eric could find any redeeming quality in the whole disturbing situation, it would have been the looks of disbelief on the faces of Governor Rose and Captain Bellview when they came closer to the *Rosemary* and saw Eric kneeling on the pier. Too stunned to even continue walking, Governor Rose had to grip onto Captain Bellview as he took it in. Bellview seethed underneath his calm exterior. After the initial pause, the two recovered and completed their walk to the group at the edge of the pier.

With flickering eyes, Governor Rose spoke first. "What . . . uh . . . what seems to have happened here?"

Lieutenant Curtis responded, "It appears that someone betrayed our nation by collaborating with pirates. Fortunately, our young friend here escaped, but someone who was never intended to be taken has been kidnapped instead—the young woman."

Governor Rose's mouth immediately tightened. He clearly had not anticipated this turn of events. Lieutenant Curtis continued, "Some half-witted, jealousy-driven coward has allowed his own pride to get in the way of Port Raleigh's best interests, and as a result, an innocent young woman was abducted."

The insults drove home to Governor Rose, who started to tremble under the verbal blows, but Captain Bellview stood firm. "Maybe we should fault the poor vigilance of an inept crew and their leader."

Samuel almost exploded at the belligerent accusation. "An inept crew? You, who have your crews idling around doing nothing, while Captain Francis is at least brave enough to stand up to the pirates even if it is with a little sloop and not a ship-of-the-line!"

Captain Bellview did not take kindly to Samuel's insults, but he held back his rage. "'Captain' Francis? I don't believe I'm acquainted with him."

Samuel replied quickly. "As we are not in the Royal Navy, we can appoint a captain as we see fit when ours is lost. Captain Francis is that replacement. And with or without the title, he has shown more nettle than you have, hiding away in the governor's mansion while he does the work you should be doing without the resources you have. Of all people, I think that you are the last one who should be criticizing him."

Captain Bellview's calm demeanor seemed on the point of bursting. His hand gripped the sword handle at his side, but he was interrupted by a soft-spoken Eric, who still knelt on the ground, facing outward. "You may have a point, Samuel, but so does Captain Bellview."

This unexpected comment immediately rendered everyone present speechless. Eric followed up by saying, "I shouldn't have been so careless to leave the ship with such a small amount of men to guard it. I especially should've realized the danger to Charlotte."

Captain Bellview and Governor Rose felt too astonished to speak, Lieutenant Curtis and Samuel both erupted with protests. Lieutenant Curtis's voice rose above Samuel's. "Captain Francis, you absolutely cannot shoulder the blame when it clearly rests on that of a traitor." He glared at Governor Rose.

"I can't take all the blame," Eric admitted. "But I know my abilities, and I know that I failed in what I could've done."

Though Captain Bellview still could not believe Eric's attitude, Governor Rose let slip a slight grin. While unfortunate that the girl had been taken instead of Eric, it at least demoralized the young man enough to reap similar results. Eric barely noticed as Governor Rose shifted plans to accommodate a new scheme.

"It takes a great man to admit an error," Governor Rose said, doing a poor job of disguising the word "man" with sincerity. "Ugly business though it is to have the young lady kidnapped, it is most likely that the pirates will negotiate a ransom for her . . . Mr. Francis," he could not bring himself to address Eric as "Captain," ". . . and as a true gentleman who has admitted his mistake, you will certainly see that the honorable thing to do would be to offer yourself up in her stead."

Samuel and Lieutenant Curtis both saw the trap that Governor Rose lay out for Eric. They also suspected that Eric saw it as well, but given his defeated condition, they worried that he would surrender without a fight.

Eric looked up at Governor Rose and nodded slowly. "Charlotte shouldn't pay for my mistake. I won't leave her to the pirates."

It pained Eric's two friends to see him in this state, but especially Samuel, who had known Eric's indomitable spirit the longest. Everything that seemed impossible to Samuel before had been overcome by Eric's confidence and abilities, but his self-assurance now appeared crushed. The loss of Charlotte took all the wind out of Eric's sails, and he appeared resigned to throw himself into the arms of the pirates, even knowing that the governor and Captain Bellview secretly wanted that the whole time.

A hypocritical smile spread across the governor's face. "It is a tough decision, but I was sure you would make the right choice. Don't worry. Your heroic action will not go without recognition. I will see to it that you are given a proper farewell before you turn yourself over to them."

"Oh, I didn't say I was going to trade myself for Charlotte," Eric retorted. His eyes, though still sunken, flickered.

"I'm sorry?" Governor Rose asked, confused.

"I said that I couldn't abandon her to the pirates, and I won't. But I'm not going to trade myself for her."

"But . . . but, how can you . . ."

"The pirates don't care for brave sacrifices, but they will try and take advantage of us with them. They might say they'll make a fair trade of Charlotte for me, but being pirates, they'll simply take me and keep both of us, which will do Charlotte no good at all."

Governor Rose was clearly appalled. Captain Bellview could not hide his shock. "So you mean to just leave her . . . ?" Governor Rose muttered.

"No," Eric said. "I'm going to go get her. Alone if I have to." His former confidence had not returned, but there could be no second-guessing his resolve.

"But . . . but . . . you can't possibly just sail on over to the Twins and expect to just snatch the girl right in front of their faces and stroll on back to Port Raleigh . . ."

"Why not?" Eric said. "Isn't that what you had someone do earlier this morning? Sail right out to the Twins and come back?"

"Are you accusing me of . . . ?" This was the first time Governor Rose realized that they guessed his involvement in the whole situation, in spite of his shallow efforts to disguise it. "That is ridiculous and absurd! If I were to try and communicate with the pirates, I wouldn't send someone to do my bidding. I would go myself. And I would go in one of Captain Bellview's ships-of-the-line, not in some paltry fishing boat, and instead of exchanging words with the braggarts, I would exchange broadsides!"

"Funny," Eric remarked. "I don't remember anyone having mentioned a fishing boat. Now, how would you know about that?"

Governor Rose realized his folly and started to sputter, but Captain Bellview interrupted him. The proud captain had recovered from his previous shock and his face had reverted to a static position. "It doesn't matter, Governor Rose. If the fool wants to go after the girl, then let him go. He won't be sneaking away from pirates this time or sneaking up on them. He will have to face them head-on. He is acting rashly, on his emotions for the young lady, and it will cost him his life, so I suggest we leave him to it." Bellview let his gaze challenge Eric's for a long moment before turning around and walking back to the carriage. Governor Rose could not enact such a comfortable exit. Still set back by Eric's revealing comment, he darted his eyes back and forth among the small group until retreating toward his carriage.

Eric, Samuel, and Lieutenant Curtis stayed silent as they watched the carriage take off. Samuel then interrupted the stillness. "I've doubted you before, Captain Francis, and you've proven me wrong every time. Would this be one of those cases?"

Unlike before, when impending action excited Eric, this time he remained solemn and he answered Samuel evenly. "Captain Bellview is right. We won't be able to sneak around them this time. Charlotte will be on one of their ships, and to get her we're going to have to go directly to a pirate ship. Such a move would be rash, and Bellview may be right that it'll cost me my life. Still, a head-on attack will also be what the pirates will least suspect."

This time Lieutenant Curtis jumped in. "They don't expect it because you don't have the resources for a direct assault, not without Captain Bellview's ships. Even if you did, you'd be up against ruthless fighters and hopelessly outnumbered. Strategically, it just can't work. They don't expect it because they don't have to."

Eric shook his head as he solidified his ideas. "Maybe I should rephrase. The pirates will be expecting a sneak attack, if they expect anything. They are also completely prepared to repel a direct assault. Since that is the case, our only recourse is to launch upon them a direct assault that is, in fact, a sneak attack."

Samuel and Lieutenant Curtis both looked to each other for help, but to no avail. Samuel spoke out, "Captain Francis, maybe you should rephrase your rephrasing, because I'm even more confused than I was before."

"I think you'll see what I mean," Eric said. He briefly laid out his plan.

Though a couple of hours earlier the Twins toasted in good spirits, this time Joshua felt anything but good spirits. Walter stood before the Twins, trembling as he realized his news had not elicited a positive response.

Joshua responded first. "What do you mean he wasn't there?"

"That's just it," the first mate responded, his voice shaking. "When we boarded the ship, there weren't no boy aboard. We done in the sailors quick enough and searched below, and we could only find a young missus."

"We sent you to get the boy, and you come back with a girl," Joshua's voice elevated. "And you expect us to be happy with this blatant disobedience?" Joshua started walking toward the first mate after unsheathing his cutlass. "Don't be surprised, then, if I come to pat your back and end up cutting out your heart!"

"Wait for it, Joshua," Jedediah spoke softly. It took significant effort for Joshua to hold himself back. Jedediah reflected on the letter. While it was annoying to have Joshua's first mate come back without the young captain, he at least did not come back empty handed. Jedediah also realized that the governor, in the letter, mentioned that he expected the boy to be in the company of a young woman, and they now had that young woman in their possession. Jedediah nodded. Maybe this was not such a big loss after all.

"Bring the prisoner, and prepare the fishing boat to go back to the harbor with terms. You will be delivering them."

Walter left, relieved that he did so with all of his vital organs intact. Joshua, on the other hand, turned to his brother, "What's going on, Jedediah?"

"If she spends time in his company, as the governor states in the letter, then she must be valuable to him. We'll offer an exchange: her for him."

Joshua smiled wickedly. "And of course we'll just keep him and kill her in front of him, just so he knows his error before he dies himself."

"It's not an accident that we're twins," Jedediah smiled back. "I'll go prepare the terms."

"And I will interrogate the new prisoner."

Jedediah retired to a remote corner of the room to write up the terms, and only moments later a couple pirates escorted Charlotte in. By now, Charlotte had recovered somewhat from the shock and despair of being taken. She stood before the ruthless grin of Joshua Willard and she barely refrained from smiling back. Her look disconcerted Joshua, but he continued the interrogation in the presence of Walter, a couple of escorts, and the out-of-view Jedediah.

"What's your name, Missus?" Joshua asked.

"None of your concern," she replied.

"True," Joshua said, unfazed, "but as a matter of courtesy I usually like to know the name of my victims before they die."

Unshaken, Charlotte replied quickly. "You aren't going to kill me yet. You don't want me; you want Captain Francis."

"So that's our grand foe . . . Captain Francis."

"That's right. And you're going to wait until you have both of us before you kill us. But it won't happen."

Joshua smiled. "So you don't think your friend will agree to be exchanged for you? I knew that he was lucky, but I didn't know that he was a coward on top of it."

Charlotte only laughed at Joshua's attempt to rile her. "I would warn you not to underestimate him, but it wouldn't help. So I can only apologize in advance for your own stupidity."

Joshua's smile disappeared. "You may accuse me of stupidity, but I know which end of the cutlass is pointy and how to locate another man's heart. And that's all that matters in this business."

Charlotte was maddeningly calm. "Nice shoes." The random compliment threw Joshua off guard. He stood flabbergasted, thinking of how to respond. He would not get a chance.

Jedediah removed himself from the darkened corner of the room where he sat. He strode purposefully to the center of the room. He immediately faced his brother and spoke as if Charlotte were not even in the cabin. "I'm heading back to my ship, and I'm taking the girl with me. Walter, take these terms and go back to Port Raleigh under a flag of truce. Once there, I want you to deliver them to the 'underestimated' Captain Francis." Walter did not dare hesitate for even a second. He took the terms and immediately filed out of the room with the other men.

"Wait, you're taking her back to your ship?" Joshua asked.

"In case of the remote possibility that Captain Francis would be foolish enough to attempt retrieving the young lady through an assault instead of negotiations. Since my ship is farther into the cove, you can trap him in by blocking the exit."

Joshua laughed. "I almost hope that he'd be stupid enough to try something like that, but I doubt it. Besides the fact that tryin' to storm your ship would be suicide, these chivalrous chumps can't resist a chance to negotiate trading themselves in the place of a fair lady."

"You still don't get it, do you? There's only one negotiation here," Charlotte remarked glibly. "You give up now or Eric will finish you off. You two have no idea who you are up against."

Jedediah turned to face Charlotte coolly, the first time she had seen him fully since he stepped out of his corner of the cabin. "And I think, little miss, that neither of you fully understand what you are up against."

While taking in the very depths of Jedediah's glittering eyes as they stared her down, for the first time since she had entered the room, Charlotte experienced true fear.

While sailing back into Port Raleigh, Walter shifted nervously at the tiller of the fishing boat. After all, he just left Port Raleigh after killing and wounding some sailors and kidnapping a girl. He felt relatively certain that his reception, even under a white flag of truce, would not be looked upon kindly. But when he looked upon the young man who was supposed to be a captain, Walter felt significantly at ease. With more confidence, Walter stepped forward on the pier and held out the paper that Jedediah had given him.

"Here are the terms the Willard Twins offer you," he said, trying to act at least somewhat official. The white flag of truce, wielded proudly by the pirate standing next to him, fluttered in a ponderous breeze. There was an unexpected pause as Walter held out the terms to an unmoving audience in front of him. After a second he waved the paper in his hand and repeated, "The terms . . ."

The young man stood forward and grabbed the flimsy paper from his outstretched hand. Walter saw anger in the boy's eyes, not a defeated anger but one of purpose. As if to drive home the point, the boy captain never looked at the piece of paper. He simply held it up—all the while glaring at Walter directly in the eyes—and then he ripped the terms into small pieces and let them flutter listlessly onto the pier and into the still harbor water.

"Sir!" Walter ejaculated. "You can't refuse the terms without even looking at them. You're dealing with the Willard Twins—they'll have no mercy on yer companion!"

"Now!" Eric's resolute voice called out in a way that Walter noted carried impressive command with it. Immediately, three small boats carrying dozens of soldiers appeared out of nowhere, surrounding the stolen fishing boat filled with pirates. "You've got that backwards, pirate," Eric stated. "I will have no mercy on them."

Walter felt a mix between outrage and perplexity. "What do you think you're doin'? You can't capture us. We're your only hope of gettin' back that little missus alive!"

"You've got that right," Eric confirmed. "Take them away and get their clothes from them." Eric then turned back to Walter, "And I'll be needing you to remove your cutlass and pistol."

Walter gasped. "Absolutely not! This is mad. Can't you see that we came here to negotiate under a flag o' truce?" Walter pointed deliberately at the white cloth dangling next to him.

Eric's patience ran thin. His sword flew out of his scabbard and the pole bearing the flag of truce tumbled in two pieces to the pier before Walter and the pirate holding the flag could even blink. The now destitute cloth lay motionless on the pier, and Eric brought his sword even with Walter's chest. "Once you start playing by the rules of war, you can expect to be protected by them."

The soldiers escorted the captured pirates to join their companions at the fort. The fishing boat, which only moments ago held filthy buccaneers, now boasted a half a dozen or so of Lieutenant Curtis and Samuel's best men, all volunteers for such a mission and all wearing the captured pirates' clothing. The only actual pirate to return to the fishing boat was Walter, still hopelessly bewildered.

As the fishing boat sailed out of the harbor for the third time that day, Eric imparted his instructions to Walter. "You are to act as if everything went according to plan and that I am in the boat with you and your crew in order to comply with the terms the Twins sent me."

Walter stared incredulously at Eric. "What in Davy Jones's locker makes you think that I'm going to do what you say? Are you going to threaten me with death? No use playin' that game with me. I'm a pirate, and under your laws, that means that I'm a dead man no matter what. There's no reason for me to cooperate."

Eric squinted. "Actually, the reason you are going to cooperate is quite simple: if you don't, then we are going to turn you over to the Twins."

Walter's face drained of its color. Being turned over to the Twins, after losing his crew members and not returning successfully with the terms required would mean a death ten times as painful as anything the citizens of Port Raleigh could think up. With a cracking voice, Walter quickly subdued and agreed to Eric's proposal. "Just let me know what I need to say."

"It's nice to see improvement," Eric smiled. By this time, the island base of the Twins slid into view as they left the reassuring shadow of the fort. "Now, one of the Twins' ships is stationed farther into the cove than the other, and I'm betting that the girl is held on the ship farthest back." Though reticent to give any information to this kid, Walter realized that one of the last things Walter heard Jedediah Willard say was that the girl would be in his ship. When he remembered this, he choked on his reply, and Eric nodded as confirmation.

Eric continued. "And now that they lost one of their ships last night, their other ship will probably be taken away from guarding the north passage and moved over to patrol the San Fernando Channel." Walter had heard the Twins give the order for the switch in patrol duties late last night, after their retreat from Port Raleigh. Again, he confirmed Eric's guesswork with widened eyes.

Samuel, who refused to be left out of the expedition, interjected at this point. "If you're right, Captain Francis, that would mean that if we somehow capture the girl from the farthest ship in the cove, we would have to go past two pirate ships to get to Port Raleigh. We may get in under this disguise, but getting back out again under it would be . . . well, it would difficult, even for you."

Eric nodded. "Most likely impossible," he said, though not in despair. "I thought it through as carefully as I could, but I'm simply not smart enough to successfully bring Charlotte back under these circumstances."

Samuel eyed Eric. "Then what are we doing?"

Ringing with determination, Eric said, "We're changing the circumstances."

Joshua Willard had already downed three glasses of rum by the time the lookout called for him. Though not yet drunk, the alcohol put him in a pensive mood, causing him to think back to the girl's comments about his shoes being nice. *They were good shoes*, he thought, glancing at them and blinking. But why had the girl brought them up? Was she being derisive? How could she know that I personally made them? Joshua burped, the reek of alcohol filling the air around him. I need to go ask her.

The call to deck interrupted his inane thoughts, and Joshua Willard never found a satisfactory answer to his casual questioning. Joshua left instructions not to be disturbed for any reason except for one, so he shook off the numbing affects of the rum and went to witness the return of Walter from Port Raleigh.

The small fishing boat took its time arriving at the ship, and Joshua Willard did not gain his reputation as the patient type, so he fidgeted on deck as the boat slid across the sea to their position in the cove. Finally, the boat approached his ship's side. Though excited to see what news they brought, he immediately put on a show of his dislike for Walter.

"What in blazes took you so long?! I see you at least managed not to get yourself caught!"

He thought he saw Walter waver at this comment, but he attributed it to the rum and shook it off. "Well?" he asked eagerly.

Walter's voice cracked with his answer. "The poor sap agreed to the negotiation, Cap'n Joshua. I've got him right here."

Joshua craned his neck see where Walter pointed. He saw a harmless boy sitting between two pirate guards next to the bulwarks with his head hung low. Visibly stunned, Joshua almost took a step back. This was the one causing all the ruckus?

"Walter, if you've let those idiot townsfolk fool you into taking some homeless kid off the streets and pretending that he's some great captain, then you'll have to sit and watch as I personally carve my name in your innards."

Walter almost laughed in his response, "Don't worry, Cap'n, this boy is the real one—there's no mistake about that." Walter's voice burst with sincerity in this last comment. Joshua also noticed the intelligent eyes of the boy look up to him after the previous statement. For a split second, Joshua almost saw something else in the boy's eyes, something beyond the destitute state he was in, almost as if he was . . .

"What're the orders, Cap'n?" Walter piped out.

"The orders are for you to shut your mouth and sit down! I'm coming aboard and then we're going to take our guest to his little lady friend."

Joshua Willard lowered himself onto the deck of the fishing boat and had them cast off from his ship. He barked orders to head farther into the cove. One of the sailors responded with a gruff "aye-aye." Joshua paid little attention to the crew as his focus drew him to the boy. He watched the boy, who sat near the stern of the boat, head downward, as if resigned to his state. Joshua nodded, pleased. After a minute or so, he decided that he could not resist a "friendly" conversation with him. He started to work himself from the bow of the fishing boat back toward the boy. Once he broke his gaze on the young captain, he found himself noticing the crew working around him. They all obeyed orders sharply, not a loafer among them. He also noticed that not one of them showed a scruffy face—they were either clean-shaven or well-trimmed. And though their clothing smelled bad, as one of them brushed past him, he did not smell the reek of body odor buildup that comes from cramped ships. Trusting to his instincts, Joshua grabbed a sailor and he removed his cutlass. "'Ere now," he said with danger in his voice, "someone want to tell me what's going on here?"

The sailor trembled visibly, but Joshua looked past him when he heard the unsheathing of a sword behind him. He shoved the sailor to the deck and swiveled to face his foe. The young captain stood before him, holding up his sword boldly, his eyes flaring. "You've been captured," he answered. "That's what's going on." Reinforcing this statement was the sound of a dozen other swords being drawn around him. As Joshua scanned the men surrounding him, he also noticed that the man at the tiller had them heading out of the cove, not farther into it.

"Drop your cutlass so that we can bind you up," the captain pressed. "Unless, of course, you'd like to make a pin cushion of yourself." Joshua tried to hide his shock at the audacity of this boy before him, but he failed. After the shock came realization, then anger.

"You're not going to make a pin cushion out of me," the Twin stated defiantly. "You need me alive to negotiate for your friend. Which is a shame, because I fully intend on fighting to the death."

The captain had not expected this. He paused to consider. "You're right; we'd like to have you alive, but I'd personally love to see how serious you are about fighting to the death, because I don't think you mean it." He motioned for the others to let up on their weapons, while he still held his out, challenging.

"You won't be able to find out," Joshua grumbled from between his teeth, "because in a couple seconds you are going to be washing this deck with your blood."

Angered, but not driven by it, Joshua stepped toward the boy, knowing that his pure physical presence should overcome any skill the lad might have with a sword. He planned to vent force into every blow he would strike, wearing the captain out until one of the power strokes hit flesh.

Joshua Willard did not realize that the captain's own anger empowered him, and he also grossly underestimated the captain's skills with a sword. The first few blows from Joshua struck fiercely indeed. Enough power burst through each one that he could have split a block of wood had it been in his path. Yet the jarring effect he hoped to inflict on his foe did not occur. The captain deflected the blows in such a way as to minimize the direct effects of the strike, though not without a price. The captain gave up footing, falling back briskly. Joshua pursued voraciously, holding his advantage while he had it, never letting up.

Just as the captain retreated past the mast, he tripped on a coil of rope and fell on his back. Though he fought impressively, Joshua needed only one mistake to defeat him. The pirate twin smiled viciously and lifted up his cutlass, about to make his last strike. For a split second he paused, thanks to a mystical smile on the captain's face. The expression did not denote the look of someone defeated. The captain took a final swing with his sword, but not at Joshua. Instead, he smashed his weapon into a cleat on the mast. The cleat sprang off the mast, and the rope that it held shot upward. The same coil that the boy apparently tripped over now entangled itself around Joshua's foot. Before the pirate could react, he found himself ripped off the deck and slammed down headfirst.

The boy stood up, deftly knocked the cutlass out of Joshua's limp hand, and ordered him tied up and the main halyard re-lashed to the mast. Joshua squinted at the thudding pain in his head. He caught one last bewildered look at the captain's face before he passed out and remembered no more.

Chapter 9
EXCHANGE

Walter barely believed his fortune at staying alive as long as he had. He recalled how the raging Joshua woke up in Port Raleigh and realized his status as a captive for the first time in his life. The heavy iron chains rattled loudly as the veteran pirate swore, cussed, and blasphemed. Walter knew that a hefty portion of that rage went his direction because of his obvious betrayal. But he also knew that underneath, most of Joshua's rage came from embarrassment—the fact that after avoiding capture all his life, the shackles on him came not by swarms of Royal Navy ships or legions of soldiers, but by the cunning of an unknown and poorly equipped sloop captain.

Seeing Joshua's wrath made Walter reticent to be the messenger who negotiated an exchange with Jedediah. Facing a Willard Twin at this moment did not tempt him in the slightest. He informed Captain Francis of his opinion on the matter, but then the astute captain quickly responded—as if according to script—that otherwise he would be chained up next to Joshua for the rest of the day and they would gather up his body later. Walter marveled at Eric's ability to find a way to motivate him to do the last thing he would ever think to do. Walter agreed to negotiate.

While on his way to see Jedediah, Walter knew that the vicious Twin would kill him for his participation in this whole affair. He harbored no shred of doubt, as he climbed on board the ship, that it would be the last conversation of his life. Walter found Jedediah brewing in his cabin, his jaw clenched, his eyes burning—clearly Joshua's crew had related to him the fate of his brother. Wasting no time, the doomed mate dispensed the terms to Jedediah: the prisoner exchange would take place the next mid-morning. They would meet at the opening to the cove in longboats. Jedediah's boat would remain deep in the cove for the duration of the exchange while the other two pirate ships were to be just visible over the northern horizon, away from the action. Walter trembled as soon as he uttered the conditions. Jedediah stewed for brief moments afterward.

"Agreed."

Walter hardly believed what he heard. He stood waiting for his mind to stop playing tricks on him. After a couple of seconds, Jedediah lifted up his eyes, bloodshot with anger, and a growl emanated from his lips. "I said, 'agreed.' Now deliver the message while you've got a mouth to do it with!"

The trip back to Port Raleigh only furthered Walter's disbelief at living to see another minute. Upon reporting to Captain Francis, he was interrogated by the young captain about Jedediah's specific reaction, down to even his facial expression and how long exactly it took for him to respond.

Walter did not know what to expect from the upcoming exchange, but he felt certain that neither side expected things to occur as planned. As they placed him in his prison cell—to his relief, far away from Joshua Willard—Walter finally had time to consider his own unenviable fate.

Eric made the terms and the pirate accepted them. Eric commanded two ships, one confiscated from pirates, the other given to him by loyal friends who trusted his nautical skills. In the distant northern horizon, he snatched a glimpse of the jutting masts of two other pirate ships sitting motionless—subdued by his word alone. Below the *Rosemary*'s deck, the jingling chains and cusses of a fierce Willard Pirate Twin finally succumbed to silence. In the cove of the first island in the Montes de Oca island chain, the main pirate ship sat near the back, limp and lifeless. All this, too, could be attributed to Eric's words and actions.

And yet, in spite of these noteworthy achievements, Eric doubted himself. True, he provided the terms, and true, they appeared to have been carried out to the letter, but in the back of his mind the thought that he was just a kid kept nagging away at him. He placed himself up against one of the most formidable pirates ever known to these people. He had charge of scores of adult men, none of whom he knew more than four days earlier. He found himself in an area and time period unfamiliar to him. He faced hostile foes not only in the sea, but also back at land in the forms of Governor Rose and Captain Bellview. All this . . . and Eric did not even have his driver's license yet.

As much as these thoughts caused him to want to turn around and disappear, one thing alone kept him plodding forward toward the mouth of the cove.

"I'm sure she's fine, Cap'n Francis," Mr. Gary said from behind. "Jedediah Willard is clever enough to know when he's been cornered. He won't risk everything to just do a young lady harm."

"A cornered man is a dangerous one," Eric replied, still looking forward.

"Are you afraid he's got something up his sleeve?"

"I'm almost certain he does," Eric nodded. "But I've got something up my sleeve as well."

Mr. Gary sniffed. "That something wouldn't have anything to do with Lieutenant Curtis taking those men and two fishing boats into the channel a couple hours before us, would it?"

Eric shrugged. "I'm just acting on a hunch, but it's one that I expect will pay off."

The *Rosemary*, followed closely by the former pirate ship, newly named the *Redemption*, crossed the channel in a couple hours and pulled up to the mouth of the cove before standing before the wind. Using a large cone made of pasteboard to serve as a megaphone, Eric advised Samuel, in command of the *Redemption*, to use a sea anchor and be ready to slip away at a moment's notice.

After some other last minute instructions, Eric hopped onto the longboat accompanied by thirty men and a somber Joshua Willard. Then, with one last glance to Mr. Gary, Eric took a deep breath and launched the boat in the direction of the cove. Coming toward him he observed the rise and fall of the oars of another longboat, the wake of which led back to the pirate ship.

The minute they entered it, Eric knew he did not prefer the enclosed feeling of the cove. He almost regretted making it the meeting spot, but he also knew that he had taken the proper precautions. Jedediah should be the one to feel enclosed.

If Jedediah Willard felt that way, he disguised it well. Even from a distance, Eric discerned the stern rage emanating from his posture as his longboat approached Eric's. Eric tried to ignore the intimidating figure. Instead, he found relief when he saw Charlotte's blonde hair move from between two large pirate guards next to Jedediah. In his own longboat, Eric saw the previously limp Joshua start to rustle.

As the two longboats glided across the final distance separating each other, Eric ordered the front of the boat cleared except for one man, who would secure their boat to the other. Jedediah neatly followed suit. Before Eric knew it, the two long boats were fastened at the bows, and the men who did the work fell back among their own.

Eric gathered his courage for the ensuing scene. After a prolonged lapse of action, Jedediah stood to his full height and proclaimed, "Well, Captain Francis, here we are together at the mouth of the cove. As you can see, I am a man of my word." His voice carried across the space in a steady manner, but underneath Eric sensed an icy blackness that put a chill through all those present. At first, Eric panicked at the pirate's confidence, but he managed to remind himself of the precautions he had taken. He took a deep breath and then, with a calm that mirrored Jedediah's, he said, "We'll see how much of a man of your word you are when you hand over Charlotte."

"And my brother?"

Eric refused to flinch. "You took first, that means you give first. Once I see she is all right, you will have your brother back." The boldness in his voice surprised even him, but he held his gaze unchanging. For a second he thought he almost saw a smile flit across Jedediah's face.

"Very well."

Though Jedediah yielded, Eric knew that it was calculation—not defeat. Consequently, Eric still prepared himself for any sort of treachery. Yet, to his surprise, his preparations could not prepare him for the one thing he did not plan on: complete adherence to his demands. Before he knew it Charlotte picked her way delicately to the front of the longboat. She switched boats and worked her way to the middle of Eric's boat, where Eric stepped up to meet her. She fell into his arms in a wave of relief for them both.

Their embrace did not completely ignore the situation at hand. "It's a trap," Charlotte whispered urgently in his ear. The spunk in her voice demonstrated to Eric that, though bedraggled and somewhat shaken, Charlotte lost nothing of her fiery spirit.

"The two ships—"

Jedediah's harsh voice interrupted her. "Now we see if you are a boy of your word."

The connotation "boy" might have had the slightest hint of condescension in it, but Eric disregarded it. He nodded knowingly to Charlotte and whispered, "Don't worry, I've got Lieutenant Curtis on the job . . ." Then he turned around and ordered Joshua released.

In a matter of moments, the shackles dropped to the floor of the longboat and Joshua glared back at his captors with a hatred in his eyes that was frightening, even considering his unarmed, outnumbered state. Slowly, he worked his way to the front of the longboat and switched boats, stealing one last venom-filled glance at Eric before climbing in front of his stone-faced brother.

Eric watched the scene with interest. At his side he felt Charlotte tugging urgently on his shirt and hissing his name. Her voice stopped and her hand froze as soon as she witnessed the scene that followed.

Once with his brother, Joshua emitted some curses directed toward the situation, vowing revenge. Jedediah did not respond, standing as still as ever while his brother muttered angrily. After a few moments, Joshua finally looked into his twin's eyes. His words dissolved as his mouth clamped shut and his eyes widened. A true, deep, and terrifying fear overwhelmed him.

"Jedediah," he murmured pathetically now. "It was Walter. The boy captured him and used him to trick me. It wasn't my fault, Jed. It wasn't my fault." By now he was groveling. Everyone witnessed the scene in silent awe.

Jedediah still showed next to no emotion as he brought his pistol and leveled it toward Joshua's face. Eric suddenly turned around and grabbed Charlotte just as the shot rang out.

A hollow thud told him the results of the action. Eric swiveled around again and stared in shock at the man who just killed his own brother in cold blood. Eric never asked a question, but he did not need to. Jedediah spoke first.

"There were two reasons I went to the trouble of getting my brother back just to kill him. One, for his idiotic blunder. I couldn't stand the thought of him dying by anyone's hand but my own after being such a fool."

Eric's expression fell while listening to a man so blackened that he would go through the inconvenience of a prisoner trade just to kill the prisoner he traded for—his own brother no less. While Eric's first thought reflected absolute disgust, his second told him how dumb Jedediah had to be to give away his collateral just so he could kill someone doomed for execution anyway.

With a motion of his hand, Jedediah called for the release of the longboats. Then he continued speaking, "The second reason was to have an excuse to lead you right into my trap." He then nodded to one of the burly pirates behind him, who subsequently raised a large, blood red flag.

"Eric," Charlotte's voice pressed.

"Wait," Eric said, holding his hand up. "He doesn't know that his trap is about to spring on himself."

After the flag raised, a pause followed, one long enough that Jedediah Willard almost wavered. Just before that happened, a flash of lights came from the heights westward above the cove, followed by a thunderous chorus of booms. This, apparently, is what Jedediah waited for, because he settled into a smug smile.

Then something happened that Jedediah did not expect. The salvo of cannonballs he expected to see tear Eric and his longboat apart never came. Instead, the cannon fire landed just behind him and his longboat. Jedediah Willard's ship, sitting comfortably at the back of the cove, suddenly found itself surrounded by the splashes of several cannonballs, with one rogue ball actually crashing through the bulwarks of the ship.

As Eric suspected going into the exchange, Jedediah had cannons placed on the high ground of the enclosing cove hills in order to rain down cannonballs on Eric's ships in the cove. And as Eric planned, Lieutenant Curtis and a regiment of his men were able to make an unsuspected strike on the pirate position from behind, take over the dozen cannons, and redirect them toward Jedediah's ship, waiting for the pirate signal before firing.

Jedediah, for all his previous calm, displayed a strained look of disbelief and anger that caused veins to stick out from his tightened forehead. The second round of shots confirmed that this was no mere accident. The two boats had drifted far enough away at this point that Eric did not hear what Jedediah said as he leaned across a seat and stretched out his hand toward a crew member. But Eric didn't need to hear what he said.

"Muskets out!" Eric called out. "Prepare for return fire." A clattering of nearby weapons showed that his men had listened attentively to his instructions before they embarked.

By the time Jedediah turned face to Eric's longboat with a pistol in hand, he looked down the distant muzzles of thirty muskets.

He displayed a surprising calm on his face as he shouted across the widening gap, "Your foresight is commendable, little captain. But controlling my pestering cannons on the heights will do nothing against the firepower of my two remaining ships."

Eric expected desperation, not more strategy. "Wrong, pirate. You know as well as I do that they're sitting in the north channel."

The succeeding boom of Lieutenant Curtis's cannons on the heights did nothing to faze the last remaining pirate twin, nor did Eric's statement. Jedediah Willard grinned and then pulled on the trigger. Eric's instincts alone saved him from the ball that whizzed past his ducking head. The return volley from the men in Eric's longboat either flew across the gunnel of the pirate longboat or embedded into the boat itself.

Eric shook off the near miss. The excitement of having Jedediah Willard on the run and trapped in his own cove prompted him to call for the prearranged signal to the *Rosemary* and *Redemption*, urging them to complete the trap by sealing off all passage out of the cove.

His signal was interrupted by Charlotte. "Eric, we've got to get out of here!"

Eric looked quizzically at Charlotte. "But we've got him on the run."

Charlotte shook her head firmly. She did not need to say anything else. Eric knew Charlotte well enough by now to know that he should trust her even when it made no sense. Forgoing the signal to seal the cove, the longboat shot across the cove waters to the *Rosemary*.

"What's going on?" he asked Charlotte as they skimmed through the water. "He's got nothing else to trap us with. I saw his two ships on the northern horizon just before we arrived."

"Are you sure you saw ships?" Charlotte asked.

"They were far away, but the masts were clear enough."

Charlotte shook her head. "I didn't hear any of the plans directly, but from where they had me locked up I could tell that all day yesterday the pirate carpenters were making rafts and chopping down the largest trees they could find, on Jedediah's orders. One of the boats was loaded with something last night and then went north."

At first confused, Eric's eyes soon widened. "I wasn't looking at the mast of ships at all. I was looking at trees posing as masts. Decoys." Charlotte nodded, trusting that Eric would naturally reach the same conclusion she had come to. Seconds later, he did. "Which means that the pirate ships are somewhere close by. They are going to surround us in this cove, just when we thought we had got the pirates surrounded."

Eric looked back toward Jedediah. His ship already had its sails set and it crawled forward. The gun ports were open. Jedediah had been ready for this exchange. Eric's eyes next went south, where the *Rosemary* and *Redemption* sat. Suddenly smoke discharged out of the south side of the *Redemption*, firing on something past the entrance that he could not see. He did not need to. It would be one of Jedediah's ships, cutting off the southern route to Port Raleigh. The trap was closing in.

Though it was an ideal time to panic, Eric's mind raced. Exhilarated by this masterful game of strategy, Eric determined that he could figure it out if he only thought it through. Once he figured out the location of all the ships, then he could decide on the best way to get back to Port Raleigh in one piece.

Jedediah's ship coasted through the cove, Eric reasoned. One of Jedediah's two other ships cut off the southern route to Port Raleigh. Where was the third ship? Possibly with the one to the south. If that held true, then Jedediah would have still left open an escape route to the north, past the Montes de Oca island chain. Eric doubted Jedediah would have left the north passage open in the hopes that he, Eric, would not think of it. He gazed northward, thinking. Then knew where the third ship would be.

By that time his longboat had almost reached the *Rosemary*. "West! Head west, before we're completely trapped in the cove. Signal the *Redemption* to come close enough alongside for me to talk to them."

As soon as Eric stood on the quarterdeck of the *Rosemary*, he saw things turning out just as he suspected. The pirate ship to the south of them ran parallel with them, firing in their direction and keeping them from heading toward the safety of Port Raleigh, waiting for Jedediah to join the fray and pick them off. Jedediah, Eric saw as he looked back, still fought past the Lieutenant Curtis's guns in the cove. If Eric wanted to push the meager advantage that he had, he would have to do so before Jedediah exited the cove.

Lieutenant Curtis, from his near impregnable position on the heights of the cove, would clearly hold Jedediah back as long as his ship was in range, and after that Eric had no doubt he would wait until there was a clear shot back to Port Raleigh before abandoning the pirate cannons and returning with his fishing boats and men. Without the need to worry for Lieutenant Curtis's safety, Eric turned his attention to Samuel.

Eric grabbed the megaphone and shouted across the windswept gap between the *Redemption* and the *Rosemary*. "He can't chase us both. Keep heading west. I'll pull up. Whichever one of us the ship follows, the other needs to go for Port Raleigh." The unspoken and obvious downfall to such a plan was that it left one ship completely at the mercy of pirates. What Samuel did not know was that Eric felt confident that his ship would be the one the pirates would choose to corner. Eric did not plan on being cornered.

The *Rosemary* immediately let up, turning into the wind blowing from the east. The *Redemption* shot past, flying west and creating a comfortable distance between the two ships.

Eric eyed the pirate ship to the south intently, every now and then glancing back toward Jedediah. At first it seemed as if the ship would just stay its course and chase the *Redemption*, the opposite of what Eric hoped for. Then it was almost as if Eric could see the pirate captain realize that as soon as he went far enough after the *Redemption*, it would open a gap for the *Rosemary* to slide into Port Raleigh.

The pirate ship stopped and came about. Eric smiled, temporarily relieved. Mr. Gary, however, struggled to mirror Eric's enthusiasm.

"Well, we've succeeded in getting him to go after the bait, Cap'n Francis, but what is the bait going to do?"

"We head north, Mr. Gary," Eric ordered. Mr. Gary's eyes brightened as he put the ship in motion again. "But don't be too disappointed if we run into another ship. One should come out from that second island any moment."

Mr. Gary spouted "How can I not be disappointed? If you're right and the third pirate ship is hidin' behind the second island, then we'd have one of the devils in front of us and two behind!"

"True, Mr. Gary, true. But not to worry. Old tricks will allow us to fight again another day."

As the *Rosemary* ran north, Eric noticed the pirate ship chasing him from behind. In relief, he also saw the *Redemption* making its way south, freely heading for the safety of Port Raleigh. Satisfied, Eric looked ahead. Not too long afterward he witnessed the realization of what he predicted to Mr. Gary. The third pirate ship crept into view, slipping out of a hidden cove at the second island of the Montes de Oca island chain.

The *Rosemary* cleared the northern end of the first island and Eric called out, "Keep close to the shoals, Mr. Gary."

Mr. Gary managed to follow through with the orders, though not without speaking his mind as he did so. "Might I ask where we're heading, sir? A pirate in front, one behind, and another one joining him soon does not make for a happy ending."

"That's because it's not an ending," Eric stated.

Mr. Gary looked around incredulously. "With those ships shutting off every available escape route, it seems like an ending to me, Cap'n Francis!"

Eric shook his head. "You of all people should recall that there are more ways of escaping to the open ocean than just by the northern or southern channels, Mr. Gary. Do you not recall the way we entered a few days ago?"

"That? You mean that tiny, improbable passage through the shoals? But getting through that was impossible . . ." He suddenly realized who he spoke to. "Cap'n, do you think you can do it again? I mean the first time was miraculous but—"

"The flood tide is in, so the timing works out. As for navigating it again, I'll be honest with you. I'm really not sure if it's possible or not, but considering the situation we're in, I'm not sure we have many other choices. I'll tell you one thing, though: I feel better giving the shoals a shot than fighting either of the two pirate ships."

Mr. Gary nodded. As had become custom, he found grudging confidence in Eric, and despite the dire situation, Mr. Gary felt calm. With a low voice, he ordered the coxswain closer to the shoals. The pirate ship to the north began to bear down hard on the *Rosemary*, eagerly set on trapping them up against the apparently impassable obstacle of the shoals.

"I'm going to the forecastle to scout the reef, Mr. Gary. I'll yell back instructions the closer we get and then come join you back here so I can take her in. For now, we can ease up on the sails a little bit." Although Eric managed to navigate the shoals before, he still felt nervous. He knew the nerves would disappear once he found himself in the midst of the action. Until then, he hoped to distract himself by scouting out the reefs.

From the forecastle, Eric scanned the shoals with a shade of familiarity and knew that the moment would soon arrive. He winced as he felt the east wind slamming against him. *That'll make the passage tricky*, he thought. *We'll have to gain some momentum to glide through the first bend and—*

Then, in the distance, he saw it: the tiny opening that would take him through the shoals. He hardly believed that a ship could fit through such a slight passage. He disregarded that thought and began calculating. His instinct for sailing absorbed all of the elements that he faced, and he nodded resolutely, swiftly returning to the quarterdeck and taking the wheel from the relieved coxswain.

At this moment of pure concentration, with the whole crew silently watching and praying, a hesitant Charlotte stepped up behind Eric and tugged on his shirt.

"Don't worry, Charlotte, I know what I'm doing," Eric said, his mind carefully measuring the distance to the passage.

Charlotte bit her lip. "I think I need to tell you something."

"Now?" Eric asked. Though not exactly annoyed, Eric felt a bit distracted. "Because I'll be happy to talk to you—"

"I saw into their eyes, Eric. Both of the twins, I saw into their eyes."

Eric's brow furrowed, but he kept his eyes on the shoals to the side of the ship. "What did you see?"

"Well, Joshua . . . he was a natural-born shoe designer."

Though the situation did not really call for it, Eric had to laugh. "One of the feared pirate twins, one of the ones that has kept a whole port cooped up for a week in terror, is a natural-born shoe designer?"

"Yes," Charlotte responded in a measured tone. She did not seem as amused as Eric. Eric suddenly flung the wheel to the right and the ship lurched eastward, close hauled with the wind and heading straight for the shoals.

"And the other?" Eric asked mechanically, his mind still focused on the job at hand. "What about Jedediah?"

Charlotte set her jaw but said nothing.

To Eric, Charlotte's silence was more worrisome than anything else. Even though the *Rosemary* now careened straight for the shoals, Eric finally took his eyes off the sea in front of him and looked into Charlotte's eyes. "Charlotte. What about Jedediah?"

In spite of the urgency of the situation, Charlotte licked her lips and stood in silence for an agonizing couple of seconds without daring to respond.

"Charlotte," Eric's voice was soft, but insistent, "tell me."

"He's a natural-born pirate."

The statement left Eric speechless for a moment as he internalized it. Though the world stopped for Eric, the *Rosemary* still plunged forward. "What does that mean?" he asked, almost in a daze. "What does it mean when you have a natural-born pirate against a natural-born pirate hunter?"

"I don't know," Charlotte responded, quickly now. "I've never heard of anything like this happening before."

The shoals loomed closer still, almost at the foot of the bow. And then it dawned on Eric. "It means that he knows what I plan to do." He suddenly seemed to see the shoals for the first time. Without hesitating, he spun the wheel sharply to the left while yelling for everyone to hold on. The *Rosemary* swung a wide arc to the north, but the shoals were close and getting even closer in spite of Eric's evasive maneuver. For a moment, the whole crew braced themselves for impact with the reef. A sudden jarring of the ship threw several sailors to the deck, and a sickening scraping sound moaned from the *Rosemary*'s bowels. For a horrifying moment, everyone thought the *Rosemary* came to an end, then just as suddenly as they came, the shoals faded away while the *Rosemary* slipped just out of reach and back into safe waters.

After an initial recovery, Mr. Gary came up to Eric and said, "What happened, Cap'n Francis? I's watching, and you was headed straight for the gap. I think you'd have made it."

Eric felt the vibrations of the scraping on the hull still reverberating in his head. Mr. Gary had to pose his question a second time before Eric responded. "Get out your spyglass and look at it carefully, Mr. Gary." By this time the *Rosemary* swiveled into the wind, standing about a hundred yards from the shoals that almost grabbed them, her sails flapping restlessly in the afternoon breeze, the water slapping in white bursts against her side. Mr. Gary grabbed his spyglass and stood against the taffrail, observing the gap as best as he could.

"By Neptune's beard," he muttered.

"What is it?" Charlotte stepped toward them.

"The passage is blocked. But it isn't reef that's blockin' it. It 'pears to be ballast . . . rocks. As if someone dumped 'em there."

Eric nodded gravely.

Charlotte turned to Eric. "Jedediah knew you were going to go for this gap? How could he?"

"I'm sure he wanted to trap me in the cove, but he also realized there was a good chance that at least one ship would escape the cove. If that were the case, he knew that I would be blocked by his ships on the north and the south. He evidently thought further than that, realizing that if I had been trapped, I might try to go back the way I came. He outwitted me. He must have blocked off this passage sometime yesterday when setting the decoy masts in the north."

"Well, Cap'n Francis, once again, you've saved us from a terrible fate," Mr. Gary remarked, still eyeing the blocked gap with his spyglass in amazement.

"Hardly, Mr. Gary. I've now run out of plans and we have pirates ships surrounding us with a reef at our backs."

Mr. Gary's spyglass went down and he immediately looked to the north, noting the approaching pirate ship with newfound fear. "What can we do?"

Eric became despondent. "Well, considering the wind, our best course of action would be to engage in battle with the ship to the north. It's the one chance we would have of escaping with our lives. But everything else suggests that we'll be torn to pieces. That one ship out-guns and outmans us ten to one. One close range broadside and there would barely be a piece of the *Rosemary* to remember her by. And if we were to somehow get past the ship, we would need to do so before the pirate ship from the south and Jedediah reached us. It'd take a miracle."

Mr. Gary's face fell. In the short time he had known Eric, he had never seen him like this. Frustrated, yes. Despairing, yes. But no matter how dire the circumstances, Eric still managed to always be thinking, planning, hoping. Now, he acted as if he did not care anymore. "Well, you've managed some miracles already, Cap'n Francis . . ." He tried to spark some hope into Eric's eyes.

Eric blinked. "There will be no miracle coming from me this time, Mr. Gary. I've been outmaneuvered."

Mr. Gary looked away from Eric and turned to Charlotte, but he received no help from her. She simply gazed at Eric with concern. Mr. Gary darted his eyes from one place to another, but to no avail. No answers presented themselves. No miracles appeared. He clenched his fists and gazed once more on the forbidding pirate ship bearing down on them.

"Go find a white piece o' cloth," Mr. Gary mumbled reluctantly to the coxswain. The coxswain faltered before passing the word along to a sailor on the deck.

Eric, in spite of all going on around him, felt absolutely alone. In spite of everything he had done and learned, in spite of his clear natural-born talent, Eric managed to still be useless. It was like a horrible curse that he could not shake. He felt empty, and it seemed as if he could neither see nor hear anyone. All on deck seemed to know better than to approach him.

Except for Charlotte.

Once Charlotte stepped toward him, his vacuous eyes finally locked in on her, and he gave her a sad smile. A last and noble, yet failing effort, to pretend that things might turn out okay. Charlotte acknowledged his effort with a pseudo-smile of her own, and he noticed a thin layer of moisture in her eyes. The two slumped down against the taffrail, and Charlotte stared straight ahead. The usually brash girl took a long moment before she could muster something past her constricting throat.

"I'm sorry, Eric."

Eric shook his head. His eyes, too, had moistened. "I got a taste of what it could be like, Charlotte. I can never thank you enough. I'm sorry that I wasn't quite up to the task."

Charlotte took a deep breath. She had a million things she wanted to say but she either could not find the right way to say them, or she didn't think it would help. She wanted to tell him that he had no fault, but she did not know how to do that in a way that he would believe her.

Men scurried around them as the two sat in silence. Someone shouted something. In the distance, they might have heard the sound of firing cannons, but they remained oblivious to it all. Finally, Charlotte spoke. "I remember first walking into your math classroom, Eric. I remember looking at you, and I knew you were special."

"Special only gets you so far, I suppose," Eric's hand waved toward the chaos in front of them.

"No. Not because of the talent, Eric. Because of you." She paused before continuing, her thoughts caught up to her now, and she felt confident that what she now said was the raw, absolute truth. "And now that I've spent this time with you, I am more convinced than ever. No matter what you were born to do. No matter what you have accomplished here, or what you think you haven't. You are special, Eric. You really are. Not because of your talent. Because of you."

Eric turned to look Charlotte in the face. His eyes softened and wet streaks traced down his cheeks from his unblinking eyes. "Thank you, Charlotte." And then, in an action that told more than any words could, the two friends embraced.

"Cap'n Francis, I hate to disturb, but . . ." the tone in Mr. Gary's voice made it apparent that he did not mind disturbing at all. Nevertheless, it took both Charlotte and Eric a moment to respond. For the short time during their embrace, they felt as if they had been removed from this foreign world around them. Finally, they turned to face Mr. Gary, taking in their surroundings once more.

"Sorry, Cap'n, but I thought you might want to see this." Mr. Gary helped Eric to his feet and pointed north. For a second, he simply stood and observed. Then Eric's mouth parted. He next swiveled south and his eyes widened.

"What is it?" Charlotte asked, as she stood up next to them. Her eyes noticed that the pirate ship to the north turned completely around and ran away fast as its sails could carry her. Charlotte then rotated and saw the anticipated ships from the south approaching in a smokescreen of cannon fire.

"What is going on?"

Eric had not recovered his enthusiasm, but he gave a sound appraisal of the situation. "There are four ships heading this way from the south."

Charlotte tried to separate the conglomeration of masts from the smoke and haze that blocked the cannon-firing ships beneath them. "But I thought there were only two other pirate ships coming after us from the south . . ."

"Exactly."

"So how did the pirates get two more ships?" No immediate response. Then Charlotte had another realization. "And why does it look like they are fighting each other?"

"Three against one, actually. The one on the right would be the pirate ship that blocked our south passage just minutes ago. Then one of the three ships fighting the pirate is likely to be Samuel in the *Redemption*."

"And the other two?"

"Looks like the fight is almost done. We should see the smoke clear any second, and I bet we'll see the Royal Navy flag show itself."

As if fulfilling Eric's prophecy, hardly moments later the firing ceased, and a white flag ran up the pirate's ship. Out of the dispersing haze, Charlotte discerned the familiar Union Jack flag that she had seen flown in the harbor of Port Raleigh.

"Captain Bellview's ships-of-the-line?"

"Looks like it. They've come to save the day." Eric spoke his line as if from a script.

"Why?" Charlotte mused.

"That," Eric replied flatly, "is beyond even my speculations."

Chapter 10

ERIC'S RETREAT

Samuel could hardly believe the high and low tides of emotion he had experienced in the last couple of hours. It seemed like only moments ago he raced for Port Raleigh, assuming that Captain Francis and the *Rosemary* had been lost to the pirates, and only hoping that he could avoid the same fate. The next minute, Captain Bellview joined him with the *Constantine* and *Metanoia*, his two formidable ships-of-the-line, and they had the pirate ship on the run. In a matter of time, he and Captain Bellview successfully hunted down the first pirate ship. With the ship subdued, Samuel hurried over to the *Rosemary* to celebrate, only to find a non-responsive Eric, an uncharacteristically mellow Charlotte, and a baffled Mr. Gary, clearly wanting to enjoy the moment, but not sure how, considering his somber company.

Samuel felt determined not to let the day's victory go by in this manner. He almost went to Eric with some direct questions, but Captain Bellview's sudden entrance on deck put a premature halt on the proceedings.

He found it difficult to know how to react around Captain Bellview. The man had behaved so proud and despicable before, yet, undeniably, he came to the rescue in the moment he was most needed. Why, Samuel could not be sure. Fortunately for him, Samuel did not need to react in any way because Captain Bellview had no eyes for anyone else on the ship but Eric. As soon as his legs stood firmly on the *Rosemary*'s deck, Bellview gaped forward, marching straight for the corner of the quarterdeck where Eric had banished himself. For his part, Eric stood apathetically, ready to receive Captain Bellview, but showing no emotion for the moment save a slight flickering of passing curiosity. Even Eric's apathy could not prepare him for the ensuing scene, however, because as soon as Bellview reached him, the proud man fell down on his knees.

Samuel lurched forward, wondering if Bellview had tripped or something, but then he halted. Mr. Gary's hand wavered in front of him, holding him back. The sight of the scene alone arrested him more than Mr. Gary's hand. Captain Bellview's shoulders were shaking. From their view on the side both Mr. Gary and Samuel saw that Bellview had tears breaching his eyelids. Both looked to Charlotte, who witnessed the scene from the other side. She observed the proceedings with as much intense curiosity as their own. Of the onlookers, only Eric seemed unaffected. He watched Bellview sob beneath him with sympathy, but as if he was only just realizing what he should have known all along.

For a long moment, time paused like a pendulum at its apex. Even the rest of the crew stopped what they were doing, though none of them knew how to react at seeing this highly regarded, decorated Royal Navy captain kneeling in front of a boy and crying so intently that he could barely keep himself from collapsing in a heap on the deck of the ship. Finally, Eric bent down at his knees and grabbed the uniformed shoulders of the man who had caused him so much grief. Captain Bellview could not look up still—almost as if he did not feel worthy to look Eric in the eyes. Finally he managed to mumble something between sobs. Though his voice was quiet, the extreme silence on the *Rosemary* helped carry it to everyone's ears. "I'm . . . sorry, Captain Francis . . . so very, very . . . very sorry."

Eric seemed to have a lot going on in his mind at this time already, but he patted Captain Bellview on the back and said, "You're here now, Captain Bellview. That's what matters."

These words guided Bellview into some deeper breaths and into gaining some more control over his body. After another minute in this position, he eventually sat back on his haunches and transferred some tears from his face onto his sleeves. Eric remained kneeling and the two looked at each other. Both were not in the mood to smile, but they exchanged the beginnings of a wry grin before their faces fell back into their set sullenness.

"I treated you poorly. And I did things not only unbecoming of a gentleman of my status, but unbecoming of humanity and the demands of civilized beings. I was doubtful, jealous, and obstinate to the point where I became obsessed. I am ashamed to admit that the kidnapping was my idea in the whole. Not only that but even after you exposed myself and the governor in our contemptible scheme, I was still hardened against you and wished for your failure."

In spite of the crowds of sailors who pressed toward the quarterdeck and the looks of shock on the officers' faces, Captain Bellview's red-smeared eyes only connected with Eric's. "But when you successfully came back with one of the pirate twins themselves, and then when you went out to face Jedediah in the exchange, I finally realized that my problem wasn't you—it was me. I was angry at myself, because I had no idea before that moment what true courage really was. And I realized that you were truly and deeply sincere about everything you had done or offered to do. You were doing everything I should have been doing, and you were doing it with a fourth of the resources I had, and all of the courage I didn't have. And what's more, you never held that against me or criticized me. You tried to call me to action, but you never demeaned my position or reputation. My pride simply kept me from seeing it, and even when I saw your true self, I was still too proud to help because it would have meant acknowledging that I was wrong, even to the point of endangering hundreds of lives, if not the lives of the whole town of Port Raleigh.

"But when you left the harbor this morning, selflessly daring to face Jedediah Willard, while I stupidly held back your two greatest resources in the *Constantine* and the *Metanoia*, I knew that I needed to change something inside of me, or I would live the rest of my life as a coward and a fake. And no matter the consequences against my own personal pride, I knew I had to help. Not that you needed the help, but because I needed this: to kneel before you, like I have, to tell you that I am sorry, which I am. And to hope that throughout my life I can somehow, in some way, elicit any of your slightest tendencies of mercy and forgiveness for the crimes I have committed."

Although the *Rosemary* stood into the wind and sails flapped, tackles clacked, waves knocked, and wind whistled, Samuel noticed none of them. For him, the whole world had suddenly become noiseless to make way for this incredible scene.

Everyone who knew Eric knew how he would respond, and he did not disappoint. After taking in Captain Bellview sitting awkwardly on his backside, his face a mess, his hair disheveled, Eric simply shook his head. "For those things you've done against me, you have no need to ask for forgiveness. I hold nothing against you. As for what you did to Charlotte . . . well, that forgiveness is out of my hands."

Captain Bellview nodded firmly while sniffing his running nose and turned to face Charlotte. "Yes, I had meant to plead for forgiveness from you as well, Miss Charlotte. I—"

"You don't need forgiveness from me. We all know you were trying to get Eric caught and not me. So if Eric somehow has the ability to forgive you for all the trouble you've caused him on purpose, then I suppose I can forgive for what you've done to me on accident." Charlotte did not seem like one who concedes anything, so she quickly added, "But only because I think Eric is an amazingly unselfish guy, not because I think you've done a whole lot to deserve your own forgiveness."

Samuel and Mr. Gary smiled at Charlotte's usual spunky response. Even Captain Bellview managed a weak smile at this point. "Of course not, Miss Charlotte. I, of all people, am very aware that I am most undeserving."

"I would hardly say that," Eric threw in. "If it weren't for you, we would have been either at the bottom of the sea or in the hold of a pirate ship right now. And then I would be the one asking forgiveness from all those crew members on board this ship for the death and suffering I'd have caused them."

Something inside Samuel churned at Eric's statement. Finally, Samuel sensed why Eric acted so strange. For the first time, Eric had been reduced to accepting one of his own failures. Samuel realized he had seen this before when Charlotte had been taken and Eric blamed himself. Yet, Samuel recalled, Eric remedied the problem himself. He successfully retrieved Charlotte and fixed the problem. But now, Samuel came to understand, Eric had again—in his mind—failed, but this time he could not fix the problem. Instead, someone else bailed him out—Captain Bellview in this case.

Samuel knew Eric too well by now to allow that comment to pass by unchecked. He almost responded, but Mr. Gary beat him to it. "'Ere now, Cap'n Francis. You'd have done no such thing as ask forgiveness from us on the *Rosemary*. We all knew what we was gettin' into when we stepped aboard for this venture, and we made the choice on our own. Wasn't you that was pushin' us. Like you've been sayin' from the start, there's risks. Well, we're grown men and sailors, and we knew the risks, but we decided to face them anyways. An' here we are in the end, safe an' sound. So don't you be thinkin' you're all so mighty as to take responsibility fer our actions," he concluded with a wink in his eye and a reprimand. "'Cause you may be the most amazin' mariner I've ever met in me life, but even you can't take that kind of credit."

Eric stared at Mr. Gary for a moment, thinking, before he finally brought his hands up and said, with a forced smile on his face, "Woah, Mr. Gary. I get enough chastising from Charlotte, I don't need to hear it from you now. Your point is taken." Eric pushed himself off the deck and offered his hand to Captain Bellview. With a sense of turning over a new leaf, Bellview accepted the hand and stood, pausing meaningfully before he let go of Eric's hand.

The mood on board the *Rosemary* from that point relaxed, and the officers discussed the details of what just happened. Mr. Gary, especially, wanted to know more about the battle that took out the last pirate ship, and they indulged him in every detail. Samuel noticed, however, that in the ensuing conversation Eric hardly spoke—that he listened detached, stewing over a still unresolved issue. Before Samuel found time to talk to Eric privately, however, Mr. Gary asked about what happened with Jedediah Willard's ship. This question, at least, drew Eric's interest.

Captain Bellview checked with Samuel to confirm the information as he related that once they passed the cove, Jedediah had finally crept past Lieutenant Curtis's guns. Bellview signaled for his other ship to keep an eye on Willard to ensure that he did not surprise them from behind, but by the time they engaged in battle with the other pirate ship, Jedediah disappeared. From Captain Bellview's perspective, Jedediah's ship suffered pretty severe damages. He would not be surprised if the pirate went slinking off to one of his hidden posts in the Caribbean.

If Eric thought any differently, he did not indicate it. After several more minutes of explanations and congratulations, the officers all wondered what the next step would be. As if on cue, everyone turned to Eric. Samuel noted the reticence in Eric's eyes and prodded, "Well, Captain Francis . . . what is our next move?"

Eric waved his hand and smiled, albeit uncomfortably. "Ha. We've got a ship full of geniuses. I'm sure you can all handle this situation."

Captain Bellview interpreted Eric's gesture as if he were tired of being the one making all of the decisions, so he graciously took over. Samuel saw it differently, however. He saw it as Eric giving up. Before

Samuel could consider it too much, Captain Bellview grabbed his attention.

"Jedediah is probably off to some unknown part of the Caribbean, licking his wounds. The other pirate ship that is still heading out the north channel will probably keep on running until the Arctic Ocean. But just to make sure, we should have one of our ships patrolling the north passage here, and then another one out by the San Fernando Channel. I think a ship like the *Rosemary* will do for patrolling the northern passage here, and then I can send the *Metanoia* to watch the San Fernando Channel, that way we can have the *Constantine*, the *Redemption*, and our newly captured pirate ship on reserve . . ."

Samuel listened to Bellview's sound advice, but instinctively slipped a glance toward Eric, looking for signs of approval. Samuel would have been surprised if he were even listening at all. Eric nodded his head listlessly at Captain Bellview's suggestions. Samuel, too, started to zone out. A week ago, Port Raleigh withered under siege, helpless in its own harbor. The pirates had complete control. Now, two pirate ships fell captured and the other two ran. One of the notorious twin brothers lay dead. Not to mention that the *Rosemary*, which should have either been captured by pirates or had its deck strewn with disease-ridden corpses by now, boasted a healthy and happy crew and proved the means of bringing the pirates to justice. Yet, in spite of this, Samuel did not feel satisfied. As he observed the hollow eyes of the young man who brought about all this success, Samuel knew that he would never be satisfied as long as Eric was not.

Eric would not give Samuel much of a chance. After the two ships had been assigned to their patrolling duty, Eric opted to go with Captain Bellview back to Port Raleigh in the *Constantine*. As they embarked, the discussion among Samuel and the other ship officers turned to the provisions they would need now that the blockade was over. As they passed the first Montes de Oca island, Lieutenant Curtis and his men joined them, informing them that Jedediah left in dire straits once he finally exited the cove. With sails tattered, and the foremast taken out—leaving him without even jib sails—Jedediah had been fortunate to slink into the open sea in one piece.

As the ship streaked south toward Port Raleigh's harbor, Lieutenant Curtis pressed Eric with questions, but Eric deftly deflected them to Samuel or Captain Bellview. So in discussing Port Raleigh's future security, they concluded—without Eric's advice—to keep the pirate's cannons stationed above the cove of the first Montes de Oca island. Lieutenant Curtis felt they could build a fort to house the cannon, since the location had proven strategic in defending Port Raleigh.

When they arrived in Port Raleigh, the first news that they heard from sailors on the pier was that Governor Rose had gathered up as much money and valuables as he could and fled with a couple of his loyal men into the hinterlands. He must have realized that with Bellview turned away from him, his last set of resources had been pulled out from under him. No one mourned for the port's absent governor, though several offered to mark a spot on a map where they thought he had gone, claiming it was on an exact southeast bearing from Port Raleigh. In no mood for revenge, or aggressive action of any sort, Eric politely declined.

The group of officers gathered at the gangplank, on the cusp of leaving the ship, to celebrate a successful day together, when Samuel heard Eric call for their attention. It was the first time Samuel remembered Eric speaking since he deferred the last of Lieutenant Curtis's questions. The group succumbed to complete silence in order to hear Eric, since his voice and demeanor had become so meek that it took every effort to hear him speak.

"You gentlemen will never know how much this experience has meant to me. But sadly, it is now time for me to go . . . to, well, to return to my native land. Tomorrow morning, I hope that I could borrow a small fishing vessel, which I'll take to the island where I first boarded the *Rosemary*. After a week, you can go back to the island and retrieve the boat, since I will have met up with my other, uh, transport from there."

While the group of men on the quarterdeck stared at Eric, shocked, Samuel noticed that Charlotte simply watched Eric give his announcement without any noticeable emotion on her face.

The inevitable protests came, but Eric staved them all off. He explained that they had all the resources they needed to protect the harbor now, and that the pirates were clearly on the run. "And besides," he added, "I think you're all under the mistaken impression that I'm the most sound decision maker among us. Captain Bellview tipped the scales today with his timely arrival. Lieutenant Curtis damaged Jedediah enough to cause his retreat. Samuel has organized and recruited crew members for the cause of our defense since we got here. I think it's clear that you're all very capable men on your own."

While this statement unleashed a fury upon the men, who swiftly denounced Eric's self-defeating speech, Samuel saw that Charlotte still watched, unmoving—her face as unreadable as a statue's. Eric smiled wanly, thanked the men again for their kind comments, but told them that he had made up his mind.

Once the men realized that he could not be dissuaded, they offered to drop him off at the island themselves, to wait with him for the arrival of his transport, to have a send off celebration from the whole town. Eric politely shot down every suggestion. He wanted no fanfare, and he had no desire to drag out his farewell. He would leave simply and quietly the next morning on a small fishing boat.

They protested in vain once more before giving their unexpected farewells to this young man they considered as nothing less than a hero. When Samuel shook Eric's hand and saw Eric avoiding his gaze, he knew he would be there in the morning to send Eric off.

The next morning, as the sun climbed over the hills surrounding Port Raleigh's harbor, Samuel saw that he was not the only one who thought to send off Eric. Lieutenant Curtis marched purposefully up the pier and stood next to Samuel, neither of them uttering a word. Then Captain Bellview greeted them awkwardly. Mr. Gary shuffled up to his superiors as the last of the farewell committee. After a few seconds of silence between the four, they noticed the same thing at once. In the distance, as the rising sun rays glittered off the rippling harbor surface, the silhouette of a retreating fishing boat told them all they needed to know. Eric had left.

Without a word, the four turned and trudged off the pier.

Not in the mood to talk, Eric also did not like Charlotte's incriminating silence. Finally, when they retired from the harbor, Eric decided to clear the air, "Look, Charlotte, you didn't have to come with me. You could have stayed at Port Raleigh with the others until the moon was just about right and then had them drop you off with me."

In spite of her previous silence, Charlotte responded with the sharpness of someone prepared to converse. "Nah, Eric. I thought I might as well join you in your retreat."

The word "retreat" had the effect on Eric that she must have hoped for. He flinched when she said it and replied, "I am not re—" and then he stopped. He became quieter. "I am retreating."

He considered this as he shifted in his seat. "You're right. I am retreating. And for good reason. Because I'm no match for this world. My pirate hunting days are over. I tried. I failed. Now it's time to go back and be the Eric I've always been."

Charlotte laughed and stood up. She walked over to the mast and held it. Looking in front of her for a while, she finally turned back to Eric. "So I guess that means you're going to go back and be the glum boy who always thought he was useless."

"Do I have any other choice? I'd always felt I was useless before, but now I've proven that even under the best circumstances I still have to be bailed out, whether it's Tina Ortiz with a math problem or Captain Bellview with his ships-of-the-line."

Charlotte rolled her eyes. "Eric, are you honestly trying to tell me that you don't think turning this place from the besieged to the attackers was useful? That you had nothing to do with the rescuing of the *Rosemary* or the foiling of that nighttime pirate attack, that you had nothing to do with the capture of the pirate ship and hundreds of pirate attackers? You honestly don't feel as if you bailed out everyone more than they could've ever bailed you out?"

Eric shrugged. "But what does it matter, Charlotte? What do those things matter if in the end I manage to get you caught and then I trap my own ship and risk the lives of those brave men? To me, the whole thing is a failure if the only reason we're not dead or captured is because we were lucky enough to have Bellview change his mind last minute."

Charlotte shook her head. If she lacked showing emotion the night before, she made up for it now. Her upper lip trembled and her jaw set as she said, "Eric, were you not listening when Captain Bellview gave his apology? Or were you too wrapped up in your own self pity to notice?" This stinging remark caught Eric's attention, so Charlotte continued. "You keep on acting like Bellview's entrance is completely unrelated to you. And yet he himself said that the reason he had his turnaround was because he saw the courage that you have . . . sorry, that you had. He said it right there, pure and simple. The reason that he came was because of you. You orchestrated your own rescue. You have due credit for Jedediah's retreat, for the capture of the second pirate ship, the retreat of his other one. It's all because of you, Eric."

Eric fell silent. He had no response.

"But maybe you're right, Eric," Charlotte pressed her advantage, "What does it matter? What does it matter if, after all you've done, you fail to acknowledge your own part in it, and in the end you make a cowardly retreat."

Another stinging blow. Charlotte was firing one full broadside after another now.

Her barrage left Eric's thought process in disarray. Up until this point, Eric had been taking credit or blame for things that he planned or did not plan. Bellview's turnaround, however, had nothing to do with his plans or lack of planning, but even Captain Bellview admitted that Eric caused his change of heart. As he mulled this over, Eric wondered whether Bellview's conversion should count as luck, or if maybe Eric could include himself in the equation.

Charlotte anticipated his thoughts because she said, "You know what's the most interesting part of all this? Captain Bellview's entrance had nothing to do with your skills as a pirate hunter. It had everything to do with you as a person—your character, your selfless acts and humility. So in the end, what saved 'useless' Eric was his tendency to just be a good person—not him as a pirate hunter." Charlotte let this sink in for a second. "Of course, that Eric is no where to be seen right now. Because that Eric wouldn't take all this time to worry about himself and how much blame he should get for things that could have gone wrong but didn't."

Again, Eric had no immediate parry for Charlotte's offensive. Again, he desired to believe it, to embrace it. A lifetime of expecting failure, however, made him reluctant to open himself fully to the possibility. So instead, he reviewed the situation and realized that whether Charlotte was right or not, it did not matter now. Eric threw out his final desperation shot. "Well, everything is under control now. Whether I get credit or not for helping, there's not really much I can do anymore. So, we might as well just head out to the island and wait for our time to go home."

Charlotte exercised some self-control in keeping herself from expressing a blistering remark. Instead, she slid to the other side of the mast and sat on the open bow of the fishing boat. With the wind coming from the southeast, her blonde hair flapped like a loose sail, and if she had not been facing forward, Eric knew he would have seen it flicking and twirling past her stubborn face. She eventually called back without turning her head, "Well, this will be a lot of fun. Once we get to the island, I'll be able to spend a full week with a surly, self-pitying companion, until we finally get to go home. All because he is too proud or scared or . . . I don't know what . . . to recognize his own achievements."

Whether he would admit it or not, Eric could not deny that Charlotte's little show had an effect on him. Deep down, all he simply wanted was someone to show pity for him, to feel sorry for him, to tell him that it was okay, that he had done his best and failed and that it was time to go home. But Eric should have known Charlotte better than that. Charlotte would not be the kind to throw out useless pity remarks. Charlotte could not stand that sort of pampering. And here she sat throwing one insult after another into his face. Well, not insult, but truth without the slightest courtesy of softening the blow.

As Eric adjusted the boat's only sail, which lay across the north side of the fishing boat, he knew that Charlotte was right. He could not leave just yet. Even if all he did was go back to Port Raleigh and sweep off the pier or coil rope for the rest of his time here, he knew he had to do it, for himself. Because the worst thing he could do after all he had accomplished would be to give up on himself.

Before Eric could voice his realization, Charlotte turned around and asked him a compelling question.

"What if you had another shot at Jedediah Willard right now?"

"What do you mean?" he asked.

"I mean, if you knew where Jedediah was right now, what would you do? Would you really still go back to that dreadful little island and wait to go home, or would you drop all of your self-pity and go after the monster?"

Since hearing of Jedediah's retreat yesterday, Eric had not given it much thought, especially because he had been so set on his own retreat. "I don't know . . ." he answered truthfully. "I, well, I think I'd hesitate, because, well, now that I know he is a natural-born pirate, it's likely that I've met my match."

Charlotte barely suppressed a laugh again. "Funny. He would probably be thinking the same thing about you considering that before you showed up he was in complete control of this place and after you showed up all of his ships were captured or run off and his own ship had to limp away."

While Eric appreciated the compliment, it caused him to wonder what Jedediah would be thinking about now. His musing led him to say, "No. No, Jedediah is too proud to consider whether he met his match." Eric based his speculation on the little he had seen of Jedediah at the exchange and Jedediah's actions the night after the *Rosemary* slipped past their blockade. "Instead he'd probably be angry. He'd want revenge. He would vow for revenge, even if he had to do something almost crazy to get it."

"Like sail right back into the cove that he left yesterday?" Charlotte asked, a twinkle in her eye.

"No. He wouldn't trap himself like that. He . . ." Eric stopped and looked at Charlotte, who for all the world could not hide the smile bursting on her face. Then Eric ducked and looked underneath the sails. He could barely believe what he saw. Though they still cruised some distance away from the island, the battered masts of Jedediah Willard's ship could be seen as clearly as if they sat right next to it.

Chapter 11

JEDEDIAH'S TRAP

Dozens of questions ran through Eric's head all at once. Why? What was Jedediah Willard planning? How could he do something so stupid? Then his next thought was, *How did he get past the patrol ship? Captain Bellview's* Metanoia *was left guarding the San Fernando Channel, yet Jedediah slipped past it? Or somehow captured it?*

Charlotte, again, anticipated some of his questions. "Well, maybe this boat will have some answers." She pointed off the port bow. Eric peeked around the mast, seeing the *Metanoia* careening toward the island.

Eric deftly adjusted the fishing boat's route into the *Metanoia's* and forced the ship's commander to turn south into the wind so that they could board. The lieutenant in charge of the ship welcomed Eric on board, though he acted distracted. Once the ship was under way again, Eric asked the officer how Jedediah had gotten through.

Flabbergasted, the lieutenant reported, "At about three in the morning, I got called to deck because one of the sailors saw lights coming from the mainland side of the channel. We went to investigate. As soon as we got closer, we realized it was a string of torches climbing over the hills of the peninsula. The long stream of torches disappeared around the west point, and we assumed it was a pirate attack making its way to the fort by land. Those hills are exceptionally rugged and full of jungle, so I wouldn't have suspected a land force to be very effective, but an attempt was being made, by a large force. We got as close to the mainland as we could and trained our guns on them, firing for an hour or so until all of the torches dispersed. By that time, dawn approached, and we were on our way back to Raleigh to report. That's when we saw the Willard ship in the cove."

The lieutenant clearly felt distressed, but Eric barely paid attention to him. He simply looked back at the mainland, and then to the island. "It was a distraction," he concluded.

"A distraction . . ." the lieutenant muttered. "But how? What kind of distraction requires the entire ship's crew?"

"It didn't," Eric responded. "It was probably only fifteen to twenty pirates. They marched with their lighted torches, then, when they got to a certain point, the first in the line doused the torch, ran back to the starting point, lit it, and marched again. All of them continued doing this until it caught your attention and their repeating march made it look like a long line of attacking pirates."

The lieutenant recognized Eric when he first boarded the ship, but he clearly had not spent enough time around him. "How can you know that?"

"I don't, but I'm pretty sure."

The lieutenant nodded. The sheer confidence that Eric exuded gave him little reason to doubt. "Then, what do we do now, Captain Francis?"

"I don't know," Eric replied. "But until then, continue your course. Whatever we do, we're going to need the help of the others."

The lieutenant muttered the appropriate orders to the coxswain and then looked back expectantly at Eric. Readjusting to captain mode, Eric formulated his thoughts before saying, "I want any available sailor not adjusting rigging to go up the masts with spyglasses observing every last movement from that pirate ship. I want to know if a pirate so much as blows his nose." The lieutenant nodded sharply, prodding one of the midshipmen into action. "And then I need to see some maps."

"Aye, aye, Captain Francis, there are some in my quarters. I will take you there directly."

Eric's roller coaster of feelings on his own competence made him pause for a single moment. If he committed to this, then he knew he was committing to the possibility of failure again. His mind faltered momentarily. He looked to his side and saw the ever-confident Charlotte. Then he knew that he would commit, regardless of the possibility of failure. Retreat was no longer an option. He nodded to Charlotte, who nodded back, then he followed the lieutenant to the officer's cabin, where he spent time alone with the large parchments spread out across the desk.

By the time Charlotte entered the lieutenant's quarters, Eric stared off into nothing with his hands resting casually on the maps below him. As she shut the door to the cabin and sat down, non-intrusively to the side, Eric faced her. "I'd take it," he said.

Charlotte furrowed her eyebrow. "You would take what?"

"The question you asked me back on the fishing boat. You asked me what I would do if I had another shot at Jedediah. Well, the answer is that I would take it."

Charlotte smiled. "Eric, I knew the answer. I can't say I was hoping Jedediah would return, but I can say that I got excited when I saw his ship." She gazed at Eric comfortably and said, "So, do you have your plan? Is that why you came to look at the maps?"

"Nah," Eric said, "I just think better around maps." He looked down at the inked lines and dots. "I still don't have the slightest clue what Jedediah is thinking. But maybe once our friends are here, we'll figure it out together."

"Are you nervous?" Charlotte asked.

Eric chuckled. "Yeah. Well, I was. You have a pretty calming effect on me, Charlotte." The two looked at each other through the dim lighting in the cabin and said nothing for a long time. Finally, Eric broke the silence, "Unless, of course, you're kicking me out of my bouts of self-pity. In that case, you have a pretty disturbing effect on me." Charlotte gave the closest thing to a bashful look as he had ever seen. "But," Eric added, "I appreciate both effects. I couldn't ask for a better friend."

"Well," Charlotte recovered, "I should hope not. I spent the night in a rum-and-pirate-stench-filled ship for you. I don't do that for just anyone, you know."

Eric grinned. "Though I'm sure you've had plenty of opportunities!"

"Captain Francis!" a voice rang out from above decks. "Captain Bellview, Mr. Wesley, and Lieutenant Curtis are approaching from Port Raleigh. The *Rosemary* is coming from the north."

Charlotte stood up and opened the door, waving him forward, "Captain Francis . . ."

"Milady," Eric countered. He offered his arm, which Charlotte gamely took, and the two proceeded to the quarterdeck.

Once on deck, Eric saw Captain Bellview in the *Constantine* heading to meet them, flanked on either side by the *Redemption* and the newly christened pirate ship taken the day before, the *Francis* (an obvious compliment that embarrassed Eric when it was announced the night before). Then, he turned to the north and saw the *Rosemary* cruising past the island that had once again become Jedediah's post en route to join them. "How did we get them to all come so soon?" Eric turned to the lieutenant.

"Ever since we were in sight of the fort and the *Rosemary*, we've had sailors holding up signal flags. The fort acknowledged first and I'm assuming Lieutenant Curtis informed Captain Bellview with as much speed as possible. The *Rosemary* acknowledged next and she came bearing down on us just afterward."

"Excellent." Eric responded, impressed. "Your name, Lieutenant?"

"Lieutenant Carroll, Captain Francis."

Eric shook his hand, and his eyes inevitably wandered toward the Montes de Oca islands. "Any developments from Jedediah, Lieutenant Carroll?"

"There's certainly some activity on the ship, but we can't be sure what yet."

Eric excused himself from Charlotte and Lieutenant Carroll and climbed to one the crow's nests in order to watch the proceedings for himself. Within the hour, all of Eric's friends found themselves congregating on the quarterdeck of the *Metanoia*. Eric stayed for one more moment above them, his mind racing in an attempt to guess Jedediah's move. Dissatisfied, he climbed down to a smiling group of adult men, with a smirking Charlotte amongst them.

"Captain Francis," Samuel was the first to say, followed with a sharp salute. Captain Bellview, Lieutenant Curtis, and Lieutenant Carroll followed suit. Even Charlotte threw her arm into a sloppy salute, her fierce smile impossible to contain.

"All right, it's good to see you gentlemen, but you can wipe those smiles off your faces because I'm just as befuddled as you are with what's going on, so I'm hoping that you've got some suggestions."

"Lieutenant Carroll gave us your explanation for how he was able to get past our patrol boats," Captain Bellview started out. "Obviously, this wasn't just happenstance. He planned out this return."

Eric nodded. "But what did he have to gain from a return? I think that, you, Captain Bellview, stated his best move yesterday when you suggested that Jedediah was going to slink off into some unknown corner of the Caribbean."

"He couldn't possibly have thought that he stood a chance against us now that his force has been reduced to one ship," Samuel threw in tepidly as the least confident strategist among them.

Lieutenant Curtis filled in the pause that ensued. "I can't help but shake from my mind the image of his ship as he limped away yesterday. He had been pretty badly damaged, and he could not have made a whole lot of headway."

Eric brightened. He stepped over to the taffrail and trained his eyeglass back toward Jedediah's ship. "Didn't you say that his foremast had been disabled?"

Curtis nodded. "Shot through completely."

Eric solidified some thoughts before turning back to the group. "What has happened is quite simple. Of course Jedediah was hoping to slink away into some corner of the Caribbean, but without foresails, how was he supposed to move eastward? The prevailing winds come from that direction, and he would need to tack, which means a lot of close sailing into the wind. Without foresails to help steer the ship, he probably would have only gone a dozen leagues or so in a few days."

Captain Bellview and Samuel both nodded in agreement. Eric continued, "If he couldn't retreat, then, what could he do? He needed to fix his ship before he stood a chance at survival. So he went as far as the San Fernando Channel, hiding to the south of it."

"Couldn't he have just repaired his ship there? Why would he take such a big risk in outnumbering himself and returning to this cove?" Samuel asked.

Eric nodded. "Good question." The maps he had recently looked at spread out before him in his mind. "Probably the main reason is that there is no anchorage off the mainland there, no friendly cove or harbor to work in, and the wind is constantly pushing toward the rocky cliffs and shore. He probably had a hard enough time maneuvering there without a foresail and waiting out nighttime. Another possible reason is that this is Jedediah Willard. When it comes to a risky, aggressive move, he'll default for the most dangerous."

Lieutenant Carroll picked up from that point. "And since he was already near the mainland, he could have afforded to drop off some men to create the distraction once night had settled in."

"Then it was just a matter of slipping over to the cove," Eric finished.

"But what is his next move?" Lieutenant Carroll asked. "Yes, he got past the blockade, but he couldn't possibly have expected to go unnoticed once he was here. Is he simply hoping that he can fix his ship's problems and get out before we close in on him?"

"Jedediah would never be that stupid," Samuel volunteered. "It will take him all day to fix that busted mast, and that is if he were doing the most simple repair job."

"You see, gentlemen?" Eric said. "Jedediah needs a cove for repairs, but he also needs to protect himself while he completes those repairs. If you were in his position, how would you hope to accomplish that?"

Eric refrained from providing the answer as the men considered his query. The realization first fell upon Lieutenant Curtis. "The cannons. The same spot that so ably disabled his ship. He will look to fortify that as his last defense until he can find a way back out into the open sea." The look of frustration on Curtis's face was apparent. "And we even left cannons there for him to use!"

Captain Bellview picked up the thread where Lieutenant Curtis left it. "If he sets up a fort there, up on those heights, we would have to take quite a few casualties if we ever hoped to remove him."

Eric shook his head. "That's what Jedediah is hoping we'll try . . . to throw ourselves against a heavily defended fortress. It will give him the advantage of time. It will give him the advantage for us to make a strategic error. More chances to find an opening and then use his repaired ship when it is least expected to make a sneak attack or an escape. With this move, Jedediah has given himself new life, even if the numbers are mounted against him."

Lieutenant Carroll then asked what most of the men there had to have been thinking. "Then what do we do? Clearly, we have the advantage in numbers this time. If we want to gather all the troops and firepower together into a massive assault, accepting the casualties and removing him at all costs, we could do so."

"I'd suggest something different," Eric replied. "I'd suggest removing the advantage of time out of his hands and taking it for ourselves."

"And how do we accomplish that?" Captain Bellview queried.

"We forget the cannons on the heights of the cove," Eric stated. "Instead, let's take away his mode of transportation."

"His ship?" Curtis responded.

"Yes. Without his ship, then he is stuck on an island. He'll have his cannons and strong position, but without a way to escape or make offensive attacks, then time will suddenly be on our side. Blockading the cove, out of distance of the cannon, would be simple. They can run around the island on their own until their supplies are gone. A surrender or a blunder of desperation would be imminent."

The thought sunk in for a moment before Captain Bellview spoke. "It is a masterful plan, but our only problem is the same as that of before. Jedediah will protect any entrance to the cove with his cannons."

"Absolutely," Eric agreed. "And certainly we'll run the risks of casualties and ship damage, much the same as Jedediah suffered on his way out of the cove yesterday. But none of that will compare to the casualties of trying to take the heights of the cove with a land force once he has the time to strengthen it. Plus we have many ships, and thus more targets to spread out the effectiveness of his shots. And finally, Lieutenant Carroll, please state what Jedediah has been doing all morning."

"Well, we couldn't see specifics, but there was considerable movement on the ship and the loading of covered items into boats, which were taken to shore."

The men wondered what Jedediah could up to, just as Eric wondered before they had arrived on the ship. "Don't you see? He's moving more cannons to the heights of the cove. He realizes his weakness just as much as we do. He knows that the more firepower he has on the heights, the better chance he has of fighting us off. He's putting all of his efforts into moving as many cannon up to his new fortress as possible." Eric smiled. "Which is why if we attack now we have a great chance of grabbing Jedediah's ship, perhaps even Jedediah himself, without much of a fight, since all his crew is engaged in moving cannon up the steep walls of the cove. If we wait until this afternoon, he will be ready for us. If we attack now, we might catch him in between points, at his most vulnerable."

As long as it took Eric to say it, it took even less time for the orders to go out. The men solidified a quick strategy and then parted for their own boats, Eric stayed on board with Lieutenant Carroll, who quickly deferred authority to him. The fleet formed and headed toward the first

Montes de Oca island, realizing that every moment that passed was precious.

According to the plan, the *Metanoia* with Eric and the *Francis* with Lieutenant Curtis surged forward, while the *Rosemary* with Samuel and Mr. Gary and the *Constantine* with Captain Bellview trailed closely behind. The *Redemption* was to keep its distance in order to be on reserve. Captain Bellview and Samuel had charge of returning covering fire on the heights of the cove once the cannons started firing. The *Rosemary* especially would be useful in getting close to the opposing fire, moving quickly and sporadically, being a pest that could draw away more of the fire from the makeshift pirate fort. Lieutenants Curtis and Carroll, on the other hand, would get closer to Jedediah's ship before disembarking a large boarding force in dozens of smaller boats. This allowed the large ships the chance to cover their offensive, plus providing the cannons from the heights dozens more tiny targets to try and hit. While they planned on plenty of resistance from the fort, back in Eric's mind he believed that Jedediah would be caught off guard, with men still transporting cannons. He felt that the cannons would not even begin to fire before Jedediah's ship had been subdued and was on its way out of the cove.

Eric knew that he based his plans on sound thinking and good strategy. He knew he had made precautions and tried to minimize the damage and casualties they would receive. Yet for some reason, as the ships rolled past the high rising walls of the island cove, he still felt uneasy. His blind spots from the last couple of outings tugged at him. He tried to dismiss his feelings as nerves and decided that a nice conversation with Charlotte would be the perfect thing for his pre-battle jitters.

Though no pirate hunter, Charlotte appreciated the excitement of an upcoming battle, with all of the anxiety and exhilaration that comes with it. As always, however, her one comfort came from knowing that Eric found himself in his element. She garnered extra comfort to have him come up to her as the ships neared their stopping point in the cove.

"Well, Eric, er, Captain Francis . . . everything seems to be in order. I've been watching the pirates on the beach with a spyglass, and you seem to have created quite the stir with your entrance into the cove."

"I should hope so. I would imagine that they are scrambling right now, probably trying to decide whether they should go to their incomplete fort or to their ship. They'll be realizing that they have just taken most of the cannons off the ship and that—with reduced maneuverability—she could become a death trap. They'll probably abandon the ship, which will make it all the easier for us to pick up."

Charlotte smiled. "This has got to be a new experience for you."

"How so?"

"You have got Jedediah Willard on the defensive." When Eric said nothing. Charlotte continued, "It's probably a new experience for Jedediah Willard as well."

Charlotte's comment sparked the vestiges of deep concern in Eric's face. He looked with renewed intensity to the ship in the cove. He looked at the ship's perfect location, just inside the cove, not so deep that removing her would be done under a lot of heavy fire. The ship even pointed out in the direction that they hoped to take her, saving them some potentially essential minutes. He glanced to the heights of the cove and noted that not a single cannon shot had fired yet, just as he had hoped, exactly as he had hoped. As he took in all of this, his thoughts shot back to the picture in his mind of the phony masts sitting on the northern horizon on the morning of the exchange, exactly as he had asked. He thought of the escape route into the small channel leading through the reefs, the seemingly perfect getaway point which happened to be sabotaged. All of these seemingly perfect situations, even brilliantly contrived; yet they backfired on him.

"Eric?" Charlotte prodded, disquieted by his sudden silence.

Eric finally responded with a soft voice of realization. "Jedediah Willard doesn't go on the defensive."

"What?" Charlotte barely heard Eric's quiet statement.

"Charlotte, you're absolutely right. Being on the defensive would be a wholly new experience for Jedediah Willard because he doesn't do it."

Charlotte now felt at least part of the concern Eric did, though for a different reason. "Eric, I don't know what I'm talking about. I'm just making trite little observations, like I always do. Don't listen to me."

Eric shook his head. "No, Charlotte. That's where I get myself into trouble, thinking that I can figure out everything on my own."

Charlotte started to feel desperate, thinking she had brought on the old, self-defeating Eric from before. "No, Eric. I don't know anything about strategy. Jedediah hasn't been on the defensive before because he had the numbers before. But now, obviously down to one ship, he'd have to be on the defensive."

Again, Eric shook his head, still thinking. "No. Not on the defensive, though he's not suicidal either. Jedediah knows how to cut his losses and run—like when he turned around his ships before entering Port Raleigh—but he doesn't know how to play a game of defense. As you yourself said, he is a natural-born pirate. Being on the defensive is not in his blood."

An exasperated Charlotte piped out, "Then what in the world is he doing right now if it isn't going on the defensive? Eric, it doesn't make any sense. You're pushing him into a corner. He has no choice but to retreat to a fort and be defensive."

"It makes perfect sense, Charlotte," and even as he said it, everything in Eric's mind clicked, as if he could see the exact thought process of Jedediah Willard. "Jedediah Willard is leading me straight into a trap."

Charlotte clearly wanted more information after this shocking revelation, but Eric slipped deep enough into his own counter-strategy that he could not pay her much heed.

"Lieutenant Carroll," he approached the officer, who turned to him smartly. "Those signals flags you used to get the others to rendezvous with us this morning. Are you able to convey other messages with them?"

"Absolutely, Captain Francis. Anything in the English language if need be."

Eric took one more glance toward the pirate ship before setting his next move. "Very good, Lieutenant Carroll. Then this is what I want you to do. Make sure that your flag signals can only be seen by our own fleet and not by the pirates; hide them by sail or however you can. Then, I want you to signal to the others that there's been a change of plans. Order Captain Bellview and Captain Wesley to take the *Constantine* and *Rosemary* to the windward side of this island. Then signal Lieutenant Curtis in the *Francis* and inform him that when we get into the longboats, all of the longboats are to follow my lead boat precisely."

After Eric finished with his instructions, Lieutenant Carroll nodded and set off to complete the task at once. Eric stood alone for a while, checking and rechecking his plans, but there remained little doubt in his mind as to what his next actions would be.

Once the signal had been given, Lieutenant Carroll approached Eric. Charlotte shuffled close enough to be in on the conversation. "The signals have been acknowledged, Captain Francis. That is a credit to you that Captains Bellview and Wesley both turned around and headed to the windward side of the island without so much as a query as to why." Eric nodded, and Lieutenant Carroll stood for a moment in awkward silence. "Not that I don't have the same faith in you as the others, but just out of mere curiosity, why the change in plans, Captain Francis?"

Eric's eyes flickered in competitive intensity as he responded to Lieutenant Carroll's question. "Because Jedediah Willard is going to see what it feels like to have his escape route sabotaged."

Eric then gauged their location in the cove and ordered the ship into the wind and the longboats in the water with all the manpower the ship could muster. Charlotte found Lieutenant Carroll in the midst of the commotion and tapped him on the shoulder. "Don't worry, Lieutenant Carroll. He always gets ambiguous when he has a good idea."

Lieutenant Carroll smiled. "I guess we'll find out together, then, Miss Charlotte!"

As the longboats disembarked from the *Metanoia*, Charlotte stubbornly found herself next to Eric on board a longboat packed with armed sailors. Eric did not dispute her presence, mainly because he knew better than to start an argument he would lose. Eric's longboat then proceeded at the head of the half dozen other boats from their ship. Soon Lieutenant Curtis followed with a half dozen of his own boatloads peeling off from the *Francis*.

At first, the group of longboats headed straight for the pirate ship, sitting like a wounded bird in front of them. As they approached, two cannon on the front of the ship, possibly the only cannons left on board, fired a couple pathetic shots toward the approaching mass of longboats. Neither of the shots fired hit a single boat. With newfound courage at this pitiful display, the oars dipped faster and stronger and the boats rushed forward, eager to take the ship.

Though the enthusiasm of the men was visibly on the rise, Eric remained stoic in the lead. He eyed the ship in front of them carefully, occasionally gazing upon the fleet of small boats around him, checking their positions. Finally, as their invading force came to within a couple minutes of the ship, and after one more harmless salvo from the two cannons, Eric detected what he had hoped to see. A small boat detached itself from the pirate vessel, filled with only a few men, and retreated for the shore.

"All boats stop!" Eric cried out. The men in Eric's longboat, confused by the call, but obedient under orders, pushed the oars against the water and brought the boat to a halt. The other longboats following them did the same. After he had all the boats at a standstill in the water, Eric ordered the boats to reverse. Silently, they obeyed, though the man at the tiller in Eric's boat managed to whisper to Eric under his breath. "Begging yer pardon, Cap'n Francis, but t'pears as if them pirates is on the run. The ship is ours to be ta'en."

Eric clapped his hand on the man's shoulder. "That is exactly what Jedediah is hoping we would think. In about a minute and a half, you'll change your mind. But don't worry. You'll get your chance to catch a pirate before the day is over. Quite a few of them, if I'm not mistaken."

Eric turned back to watch the ship. His mind calculated where their longboats would have been if he had not ordered the stop. *Right about now*, he thought, *we would've reached the side of the ship. Now, we would've boarded. I'd have gone aft and sent several patrols down the fore and midships hatches, right about now.*

Charlotte, who watched Eric through her breeze-caressed, wispy strands of hair, said, "When, Eric?"

Eric nodded toward the ship and said, "Just about now."

A pause of several seconds passed before the most magnificent explosion that Eric or any of the others had ever seen rocked the scene. The pirate ship, which one minute had been a large, albeit damaged fortress of wood on the water, had in an instant been decimated to splinters and consumed by succeeding balls of red, engulfing flames, spiraling in mad fury as they expanded and devoured the ship, rocketing any obstinate pieces out of its path. It seemed as if all of this occurred in silence, but really only a split second later the resounding boom and succeeding roar of the explosion traveled across the water to Eric's ears, followed by the crackling of ferocious flames. After a moment's hesitation, the

strewn pieces of the now nonexistent ship sailed through the air, landing in broken piles everywhere within a half mile radius.

Most of the men flinched and then gazed in dumbstruck awe at the
firestorm in front of them before they realized that the explosion had
been meant for them. With that knowledge in mind, their widened eyes
could barely remove themselves from the blackened wreckage scattered
about pathetically in the clear Caribbean water, which ably doused the
vestiges of flame clinging to the wood.

Where the crew members had fallen inactive, Eric became all
action. Lieutenant Curtis's longboat approached his own, and he called
out the orders. They were to go to the beach and attack Jedediah's crew
there. They would go in two prongs, one to the north of the pirate
landing and the other to the south. Thus trapping the pirate crew, they
would close in on them and finish them off until they surrendered.
Lieutenant Curtis was to take his crew to the south and move north, and
Eric's longboat would lead his group to the north and then move south.

Some confusion ensued as Lieutenant Curtis separated himself
from Eric's boats and Eric imparted instructions to his own little fleet.
The longboats re-positioned, and amidst the disturbance, Eric deftly
transferred onto a tiny dinghy with only a couple of men at the oars.
By the time Eric directed his abandoned longboat where, specifically, to
make its landing, Charlotte noticed he had left. She swiveled toward his
voice in the dinghy. "Eric, where are you going?"

"Stay with the main landing force and hang back behind them
once they start their attack. It won't be long, Charlotte. The pirates
won't put up much resistance without their leader."

Though Charlotte felt confused and upset by Eric's sudden absence,
she thought about what he said. "Without their leader? Eric, what are
you saying?"

"This was all a set up, Charlotte—one to trap me. Just like with his
brother, he doesn't care what he loses, as long as it can lead to defeating
me. He doesn't care about his crew or his ship. He planned on abandoning them this whole time, so the fighting shouldn't be too bad once
his men figure that out. I expect they'll give up once they realize they
are surrounded and their leader has left them. You should be safe if you
hang back a little." Eric's dinghy now separated itself from the rest of
the boats, heading for the northernmost corner of the cove.

"But what are you doing, Eric?" Charlotte called out over the noise of the dipping oars that propelled her away from Eric.

"I'm going to find out what happens."

"What do you mean, 'what happens'?"

"When you place a natural-born pirate hunter against a natural-born pirate."

Chapter 12

PIRATE HUNTER
VS. PIRATE

Eric chose not to watch Charlotte's reaction, as he sensed it would not be a kind one, so he turned around and encouraged the two men rowing the small boat. While digging his oar into the ocean, one of them piped up.

"I may be mista'en, but is yer honor lookin' to hunt down Jedediah Willard hisself?"

Eric nodded, steering the boat for the very northern nook of the finger-like cove.

The other oarsman jumped in at this point. "We ain't much a fight'rs, Cap'n Francis, sir. We're more a jes yer common sailor type. But we've seen yer bravery, an' we're with ya to the end wid this one!"

Eric nodded once more. "Thank you for your support."

Minutes later, the dinghy scraped onto the sandy shore. After the two sailors tugged the boat farther up the beach, the three did a weapons check. Unlike his first battle, Eric had the wherewithal to grab two pistols and a rapier sword while still on the *Metanoia*. The other men carried cutlasses and a pistol each. Eric had the sailors load their pistols while he surveyed the situation. Using the calculating mind that Eric could only explain as instinct, he figured that Jedediah separated himself from his crew as soon as the longboats approached his lame duck ship. Eric scanned the shoreline, seeing that the jungle broached it at all points except for a rocky ridge that dropped into the water and cut a swath in the greenery of the island. Eric knew that Jedediah would have stopped there to witness the explosion. Once the explosion had occurred, he would have moved on.

171

Eric checked the cove. But from his angle, the pirate would have been unable to see that Eric and the others had not fallen into the trap. He would have continued his retreat, but in a confident stride, quick but not panicked. He would likely stay among the tangled branches of the jungle, away from the beach, where it would be possible to be sighted by the ships that would finish off his crew. Eric's eyes traveled along the jungle-edged cove, estimating the potential path and time frame, trying to account for the difficult path of the dense trees.

"Very well, sailors," Eric finally spoke out. "Jedediah should be coming this way any minute now. Because there are a few paths he could take, we'll need to spread out to find him. Once you sight the him, fire your pistol, and we'll join you. Do not fight the pirate until the rest of us are there. Do you understand?"

The sailors nodded grimly. "Very good. I want one of you in charge of the beach area, and then the other within his sight at the edge of the forest. I will take the inside of the jungle area."

Eric neglected to tell the men that neither of them would ever see the pirate, nor that he did not even expect them to participate in the struggle. Part of the reason he kept them from helping him take on Jedediah Willard came from being afraid that any unforeseen error on their part could tip off Jedediah to their presence or cause them to become collateral damage or a hostage. The other part that kept him from including them derived from something that Eric could not easily explain. He simply felt as if the meeting between himself and Jedediah should not be fettered by outside influences, but simply the two of them with their natural inhibitions and abilities.

Either way, Eric left the two sailors on the beach area and scrambled into the forest, past vines, palm plants, and fallen trunks. After a short walk, the ground sloped upward into the hills of the island. Eric knew that Jedediah would not head for the hills just yet. He would round the cove first before he attempted that. So Eric backtracked slowly until he found a faded animal trail in the spongy island ground. *This is it*, he thought. He discovered a clump of trees standing next to the trail and hid himself behind them.

As he stood there, he mentally calculated how much longer it would take for Jedediah to arrive. *Less than a minute*, he told himself. He checked his pistols and they were ready. He fingered his rapier. In his mind, he pictured Jedediah working his way through the jungle. He realized that the pirate would probably have his pistol out. *The rogue may be a lot of things*, Eric thought, *but unprepared is not one of them.*

Eric knew that the element of surprise would allow him to shoot before Jedediah could, but that might expose him to Jedediah's return fire before going down. Eric decided that he had to disarm the man before he let any shot come, so he tucked one pistol in his belt, leaving one hand gripping the rapier and the other hand on his other pistol. Just as he made that determination, he heard the squelchy sound of approaching footsteps. Eric had no question as to whom they belonged.

The sound alone justified everything Eric already guessed. It was a confident, unsuspecting gait, moving briskly along the slight path, not making a lot of noise, but not being careful about the noise either. Eric gripped the rapier handle in his left hand, let go of everything else in his mind, listened to the impending footsteps, and in the right moment, he struck.

The rapier rang sharply against the metal barrel of a large pistol, and Jedediah Willard, in complete shock, dropped the weapon and sprang backward, tripping against a fallen tree branch. Eric snapped out of his hiding spot, his rapier trembling in exhilaration in his left hand and the pistol pointing deftly at the pirate on his right.

Neither spoke a word as they stared each other down. From all appearances, Jedediah Willard rushed through a wide range of emotions, starting at mild alarm and evolving to shock once he recognized his assailant. Eventually the cunning pirate settled with a disconcerting though slight smile before he spoke.

"Captain Francis, alive still. Either you weren't smart enough to fall into my trap or you were too smart." He eyed Eric and chuckled, though not as comfortably as he could have in a different situation. "Too smart, I guess. Always a game of chess with you."

If Eric thought it prudent, he would have agreed with Jedediah. Even now he could tell how the man calculated his odds of survival and his next move. Eric knew the pirate, knew his actions, knew his motivations, knew it all too well to wonder what went on in that mind of his. Eric also maintained awareness of the absolutely despicable, detestable, murderous nature of the man. He had no doubt that the man, while contemplating his escape, also contemplated Eric's painful demise.

Eric knew one more thing. He knew he could kill him in an instant. He did not need a moment of moral decision. His nature centered on hunting down a pirate, and the man before him was more pirate than any other person he would ever meet. He could kill him. The only thing Eric considered was how to best accomplish it.

"You must be pleased to see that I both killed my brother and blew up my ship in trying to catch you."

Jedediah was stalling, trying to salvage enough time for some kind of opening for escape. While Eric recognized this, he also needed a moment to assess the situation. He could shoot Jedediah in the head and that would be the most detrimental, but he also remembered not to underestimate his opponent. The head can dodge much quicker than the rest of the body, and then it would simply be a guessing game as to which direction the head would dodge once Jedediah registered the falling of the flintlock hammer.

Eric decided that as long as he tried to figure out his own best move, he might as well play along with Jedediah in the stalling game. "What I'm pleased about is that your murdering days are over, whether it's murdering your own family or other innocent people."

Eric felt confident that he could shoot the pirate in the body, but disabling him instantaneously would not be guaranteed. With his other pistol loosely hanging in his belt, Eric assumed he could grab it before Jedediah could retaliate. If not, he could defend himself with his rapier well enough.

Jedediah must have sensed that Eric was wrapped up in his thoughts, because he forced a cautious smile. "Don't be ridiculous. You could never shoot an unarmed man."

Eric did not smile back. He responded in as serious a tone as he ever voiced. "Until your brain is no longer working, you are most definitely armed." His finger started to squeeze the trigger, the barrel aiming straight for Jedediah's heart.

"You're left-handed," Jedediah stated suddenly. The mere fact of the matter caused Eric to loosen his grip. He realized that Jedediah was thinking out loud, his mind racing up to the very last seconds of his life. "You knocked the pistol out of my hand with the sword in your best hand, your left. That means the pistol you are aiming at me right now is not in your best hand. Certainly you'll be an excellent shot with both hands, but I have a slightly better chance with the pistol in the hand that it is in right now. You might consider switching hands, but that split second between hands will give me all the advantage I need."

"Then again," Eric said coolly. "I might be ambidextrous."

Jedediah gave a reluctant nod. "You could maroon me on this island and set a patrol boat to ensure that I don't try to escape. Marooning is a common and devastating punishment for a lot of known pirate offenders. Nothing worse than knowing that you're going to starve to death or to be alone for the rest of your life thinking back on your crimes."

Eric almost smiled. "Not that I don't appreciate your creativity, but death by my pistol or marooning is all the same, except that one is more certain than the other. So I'm going for that." With that, Eric squeezed the trigger and the pistol fired.

Eric could not be certain at what point Jedediah Willard planned on using the branch at his feet, but the fact that he started kicking it right as Eric finished his last statement meant that he had not reacted to the shot, but instead anticipated it. Even so, the kicking of the branch was a desperation move and they both knew it. The odds that it would harmlessly fly past Eric, ungrazed by ballshot, reached beyond reasonable calculation. Yet a miniscule chance remained of it disturbing things enough to save Jedediah's life, and Jedediah's impossible chance paid off.

Just as Eric fired, the branch soared in front of the barrel. The ball showed little mercy for the offending branch, repelling it back to where it came and scattering the broad end of it into pieces that dashed everywhere. Even still, the spherical piece of lead never found Jedediah's flesh. And in the aftermath, through the slight haze of the powder shot, Eric saw the pirate scrambling to his feet and tearing through the path that he had previously been on, heading east.

Eric had limited time and target, with Jedediah now dodging between trees and plants, but as soon as the first pistol had misfired, his next one materialized. Even though he did not discharge it with his favored left hand, as Jedediah astutely noted, the shot successfully thudded into the only visible patch of Jedediah's body, his right arm.

This shot only produced a grunt from the retreating pirate, doing nothing to slow him down. Regardless, as soon as Eric's shot met its target, he jumped into the undergrowth and followed the crashing sounds of his quarry. The chase progressed painfully slow as the two scurried around, above, and underneath thick growths of plants, panting heavily, trying to make up distance on the few open spots in their paths.

Even though Jedediah, by nothing more than great fortune, had kept himself alive, his situation still left him in a grave state. In spite of this, the pirate's retreat showed signs of being more deliberate than desperate as he moved in a measured but not panicky speed. Eric realized that this unseen force that made so him difficult to capture must have been an expectation of survival. Hoping to curb this motivating factor, Eric called out to him in the couple of spots where he could make out the pirate's figure in the brush ahead, "There's no place to go, Jedediah. We're on an island. Sooner or later, you'll have to turn around and face me!"

"I'll face you when I'm good and ready," a growling voice responded one of the times. "But first I'll get off this island and come after you on my own terms." His voice then darkened. "And then you will die."

As Eric scraped past clinging leaves and branches, he perceived that Jedediah actually felt as if he might get off the island. The pace of his retreat did not reflect the random fleeing of a cornered man. His retreat had purpose. Eric watched Jedediah start to ascend the main hills of the Montes de Oca island, and the young pirate hunter smiled while wiping sweat off his brow. *Now*, he thought to himself, *you'll see how it feels to have your carefully thought out retreat sabotaged.*

After fifteen minutes of a grueling uphill march, with the two still within shouting range of each other, Eric watched as Jedediah crested a saddle in the steep hills, giving him a view of the other side of the island. Eric stopped and observed. He saw the pirate, with his right arm slumping against his body, scanning the scene below. It took a split moment of realization before a crescendo rumble emanated from his throat, climaxing into a roar of rage. Jedediah swiveled around, blazing eyes searching for Eric, then he instinctively started to reach for his cutlass. But even by that movement he became frustrated, since his arm could not reach across his body due to the injury he had received. Eric had shot the pirate's favored arm.

As soon as Jedediah grasped that each of his options was being exhausted, he desperately threw himself onto a small boulder and hurled it downwards. The boulder tumbled for a few rotations before tangling up in the undergrowth and jarring to a stop. Jedediah cast his eyes around, looking for more potential weapons. Seeing none, he scurried farther up the ridge. Eric reached the crest of the saddle in a short time, and the view only confirmed what he speculated.

Anchored on the windward side of the island sat the final pirate ship, the one that had fled north the day before. Surrounding it, clearly having subdued it, were the *Constantine* and the ever-familiar *Rosemary*. Jedediah's frustration could be understandable. His carefully thought out trap, which required a heavy sacrifice of his flagship, had turned on him. And now his only venue for escape had been removed from under his feet. This left him cornered on an island, alone and forced to finally turn to—as he had always avoided before—the defensive.

Yet even a cornered prey could be dangerous, Eric knew. And Jedediah still might prove resourceful in his desperation. As a precaution, Eric reloaded his pistols and placed his rapier in its sheath, though he checked to make sure that it could easily be removed if the discharged pistols were not enough. Then he sucked in some air and sprinted up the ridge to finish the job.

He could not see Jedediah in front of him, but the boots scraping on the rocks and an occasional grunt told him that the pirate was close. Forward progress, for both of them, required burdensome labor. From the saddle, the ridge shot up into the air, vaulting out of the jungle into a razor-thin, rock-studded edge. While Eric started out on just his feet, the higher up he went, the more he relied on his pistol-laden hands to aid him in climbing. Still, he knew he was getting closer, and he knew that Jedediah had to be desperate. Finally, there would be an end, and Eric would see if he got to fulfill his natural-born destiny . . . or, he amended his thought, if it would defer to the pirate.

Then Eric heard the scraping above him stop.

Eric rounded a bend and saw that the ridge traced a line right past two mammoth towers of rock. Though easy enough to follow the path, Eric knew at once that it had now become an ambush point.

Knowing that fact was one thing, but doing something about it was not quite so simple. The monolith rocks did not provide any other access around them except through the path down the middle. This meant that all Jedediah had to do was hide behind one of the towers and wait for Eric to come, then stab at him from behind as he passed. Then again, if Eric could guess which rock the pirate stood behind, he could simply walk up that side of the rock and fire on the waiting enemy. If Eric guessed the wrong side, however, he would leave his back just as exposed than if he had no idea there was an ambush waiting for him at all. It would be just as fatal.

Eric tried to focus on the scene in front of him as if he were Jedediah. Which side would make the most sense? But the two towers of rock seemed nearly identical. Eric could not see an advantage to one side over the other. Then Eric's mind really started to run. He knew that Jedediah's arm, his right arm, was wounded. That would mean that he would be wielding his cutlass with his left hand. If he were hiding behind one of the towers, he would probably want to hide where he had more room for his left hand to maneuver, which would be the tower on the left. That made sense, but his previous encounters with the pirate made him hold his ground still. The times where Jedediah had bested Eric had been when he anticipated Eric's strategy and then adjusted his own strategies to match. What if Jedediah anticipated that Eric would figure out which side would be easier for the uninjured left hand and so he then hid on the other side?

Eric squirmed a little bit at this uncomfortable thought. He reexamined the gap between the towers, wondering if he might be able to just take a peek at both sides. Even as he thought it, however, he realized that it could not work with that particular layout. That was simply a guaranteed way of getting stabbed. If he wanted any chance at completely disabling Jedediah, he needed to commit to one side or the other. Not committing would put him at just as great a risk, if not more. Eric ran the scenario through his mind again, then tried something.

"I know you're waiting for me, Jedediah, just as your ship was waiting for you. Of course, that didn't work out very well. Maybe you should just drop your cutlass and give in."

Eric, of course, did not expect Jedediah to do any such thing. He did hope, however, that he could elicit some type of reaction from Jedediah. Anything. Even if he gave no verbal response, he might shuffle his feet, or maybe even sneeze, or, well, anything. Anything that would betray which side he had committed to. After a long pause, Eric heard nothing. He tried again.

"Once I realized that you were leading me into a trap in that cove, I wondered why you would blow up your own method of transportation just to kill me. That would mean even if you succeeded, you would have left yourself trapped on the island. Then it was obvious. Your ship that fled to the north yesterday, we had assumed that it was gone, but I realized today that of course you'd have had a rendezvous point in case of separation. Where else would you rendezvous but nearby, in the event of the need for a counterattack? So, even though you hadn't had contact with the ship, due to the limited sailing abilities of your own boat, you could count on your last pirate ship to be waiting for you at the rendezvous point on the windward side of this island. Once I figured this out, it was a simple matter of sending a couple ships around the island to neutralize your last resort. So as you can see, I've defeated you at every turn. There's no need to drag this out any longer. You might as well show yourself."

Eric threw out this last piece of bait, where it hung in the tense air. He hoped to tap into the pirate's emotions, get him angry enough to be pushed into a response. Obviously, Jedediah lost his cool on top of the saddle—his rash boulder shoving was a prime example. Yet Jedediah's retreat up the ridge must have given him enough time to collect himself, because as long as Eric waited, he received nothing in return.

The air hung completely still, not even a breeze to push away Eric's stale conversation. For a brief moment, Eric wondered if he guessed wrong and that Jedediah might be farther up the ridge. One look at the situation, however, removed any doubt. A desperate Jedediah would not pass up an opportunity like this. As the best option for survival, Eric felt assured that Jedediah took it. He simply had no way of knowing which side of it the pirate took.

Finally Eric realized that it would all come down to chance. Either side could have been chosen for any number of reasons. It would simply come down to when Jedediah stopped anticipating and actually made his decision.

Eric almost laughed at himself then. So it came down to this? A fifty-fifty chance?

At this point, however, Eric felt certain that he would never get a better chance at Jedediah. If he left to get help, Jedediah could retreat and hide for months on the island, figuring out a method for escape and revenge. If Eric waited until dark, his choice of using pistols would be at an even greater disadvantage. Eric needed to choose now and act now. He took one last moment of thought and then made his decision.

I will go for the right side, he told himself, rationalizing that Jedediah might have only had time to think of taking the preferred left side and then counter once with anticipating that Eric might guess that move. Even as he reasoned it, however, he recognized how flimsy any rationale seemed at this point. He simply walked into a fifty-fifty situation . . . but, he comforted himself, at least he did so knowingly. With that, he cocked his pistols and strode forward onto the tiny path leading between the sentinel rocks.

The sound of his steps betrayed his movement, but he knew that it would not matter. If right, he would have a clean shot at Jedediah. If wrong, he would be caught from behind. These things would happen whether or not Jedediah heard him coming, so he stepped forward with more vigor. Once he fell under the shadow of the gated rocks, he was tempted to pause and try to scope out both sides, but he sensed that vacillation would get him nowhere. He committed to the right side, trained each pistol in front of him, and placed pressure on the triggers. Then he stepped.

It only took one step for Eric to realize that he chose the wrong side.

The small alcove behind the rock lay empty, and not a second later a sharp point thrust itself in his back, tearing through his shirt and pushing the skin back until just before its breaking point. The discomfort was deliberate, but Eric could at least be relieved that the pirate had not taken advantage of the opportunity to sink the point all the way through his soft skin. Why, though, was not clear to Eric.

"Toss the pistols!" a vicious voice spat between clenched teeth. This was not the calculating Jedediah that Eric had seen at the exchange. This was not even the smiling Jedediah Eric had seen on his back in the jungle, only seconds away from being shot. This was an enraged Jedediah, and Eric sensed that he cared nothing for Eric's life. In fact, he even cared nothing about gloating in his victory because Eric had taken any positive from behind the victory. So why Jedediah had taken a moment before plunging the cutlass into Eric's back went beyond Eric's understanding.

One thing Eric did know. Jedediah would not play any games, nor would he permit any perceived strategy on Eric's part. Eric knew even the significance of wording. He did not tell Eric to drop the pistols. Dropping them would leave them too close to Eric for Jedediah's comfort. So Eric preserved his life for at least a few moments longer by tossing the pistols into the alcove in front of him, where Jedediah should have been hiding. They clanked loudly on the stone floor, well out of Eric's reach.

Eric could not tell for certain, but it felt as if the pressure against his back let up, if only in the slightest degree.

Jedediah spoke again, once more measuring his words carefully. "If I see that hand go anywhere near that sword of yours, then I won't hesitate in chopping your body in half."

Eric believed him—believed every last word. And he still wondered why the pirate had yet to kill him.

"Now, no games, no playing. Tell me who you are." The intensity in Jedediah's voice scared Eric even more than the situation he found himself in.

Confused, he muttered, "Eric Francis . . ."

The cutlass suddenly pierced his skin. Not a whole lot, but enough to start the flow of blood. Eric twitched but made no sudden movements. "You're smarter than that. I don't want your name. I want to know who you are!"

Eric began to catch on to what Jedediah asked. But he felt unsure of how to answer. "What does it matter?" he asked sincerely.

"Before you came, I had been unrivaled. Given the right amount of men, there were no limits to my abilities. But once you showed up, predictability was lost. I no longer know whether I have the advantage going into a situation. I can fix that by killing you here and now, but first I want to know who you are. Who are you, and should I expect to see more like you?"

Now it made sense. Jedediah Willard would kill him. But first he had to know if he could be safe or if he should be on guard for more enemies like Eric. The advantage to Eric here was minimal. Jedediah had no intention of keeping him alive, and if he tried to bargain for information, Eric sensed that Jedediah would stick true to his words: no playing, no games. The only advantage this gave Eric was time . . . and he would use it. He responded honestly because he felt that Jedediah would detect any deception. As he responded, he also thought through his situation with every angle left to him.

"Hunting pirates is what I was born to do, Jedediah. I'd never been in a ship, or even on the ocean more than a week ago, but that girl, Charlotte, she recognized my natural-born ability, and she brought me here so that I could test my abilities. I don't know if there are more like me. I suppose if there were it's possible that they would also come against you, though I really don't know enough about it to say."

The pressure of the cutlass loosened again, this time allowing for the trickle of blood to increase slightly, but Eric felt relief by the extension of life that it indicated.

"Now we're getting somewhere, Captain Francis. Mark my words, if you keep talking openly like you just did, you just might spare your life a little bit longer. Now, will this girl Charlotte be able to tell me some of the information that you don't know?"

A desperate thought popped into Eric's head after Jedediah said, "Mark my words." That phrase rang out as the truest thing about this whole conversation. Eric trusted—just as Jedediah expected him to trust—every word leaving Jedediah's mouth. That brought him back to the second thing that Jedediah told him as soon as he placed the cutlass to Eric's back.

"Charlotte knows a lot about people's natural-born abilities, but she doesn't know everything. She didn't know what would happen when there were two people with such equal abilities coming up against each other. But certainly, she knows more than I do. I doubt that she has seen others with the same talents as me, though, or else she probably would've mentioned it." The cutlass now only hovered above his back, not even touching it. Before Jedediah could give a follow-up question, Eric beat him to it.

"Now, what did you say would be the repercussion if I reached for my sword?"

Jedediah clearly did not expect this question. He immediately suspected Eric was up to something. "I said," he said evenly and clearly, "that I would chop you in half."

"That," Eric said, still as motionless as a statue, "is what I hoped you said."

The following actions happened within a split second after Eric's statement, but with so much riding on their outcome, for the two opponents it took place in slow motion. Eric's right hand immediately grabbed the handle of his rapier and thrust upwards. He did not dare reach for the rapier with his left hand because he knew that there would be no time for his hand to cross his body to his waist before Jedediah would notice the movement and strike. Instead, Jedediah saw Eric grab the rapier handle with his right hand, and the pirate drew back his sword in order to gather momentum for a blow that could potentially sear through most of Eric's torso.

In this tenth of a second, Eric did not maintain his grip on the rapier handle. Instead, his body dropped to the ground while the rapier rocketed up, out of the sheath, and into the air. The result of this action allowed Jedediah's cutlass swing to arc directly into the open space between Eric's dropping body and the upwards-flying rapier, just missing the top of Eric's head and managing to connect with the upward-flying tip of the rapier blade. Once the cutlass passed over his head, Eric sprang back up in the air and his left hand reached out and deftly grasped the rapier handle as it spun around from the blow it received from Jedediah's swing. Then, in one motion, Eric brought the rapier screaming down. Before Jedediah could recover from his forceful miss, Eric's rapier fell down on Jedediah's last good hand, causing the cutlass to crash to the ground and Jedediah to jerk back his arm.

Jedediah's body trembled as he nursed his hand in complete confusion and shock. It took both of them a moment to realize what happened, because only a split second before, Jedediah held complete command of the situation. Now the entire situation had been reversed.

Eric barely believed what had happened himself, but he stood resolutely with his rapier outstretched toward Jedediah's chest. In that moment, Eric could have explained it to Jedediah. He could have explained that Jedediah had said that he was going to chop Eric in half. If the pirate had said that he would stab Eric, then Eric would not have had the time to make a move—one thrust would have ended it all. But Eric had to trust Jedediah's words and that he would take his arm back to swing into a hard chopping motion. Then Eric also could have explained to Jedediah that the single distinction between stab and chop meant that Eric could control when Jedediah attacked, and it also meant that he knew how Jedediah would attack. And that distinction gave him just enough time to both duck and remove his rapier, leading to disarming the pirate once and for all.

These are all the things that Eric could have explained to Jedediah, but as the wily pirate cradled his bleeding hand, he must have thought back on the last thing that Eric said before the incident, and his cunning mind filled in the rest of the details. His look alone told Eric that he knew how he had been beaten.

Before either of them could plan out his next move, Eric saw the realization on Jedediah's face that not only had he been beaten, but that he was about to be killed. The pirate was aware, ever since Eric shot at him down by the beach, that there would be no negotiating out of this one. Eric saw Jedediah take an unconscious step backward. Almost, Eric had pity for him. His slumped right arm, his bleeding left hand, the look of certain death, an end to his very life, bursting across his face. Eric almost had pity for him, but not quite. Eric felt as strongly as ever that what he said earlier resonated with truth: as long as Jedediah's brain was working, he was armed and dangerous.

A new expression fell across Jedediah's face after one more shuffle backward, and with ease, Eric voiced what he knew raced through Jedediah's mind. "You know that I am about to pierce you in the heart. And you know that you are in no position to match me, especially without any weapons. So you know that you will die. And now the last thing that you're thinking is that as long as you're going to die, you're going to try to take me with you. You're going to charge me and try to deflect my blow as best you can. Even though you know that the wound I inflict on you will be fatal, no matter how much you can deflect it from a direct blow to your heart, you're hoping to extend your life just enough so that you can barrel through me, land at the spot where I tossed my loaded pistols, and take two final shots at my head before death seizes your limbs and then your brain. And you are hoping that the last image in your soon-to-be-lifeless eyes will be me falling to the ground and joining you—your final consolation in a lifetime of evil."

As Eric accurately delineated each of Jedediah's desperate thoughts, Eric saw a semblance of awe overcome the man's visage. By the time Eric wrapped up Jedediah's final vision, the awe transformed into a smile. "Well then," Jedediah grunted, "since we know each other so well, let's stop thinking and start acting. Let's see if your sword will stop me in my tracks or if I'll be able to drag you into death with me. No more surprises."

Eric had time for one last thought as Jedediah lunged toward him. He thought that it would be nearly impossible for him to stop Jedediah in his tracks. Fired with adrenaline, the man still maintained almost all of his physical ferocity in spite of damage to his two arms. Eric knew that trying to adjust his thrust to match Jedediah's deflection and still pierce him in the heart would be nearly impossible to predict since it could come from any angle.

So, without any delusions, Eric simply hurdled his rapier forward with as much force as he could into the oncoming body of Jedediah

Willard. The last thing that Eric saw before being enveloped by the large mass was his rapier bound tightly, up to its handle, in the chest of Jedediah—clearly a fatal blow. Yet as Eric crumbled beneath the large body, he knew that he just missed the heart, if only by inches, and that Jedediah might have a chance at a couple more seconds of life.

Jedediah rolled over Eric, leaving him with the breath knocked out of him. Facing away from where he tossed his pistols, Eric could not be sure whether Jedediah rolled close enough to grab them or if he even had enough strength left in his mortally wounded body to aim and shoot. Eric tried to muster the strength to move, to see if he could at least watch his own fate unfold, but before he could even budge, his body was shaken to the core by a pistol shot that cracked the air around him as if lightning had struck. It was closely echoed by another one.

In a surreal moment, Eric tried to determine whether he felt his skin being punctured at any point by the metal balls from his own pistols. He was unsure what being shot would feel like and at what point his body would realize where it had been hit, at what point death would overtake his body.

But Eric could not feel anything, though the sound of the shots, he knew, were as real as anything else he had heard in his life. Since his sense of touch failed him, he finally lifted his head up and depended on his sight. A quick scan down the length of his body showed nothing, and then his eyes drifted off of his body and down a short slope to see the body of Jedediah Willard, unnaturally contorted like a V from his waist, Eric's rapier blade uncomfortably keeping him from resting his back on the ground.

It only took a short second, but the scene that his eyes swallowed told him several amazing things. The side of Jedediah's head, above his ear, had a gruesome musket ball wound in it. Closer inspection showed yet another shot in the pirate's chest, opposite of the rapier handle, a pool of seeping blood marking the devastated place.

That explained the end results of the shots. But what amazed Eric even more were the pistols bound tightly, in a literal death grip in Jedediah Willard's hands. No smoke emitted from them, and, Eric noted in amazement, they were still cocked—just as he left them when he tossed them. That meant that Jedediah, though his fingers rested impatiently on the triggers, had not fired the shots at all.

Just as Eric realized this, he heard some shuffling behind him. The shuffling belonged to two sets of feet. One pair approached Eric and the other went toward Jedediah. Eric swiveled his head and looked, shocked, into the face of one of the sailors that went with him to the beach. The sailor's look mirrored his own, still trying to take in the situation and breathing heavily.

Though he looked exhausted, the sailor still gathered enough air to exclaim, "Are ya alright Cap'n Francis, sir?"

Eric started to sit up, his body finally catching up to the speed of his mind. He glanced at the other man checking on Jedediah and saw that it was the second sailor from the beach. He did not say anything for a second before finally nodding slowly, then more vigorously. "Yes. Yes, I'm fine." He shook his head, then added, "Sailor, I don't believe I ever caught you or your companion's names."

The sailor looked relieved that Eric could answer. "Nathan, sir. And that fellow there, he's Paul." After a pause, Eric's bewildered look convinced the sailor to fill the missing details. "We was patrolling our spots on the beach, sir, and then we heard the shot and the rustlin' through the woods, as t'were. Well, we knew yer orders were to wait fer a discharged pistol as the sign to join you, but you were already gone, sir. We assumed that you'd be chasin' the pirate and we knew it were our duty to help you, so we chased after ya. Long and difficult chase too, I might add. Us sailors are in shape enough for climbin' around on a ship, but a long distance run is sure to tire us quick enough. But we didn't want to let you down, Cap'n Francis, so we kep diggin' fer more after we had given all we got." As if to emphasize this point, Nathan paused to gasp for some more oxygen before gulping and continuing, "Finally, we just made it up this ridge and to this gap in the rock in time to see that crazy Willard bloke divin' at you, see you stick him right through with yer rapier, and see him roll across the ground an' reach fer them pistols with the last bit o' energy he had left. Well, we knew we didn't have loaded pistols fer nothin' and . . ."

Nathan did not need to finish. Eric slapped him on the side of his arm. "Well, Nathan and Paul, congratulations. You two just killed the biggest terror this Caribbean has ever seen."

Paul squatted down next to the pirate's body and, between heaving breaths, he spoke for the first time. "I'm thinking that yer sword did the killin', sir. Our shots were just speedin' things up a bit."

Eric laughed, partially at Paul's comment, but mainly at the situation. For all of the predicting and mind reading he and Jedediah had done, neither of them could have foreseen this result.

Paul seemed satisfied that the rogue was truly dead and stepped away, and Eric noticed one last thing that escaped his attention before. As a direct contradiction to Jedediah Willard's final words, he saw the last look on the pirate's face just before the musket ball to the head finished him off. Jedediah Willard held a look of surprise.

Chapter 13
USEFUL ERIC

As the small dinghy rode over swells toward the *Rosemary*, Eric barely remembered the events between leaving Jedediah's body on the ridge and descending with Nathan and Paul to the windward shore guarded by the *Constantine* and the *Rosemary*. After Samuel, Mr. Gary, and Captain Bellview saw them waving their arms on the beach, they sent the dinghy to transport Eric and his men back to the ships. Picking them up off the shore had not been simple, since the waves crashed into the windward side of the Montes de Oca island with an intimidating fierceness. Still, when they finally got past the breakers and to the anchorages of the *Constantine* and the *Rosemary*, cheers of jubilation broke out from everyone at the news.

After ensuring Eric's safety, they sent a party of men back up to the ridge, guided by Nathan, to retrieve the body of Jedediah Willard. By the time they retrieved the body, the final captured pirate ship had been overhauled and prepared to sail, and it joined the *Constantine* and the *Rosemary* around the southern tip of the island, heading back to the cove where they left Lieutenants Curtis and Carroll. Upon entering the cove, their small fleet received a cannonade salute from the ships and cheers from the soldiers on shore, where they secured and transported the prisoner pirates to the ships in small boatloads.

While Eric appreciated the accolades, he still found himself unsettled as he observed the dinghy that detached itself from the shore and headed his way. The receding sunlight drained the color out of the water and island, transferring it to the clouds in a beautiful spread of fiery orange and dark purples.

Eric did not notice the display forming above him, only the approaching dinghy, which by now boasted the gray silhouette of a young woman near the bow of the boat, looking in his direction. Eric knew that he had abandoned Charlotte at a crucial moment in the day's activities. While he had no regrets for his action, he cringed at the wrath that could only come from Charlotte as a result of his decision. The dinghy finally pulled up to amidships and the sailors helped Charlotte climb on board. Eric went from the quarterdeck down the stairs to amidships and by the time his foot had settled off the last stair, Charlotte emerged from the side onto the ship.

She gazed around uneasily, almost jittery. Her trembling eyes filed past each sailor, and then as Eric stepped forward, she saw him.

"Eric." It was a breath, a thought turned to sound that barely escaped her lips. But Eric heard it and it jolted him. He expected a typical Charlotte berating, but before he could even think any further she staggered over to him and fell into his arms, gripping him tight.

Neither said another word for what seemed like minutes. They just held each other, and Charlotte kept her head buried in his chest. Not until Eric felt the moistness on his shirt did he realize that Charlotte had been crying. Still taken aback by a Charlotte that he had not known before, he held her tighter still. Though in a cove filled with activity and on a ship amid all of the bustle of one preparing to anchor, Charlotte and Eric were alone with each other.

Finally, Charlotte's muffled voice spoke through his shirt, "I'm sorry."

"No, I'm sorry," Eric gazed forward at nothing.

"I know you knew what you are doing," she started to lift her head up, "and I even encouraged you to face down Jedediah because I had full confidence in you. But when you left and I watched you go . . . well, I am still human after all." She made a noble effort to smile through her drawn face. "I wondered, I . . . I had these obnoxious doubts, and I imagined the worst . . . I wondered if that was going to be the last time I would ever see you." As she finished talking, her already moist eyes renewed their teary reservoir.

"I shouldn't have left you like I did," Eric said. "I should've told you on the boat."

Charlotte shook her head, wiping her eyes. "You did everything right. Look around you. You've amassed a fleet here. It was nothing you did. I just . . . I've just grown intensely attached to you, Eric, and even though I knew I needed to let you go, it was hard to do."

Eric about contradicted her to tell her how he still could have gone about it differently, but she saw his expression and cut him off. "But now, here you are all safe and sound, not a scratch on you. I don't know what I was worried about."

Eric laughed, his body still sore from the impact of Jedediah's body rolling over his and a small itch on his back where Jedediah's cutlass point had punctured his skin, "Well, not too deep of a scratch, at least."

"And . . . Jedediah . . . ?" Charlotte then ventured.

"Gone. Done." He pictured the frozen expression on Jedediah Willard's face. "Dead." His mind reviewed the whole experience and it exhausted him just thinking about it. Charlotte read his face, and he eventually noticed. So Eric grabbed her hands and led her up to the forecastle. There, the two sat against the railing and he told her everything, every last detail, every thought. He spoke with her until the stars dominated the black sky. Then they sat in silence for a while, glancing up at the stars.

They both tracked the moon rising past the high hills of the cove into the night sky. Eric looked at Charlotte and wondered if she could tell what he was thinking. Never one to disappoint, Charlotte removed her glance away from the moon's pitted face and turned to Eric. "I just think that I should tell you that, with those two sailors coming to your aid in the last second—"

"I know," Eric interrupted. "They didn't just bail me out. It wasn't just luck that I defeated Jedediah." By the halting tones in his modest voice, Charlotte discerned the difficulty of Eric's admission, but he voiced it anyway, saving her the trouble of doing it for him. "First of all, I defeated Jedediah already—he was only trying to even the score. And second of all, I remembered what you said about Captain Bellview, that it was because of me that he showed up to save the day. Well, those sailors told me that they were with me because of the bravery that they had supposedly seen me use. They even said that, when they were chasing Jedediah and me, they didn't give up because they didn't want to let me down. From that, Charlotte, I have to admit that their role in this whole affair can be at least partly attributed to me."

Charlotte must have been smiling, but Eric felt too embarrassed to check. She fell quiet before speaking out. "Eric, if you keep on figuring stuff like this out, you're not going to have any use for me anymore." Eric nearly protested, but Charlotte continued, "The other interesting thing about the whole experience is that, once again, the thing to save you was not necessarily your skill, but your personality. The men admired your character, and that is why they helped you. Jedediah may have had all the pirating skills he needed, but his men never would've searched him out to help him on their own. They didn't admire him; they feared him." Charlotte gazed upwards musing. "Now we know that's what happens when you put a natural-born pirate against his greatest foe, Eric. Identical skills, but the victory goes to the better person."

Eric let this sink it. He realized that the truthfulness of her explanation left nothing for him to even add or detract. After a long while, he finally reasserted his gratitude for her insight.

Charlotte let more time pass in silence before saying, "Well, looking up at that moon reminds me that time in this place is limited."

Happy to move beyond a conversation entirely about himself, Eric gauged the current phase of the moon, "Yep. Only a week more." He thought for a moment before adding, "Only a week more and then it's back to math class, driving tests, and," his voice lowered, "mediocre Eric."

Charlotte eyed Eric curiously, the moonlight painting his face with an unnatural white glow. "I said that time in this place is limited. I didn't say it had to be for you."

Though Eric had been studiously scanning the dark night before them, this comment forced his eyes back to Charlotte's. "What do you mean?"

Charlotte reluctantly spoke, "You don't have to go back, Eric." Her voice hovered between them earnestly. "This doesn't have to be a glimpse. If you don't go back to the island where we came, you can stay and live in a world where you are the master of your own natural-born talent."

Eric's eyes widened. He had never anticipated this option since, in his mind, the whole experience had been temporary. For a brief moment, the thrill of having a daunting pirate foe in front of him, or standing at the helm of a ship just as it is preparing to engage with another, or feeling the weight of a sword balanced perfectly in his hand all rushed through his mind—that was what he had been born for.

The thought coursed through his body with every deep breath. What more could life offer than to be the master of that fate you were born for? How could he choose anything else? To command men who respected and trusted him because of his knowledge, to pore over maps and discover stratagems, to smell the sea air and feel the tug of currents and swell of the open sea—could he ever be truly happy with anything else?

And then the moment checked. Something in the back of his mind pushed to the forefront. While completely satisfied with the new friends and colleagues he had formed, Eric valued the small group of people who knew him when he considered himself useless—and they loved him regardless. "And my family?"

Charlotte looked at him wistfully. "Even if I had the ability to bring them here, they wouldn't belong. Theirs are all different worlds, different times. If you chose to stay, you would choose a world for which you were born but a world without your family."

The thrill came to a stop. "What about you?"

"I'm here now, it is true. But I can't stay, Eric. I don't belong here either. This is your world. And once I went back, there would be no coming to see you, since I can only travel to worlds with the person . . . and you'd already be here. I'd go back and stay. My place is with my family."

Eric allowed his mind one last glimpse into the world that could be his—the ships, the wind, the chases, the excitement—and then he let it drift across the horizon of his mind. He glanced at Charlotte and even managed a wry smile. "A world without my family is no world at all . . . even if I'd be unexceptional there."

Charlotte eyes reflected the whole of the night sky as she responded, "I thought I knew you well enough to guess your answer, but I had to give you the option." She looked around at the ship and noted, "I'm sorry that you will have to leave it all. It must not be easy." Eric said nothing, so she ventured, "But at least you can keep me company when we go back. I would have missed you terribly."

Though at peace with his decision, Eric could not quell at least one pang of regret. "I think the hardest part will be to go back knowing that I could have been useful."

At this comment, Charlotte shook herself out of a subdued mood. "Have you learned nothing on this whole adventure? Even now you'll make that ridiculous claim that you are useless."

Eric quickly went on the defensive. "No, I very, very much appreciated this experience. It showed me that I'm not destined to be useless. But you have to admit that I won't be chasing down any pirates as soon as I get home."

Charlotte shook her head condescendingly. "I guess I can still be of some use to you now. This takes us back to a conversation we had a long time ago. How many people are actually born at the right time and situation for their natural-born talent to be useful?"

"Not many," Eric granted. "But I think I am particularly useless. Ryan Thompson, for example, isn't anywhere near the right time or place for his buffalo hunting natural-born ability, but at least he has a football field, where that talent for throwing accurately and quickly can come in handy. There isn't a sport at my school that requires fencing skills or outmaneuvering someone in a boat."

Charlotte rolled her eyes. "It's a good thing I like you or else I probably wouldn't have the patience for this. You don't just need to have the perfect skill that will match just right with a certain activity, Eric." Charlotte sighed, and then, as if she were demonstrating the greatest amount of patience she could muster, she approached the conversation on a different tack. "What do you think George Washington was naturally born to do?"

Though the question came a bit out of the blue, Eric had a quick answer. "Be a general?"

"No," Charlotte replied, "In fact, if my history teacher taught me correctly, he wasn't all that great of a general, as far as tactics go."

"Be a president of a country?"

"Nope. From what I understand, he never was too enthusiastic about being a president either, which wouldn't fit for someone offered an opportunity to fulfill their natural-born talent."

Eric groped for a minute. "Well, Washington was one of our greatest heroes so you'd think he'd have some pretty awesome natural-born ability. Let's see. Wait a second, you're probably trying to make the point that he wasn't in the right time or place for it, so . . . oh, I know. A king or a ruler!"

Charlotte shook her head. "He was offered the opportunity for kingship and he turned it down. I'm betting if it was his natural-born talent, that would not have been such an easy thing to do."

"You've studied up on him, haven't you?"

"Washington is a pretty interesting case study in natural-born ability."

Eric let his mind touch on some random ideas before he gave up, exasperated. "I'll throw out these last guesses, and then you have to tell me: Pope, Pharaoh, or dogcatcher."

The "dogcatcher" guess threw Charlotte off a bit as she denied his answers, but Eric just shrugged to show her that he really had no idea. She continued. "George Washington, as has been passed down from generations of natural-born talent seers, was a natural-born point guard."

"Point guard?" Eric imagined in his mind a soldier guarding a certain station. "What kind of point would he guard?"

Charlotte took a deep breath. "He wasn't born in the right time for his ability, Eric. Think more modern."

Eric tried again, and then it dawned on him and he looked at Charlotte. "Point guard . . . you mean in basketball? He was naturally born to be a point guard on a basketball team?"

Charlotte nodded deliberately.

"But a point guard . . . that's not even close to maintaining an army in a war or being the head of a new national government."

"On the surface, no," Charlotte responded. "But think more broadly. What skill would a point guard need to have?"

"Dribbling? Um . . . passing? Am I missing something here? Did Washington show tremendous passing skills with cannonballs or something?"

"Now you're being silly. Those are specific talents. Step back more."

Eric thought about some of his favorite basketball heroes and then focused in on the point guards. At first he just thought about the distinct basketball skills they had, but then he thought about a point guard's job broadly. He slowly nodded his head. "The team leader. He directs the plays on the court. He finds the right people for the right job. He communicates the team's needs to his players."

Charlotte allowed a smile to come across her face. "Now are you starting to see? That man in the late eighteenth century, over six feet tall, athletically built, dexterous, was meant to command, not an army, but men on a court. He was meant to be a leader, not of a new emerging nation, but of a group of other guys in a game. George Washington was not born in the right time for his natural-born ability. But I'll tell you one thing: I'm sure glad he wasn't. Because, as entertaining as he probably would've been to watch at the head of a pro basketball team, I think that he proved much more, well, useful as one of the founding fathers of this nation."

Charlotte's lesson hit home pretty hard. Eric finished making her point for her. "And it wasn't his skill in shooting a ball or running a court that came in handy. It was his leadership skill, the only real relevant skill from his natural-born ability. And he put that to use in the best way he could." Eric allowed this thought to rest in his mind for a while. "Wow. That is truly inspirational, Charlotte."

"Now do you see why it irritates me when you claim that you are useless?"

Eric smiled. "Yeah, I guess so."

"Now can we talk about how you could be useful?"

A whole new world opened up to Eric as he considered his abilities. "Let's see, maybe a cargo ship captain . . ." but then he threw the idea out as soon as he thought of it. Not enough excitement for him or his talent. "No, no. Um . . . maybe a geographer of some sort." He knew that he really liked maps, so that might be fun. But again, he didn't quite feel as if that tapped into his true talents. Then he thought of one that he really liked, "What about a detective or a marshal? Chasing down criminals. Not in the ocean, granted, but it would all be about outsmarting my foes." He liked the idea even more when he voiced it.

"That," Charlotte said, "is a great one. And there are plenty more for you to consider as you get older. Sooner or later, if you don't give yourself in to a life of uselessness, you'll find something that may not be your natural-born ability, but that you'll still be really good at, whether it's a detective, a marshal, or something else."

Eric allowed a long silence to tuck in around them as he soaked in this new life that Charlotte opened up before him—a life where he was useful. And he liked it.

"Charlotte," he finally said. She turned to him. "I'm ready to go home."

As ready as he might have been, the two still had a week before the moon reciprocated its cycle to the phase that would take them home. Eric took advantage of the time to bask as much in this world where he excelled as he could. He counseled often with Captain Bellview, Samuel, Lieutenant Curtis, and others as they arranged the new fleet of Port Raleigh. He also, at the insistence of those same men, aided in creating the type of defenses that would protect Port Raleigh from just about any pirate attack in the future. There was even an interesting episode involving the self-exiled Governor Rose, one which time and relevance will not permit an account of here. Regardless of what he was doing, Eric relished every moment, using all of his spare time trying to put his talent to use. Charlotte shadowed him everywhere, providing silent support—and spunky responses—when appropriate.

Before they knew it, they were giving their good-byes to their friends. Captain Bellview and Lieutenant Curtis managed to get the whole of Port Raleigh out for the occasion, the guns from the fort gave out sporadic salutes, and the men that had served under Captain Francis lined up for his final inspection. While a moving moment for Eric, he also found it embarrassing. He tried to hurry up the ceremonies as much as possible before he finally boarded the small fishing boat loaned to him.

There he said good-bye to a teary-eyed Mr. Gary. He shook the hand of Lieutenant Curtis, who nodded with the utmost respect. He firmly held the hand of Captain Bellview, who held back emotions as he thanked Eric for his mercy, and then he shook the hand of Samuel, who appeared to not know what he could possibly say to the man that had saved him and had been his close friend. So he said nothing and instead tugged Eric into an embrace. They clasped each other for a long time, but there was a brotherly comfort to it that consecrated the moment in their memories.

All of the gentlemen had respectful words for Charlotte, who received them politely, but impatiently. Her attitude only endeared them to her further.

Finally, the others stepped off the fishing boat, and, trusting to a steady breeze that hailed from the east-southeast, they pushed off the docks and left Port Raleigh for the last time. Eric gazed longingly at the ships lining the harbor: the stately *Constantine* and *Metanoia*, the converted pirate ships *Redemption*, *Francis*, and *Charlotte* (a homage which

Charlotte outwardly scoffed but inwardly treasured). And finally, Eric looked longest at the small sloop, humbly nestled amongst the other dignified merchantmen and ships-of-the-line, the *Rosemary*. Eventually, as they rounded past the cape that held the fort, the sloop disappeared from sight and Eric managed to face forward.

The cruise to the small island that marked their entrance into the world passed mostly in silence, though not an awkward one. It was a silence of satisfaction. By the time they reached the island, the sun had just disappeared below the horizon, and twilight encroached upon the open, cloudless sky.

With all the skill of someone in his element, Eric anchored the boat in the precise spot where he and Charlotte first tumbled into the ocean, a stone's throw away from the *Rosemary*. There they waited and discussed the future of Port Raleigh and their friends, speculating on what was to come. They did this until night fell completely, and then they started to talk about home and school and their families and speculated on their futures. After quite some time of this kind of talk, Eric gazed at the horizon and sensed, if not saw, a slight halo of light. "It's time," he announced.

Charlotte shifted so that she sat in front of him and grabbed his hands, looking deep into his eyes. He could tell that she was smiling, even though his eyes did not even dare to leave the grip of her gaze to check. The moon started to rise from its resting spot—its weak, white light fighting across the distance to glimmer off the black, lapping ocean water. As the two held hands and concentrated, Eric allowed his whole experience to flash through his mind as one, quick extended thought. Quick as it may have been, the review of these events presented Eric with a revelation and a question that had eluded him this whole time.

Charlotte must have noticed something had changed because she murmured, "What is it?"

"I just realized," Eric said, his voice no louder than a whisper, "that when we talked about my victory over Jedediah, you mentioned that the two of us had identical skills. But that's not true. The skills of a pirate hunter and a pirate are different. Sure, we might anticipate the other person's skills, but our skills are not identical."

Charlotte almost smiled. "Are you accusing me of being a liar or just inaccurate? I'm not sure I'd like either!"

Eric continued as if Charlotte had not said a thing. "But then I wondered if you really meant what you said: that we had identical skills. To have identical skills, it means that we'd need to have the same natural-born ability. If that's true, it'd mean that this whole time I've really been a natural-born pirate and have used my piracy abilities for capturing one of my own kind, and you simply generously framed my ability as being a pirate hunter, even though it wasn't the case . . ."

Charlotte somehow held back her growing urge to smile, "Or Jedediah was a natural-born pirate hunter and he used his ability to read pirates and their strategies to make him a formidable pirate in his own right."

"So the question is," Eric followed up, "about which of us did you lie?"

"Eric," Charlotte said, "when I told you that you were a natural-born pirate hunter, I said that I was not lightly playing around. And I wasn't. I take my own ability, and the trust that goes with it, very seriously. But just as your personality enhances your natural ability, it is my personality that has me look beyond just the natural-born ability of the person I'm looking at and take into account the character of that person as well. While your abilities or Jedediah's abilities might have been naturally born to be either a pirate hunter or pirate, your personalities fit better with one or the other. Whether you were naturally born for it or not, Eric, you would've made a terrible pirate. You're just too darn nice and you have no selfish ambitions."

As soon as Charlotte imparted this explanation, Eric realized why he continued to trust her. It was silly of him to doubt her now. They sat for a moment of understanding as the moon attempted to complete its climb into the night sky. Eric knew he had a tiny bit of time left, so he figured it could not hurt to prompt one more question. "So," he asked, almost sheepish in his digging, "which is it? Pirate hunter or pirate?"

Now Charlotte's inevitable grin tore across her face. "Eric, does it really matter?"

Eric settled into a smile with a sigh. He knew that he was satisfied with what he knew now, with the person whose hands he held now, and just before the moon flicked its waning crescent tail above the horizon, he quipped, honestly, "Nah. It doesn't matter."

Discussion Questions

1. Why does it not matter what Eric's true natural-born ability is?

2. What, ultimately, marks the difference between Eric and Jedediah Willard?

3. What specific things contribute to Captain Bellview's dramatic change of character?

4. What role does loyalty play in the story? Which characters demonstrate it and under what conditions?

5. Is the friendship between Charlotte and Eric one-way or does it benefit both?

6. List out some natural-born abilities that you have. Under what circumstances would they be most useful? How can they be used now in your current situation?

7. What, if any, is the connection between usefulness and someone's natural-born ability? How useful is Jedediah's natural-born ability and for whom? What about Charlotte's and for whom? Eric's? Other characters'?

About THE Author

Marty Reeder lives in Smithfield, Utah, with his wife and five children. He teaches creative writing and Spanish at the local high school. Though not a natural born pirate hunter, he taught sailing at Scout camps for many years and uses his history degree to fuel worlds of piracy and compensate for perhaps being born in the wrong time and place for his passions!

SCAN TO VISIT

WWW.MARTYREEDER.COM